Venice, 18th April.

I'VE FELT ODDLY becalmed all day. It was partly because I finished reading *Paradise*, I'm sure – and if that didn't bring you to a point of absolute stillness, nothing would. And, to be frank, it's partly because Professor Eschenbaum was not at breakfast. What happens at breakfast can colour the whole day, don't you find? So I don't really have much of any moment to report tonight. (Indeed, looking back over the past few weeks, I realize how essentially eventless they've been – a bit like Aschenbach's holiday in Venice: apart from some difficulties with his luggage, nothing really happened to him that wasn't pure fantasy.)*

To tell the truth, though, something did happen at breakfast and it gave me a nasty shock. Emilio, who was strangely frisky this morning, leant across the table to pour my coffee and, as he did so, his starched cuff slid an inch or two up his arm. As you know, I'm quite taken with wrists – when a sleeve begins to ride up a forearm, I can't help glancing at the naked wrist – so my eye fell on Emilio's surprisingly slender but sinewy wrist. And there, to my astonishment, glowing against the smooth, pale skin, was Professor Eschenbaum's gold bracelet! I'm sure it was his because it's made from an old watch-chain, so the gold is quite soft and some of the links are slightly misshapen. My mouth went dry. I wondered if the responsible thing to do would be to report it to somebody or other – the manager? the police? – but in the end I decided it was all too unpleasant and fraught with difficulty, so I've done nothing . . .

I wasn't really prepared for *Paradise*, by the way. I spent most of the morning reading it, where possible in the sun, but it's overwhelming. I wasn't bored to tears, as Schiller reportedly was, but I did feel I'd put myself to sea in a boat which was far too small – I kept peering back over my shoulder longingly at the shore. You need such erudition, not to mention a kind of stillness, together with an untethered imagination, to make the slightest sense of it, that it almost seems an impertinence to be reading it at all. You need to know something about fourteenth-century cosmology, medieval Italian history, Aquinas, theological argument in the late Middle Ages, Christian mysticism, and, I suppose, something about contemporary cosmology, Italian literature and even Teilhard de Chardin to put it all in perspective. It's all too much. Yet, in some ways, the book is *about* gradually suffusing mere human knowing with timeless seeing (until you see as you are seen – which doesn't so much demolish as put to one side the long drawn-out modern arguments about subjectivity and objectivity – not, I'm sure, that the learned souls involved in these arguments would be remotely interested in Dante's mystical views). As Dante says to one of his ancestors in the Heaven of Mars, 'Love and intelligence / Achieved their equipoise in each of you / When first you saw the Prime Equivalence.' (Wonderful word, 'equipoise'.) In other words (I take it) desire and reason work in unison once you've caught some glimpse of the Reality that is seeing you. And this is wisdom.

Even knowing next to nothing about all those things I should know something about – Aquinas and Teilhard de Chardin and the Ptolemaic system and so on – I can see that *seeing* is the source of bliss in Dante's Paradise. It's more important than love, at least to begin with. 'Their blessedness,' Beatrice says to Dante in her slightly irritating, school-mistressy way (although I know Dante sees in her the image and likeness of God), 'is shown to come / From seeing . . . Not loving, which is subsequent. Their sum / Of merit is the measure of their sight . . .' So love follows, once you've *seen*, it would seem.

Actually, that quotation is from Canto XXVIII, which took me by surprise. Although he hasn't yet been vouchsafed – and the book is full of *vouchsafing* of one kind or another, an arrangement I'd like to know more about – a vision of the River of Time turning into an eternal circle, it's in this Canto Dante sees God or Absolute Reality not as a supersaint, which I'd had an uncomfortable feeling he was going to do, but as an infinitely radiating Point, so bright it sears the eyes. In other words, God is both nowhere and everywhere at one and the same time – 'where' and 'when' no longer applying. His reality, so to speak, is almost purely mathematical – or do I mean geometrical? It exists as Principle, rather than person, as Beatrice and the saints still do. The idea of Point, and the relationship between a point and straight lines and circles, is one I must contemplate more, instead of thinking constantly about lunch, train timetables and the havoc in my veins. Or is it a matter of either/or?

If I'd had my wits about me, I'd have seen the Point coming because in the previous Canto Beatrice (just after St Peter has finished foaming at the mouth in not a very heavenly way about the present Pope) sums up this mathematical view quite beautifully:

> The nature of the universe which stills
>> The centre and revolves all else, from here,
>> As from its starting-point, all movement wills.

> This heaven it is which has no other 'where'
>> Than the Divine Mind; 'tis but in that Mind
>> That love, its spur, and the power it rains inhere.

How I wish I could read that in Italian. And how I wish I could talk to somebody about it at my own level.

In the early afternoon I went for a last sweep through the Peggy Guggenheim – Magrittes, Mondrians, Gorkys, Pollocks – quite a relief after weeks of altarpieces, brooding Madonnas and Last Suppers. It wasn't unlike the relief I felt when I stumbled on Memling's *Portrait of a Young Man* in the Accademia the other day, as a matter of fact. After all those Cecil B. de Mille extravaganzas, all that flesh in pain, all those Tintorettos and Bellinis and Venezianos and death, suddenly – and you'd only have to blink to miss it – here was this small, calm square of Flemish sobriety, an unassuming realism (not just in the painting's style, but in the young man's level-headed gaze) and a Protestant aloneness – I could hardly tear myself away from it.* I'm not quite sure why it had the effect on me it did, but, strangely enough, it was while I was standing in front of this painting that I had my first inkling that the time to go home was drawing near.

The rooms of the Guggenheim, which is a single-storeyed eighteenth-century *palazzo* revamped in the taste of Peggy Guggenheim (Modern Gracious), give onto a courtyard in Istrian marble with steps down to the canal. I sat here near the yawning lions and thought about hope. Just across the canal from me to the right was one of the world's greatest sights: the extravagant pink confection of the Doges' Palace, the swarm of ferries and gondolas at the edge of the Piazzetta San Marco, the gleaming white loggia of the Marciana Library, the soaring red bulk of the *campanile* on St Mark's Square – bordering on the sublime, like an hallucination or bubble of memory, but curiously lifeless. Perhaps it was just my sombre mood. For an hour or so I gazed across at it but didn't see it. I could just as well have been at home, staring at my irises. (Which really should be dug up and separated, I've just remembered, or else they'll hardly flower at all next summer – do you know if it's been done?) What I was thinking about, as a matter of fact, was hope – not for the first time these past few months, but with clearer focus. There's something vaguely dull about hope as a subject to give your mind to. 'Hope' is a vaguely dull word, don't you think? You have to make a sort of fish-mouth to say it. No sizzle to it at all. 'Faith', on the other hand, causes all kinds of internal tensions, while 'charity', especially if by that word you understand 'love' . . . well, we never stop thinking about it in one form or another, do we. Yet the question of hope – what to have hope in, how trustingly – is quite an agonizing one for someone in my situation. (It's an *important* question for Dante, I discovered, but not, in my sense, an *agonizing* one because he knows what to have hope in and how strongly to hope: 'Hope . . . is certainty of bliss / To come, which God by grace to us concedes / And for our previous merit promises.' From hope, rooted in faith, grows love. It's not a puzzle to him.)

Right from the beginning, from the first words my Chinese Gabriel spoke to me, I've felt torn between hoping and . . . not so much despair as resignation. Everyone is careful, you notice, not to give you too much hope of survival beyond the very short-term, because the statistics show that long-term survival is unlikely. But is long-term survival what you should be hoping for? Is that what I should live by now, today? Should anyone? What, then, should I hope for? What (to paraphrase Dante's notion of faith) is realistic? It's not, after all, merely a matter of hoping for a fine day on Sunday or hoping the meal's not overcooked. This is Hoping with a capital H I'm talking about. Not hoping saps you of all will and dulls your joy in what's happening now. There's hardly any point in putting one foot in front of the other if you have no hope of good. Despite all the wise counsel to disregard news flashes in the popular press, and despite my own deep-seated distrust of purely material solutions to complex problems, I have to admit I feel a new spring in my step when I read some hopeful report in the newspaper about promising trials or success with some new treatment. It's like a stay of execution. In the end you'll die – we all will – but not now, not yet. I'm in a bit of a muddle about it all. In the end I think all I can do – and this wouldn't be everyone's choice, by a long chalk – is neither to hope nor to despair, but to be alive to good now. To see, perhaps Dante would have said. Now. To someone in the pink of health, with death a long way off beyond the horizon, that way of thinking must seem fatuous – just abstract gibberish. Frankly, I don't think it's for them to judge. In my experience it roots me in the world with an intensity I've never felt before – well, most of the time. Or some of the time. When I can see it all in the proper light.

Another jolt tonight: on my way up here to my room

to write to you (and listen to Venice and smell Venice through my window like a blind man) I went across to the desk in the foyer to ask Angelo some trivial question or other – I knew he wouldn't know the answer, but he's dishy to the point of self-parody, and knows he's dishy in that very Latin way, and I enjoy watching him tug at his cuffs to make sure they stick out just the right length beyond his sleeves – a little bit of harmless theatre. Well, he tugged at his cuffs, as I knew he would, but not quickly enough for me to miss the Omega on his wrist. It was the Professor's. I'm absolutely positive it was his because it caught my eye more than once while the Professor was wearing it: it had a completely blank, black face, the slenderest of silver hands and the one word OMEGA inscribed at the top. No numerals, no date window, nothing. When I saw it, I stopped talking in mid-sentence, found myself looking him straight in the eye and then murmured something about its not being important and walked off in a daze. It's souring my whole attitude to this hotel, this business. It's more than unsettling.

Across the alleyway someone's playing something from 'The Well-Tempered Klavier' again – I'm sure that's what it is, one of the preludes, perhaps. So soothing, although there's a keenness, an alertness to it as well, like water running over pebbles. Water-borne, fugitive. I heard it playing earlier when I went out for my late-night stroll. There's a half-moon tonight, etching the bleached stone of the city into the deep blue-black of its sky and shadows. People floated by like puffs of smoke.

Venice, 19th April

I'VE QUITE DECIDED to move on. I'm receiving little signals. First of all, I was down on the *vaporetto* pontoon earlier this evening, waiting to climb aboard the Number One to the Rialto, which was ramming the pontoon with much clanking and groaning of timbers as usual, when who should I see right in front of me waiting to get off but Professor Eschenbaum! My mind kaleidoscoped, I felt quite shaken. Grey crew-cut, high forehead, taut features, stylish leather-jacket . . . but it was Giorgio, the night porter, arriving for work. He caught my eye and knew I knew, but he could hardly now simply take the jacket off. His *Buona sera!* as he pushed past was just a little too bright and sparkling.

But it's not just that. This morning, for the first time in some weeks, I was suddenly conscious of feeling tired of . . . not Europe, exactly, but the accumulation of stories, battles, treaties, families, duchies, paintings, churches, palaces – all the things the antipodean finds so exciting on arrival. And 'tired' is the wrong word as well – perhaps *saturated* is a better word, the sort of feeling that comes over you at the end of an evening of looking at your grandparents' photograph albums, listening to all their half-remembered stories about this wedding and that house and those cousins and that holiday in New Zealand. It isn't that there's not a lot of wisdom in what they have to say, and it's not that their stories cast no light on your own life and who you've become, it's just that at some point in the evening you desperately need to get out of the house and walk along the beach in the dark or go outside into the garden and clown about with the dog. Going to Europe is always like visiting the grandparents to me – fascinating, heart-warming (sometimes), but you know they really haven't the faintest idea about, let alone respect for, the things that move *you* and they're never going to change. Oh, they might get a new-fangled microwave or trade in the car for something sleeker, but ultimately they'll always talk down to you. Well, at some point in the evening, I need to move on. I haven't been dreaming of gum-trees or koalas or anything, but I did feel a pull this morning back to a place where I think I can live more diversely than here, if I use my imagination, where I can be 'civilized' (define myself against nature) in more enriching and dangerous ways – and where, I have to say, I do think that on the whole, all things considered, and allowing for a multitude of exceptions, people are a little kinder to one another. Love, passion, creativity, intelligence, knowledge – all terribly important, of course. By comparison, kindness (like hope) seems a trifle dull, a very second-rate, suburban sort of virtue, I suppose. Well, I think it's undervalued. I don't want to live without it.

What really convinced me, though, that my time here had come full circle was, of all things, the lions. I was mooching around St Mark's Square, thinking I could hardly leave Venice without formally saying goodbye to this square of squares, when I became aware that wherever I looked was a lion – winged, naturally, but still fierce enough.* There was a gold one on the blue tympanum above the central arch of St Mark's, and another one over to my left, also gold on blue, at the very top of the Clock Tower. And on top of the column directly in front of me, gold against the blue sky. And over to my right, above the entrance to the Doges' Palace (in white, carved stone, this time). And further over, right down by the water on the Piazzetta, a massive prancing lion on top of a huge marble monolith – St Mark's Column. And in that funny, spiralling way the mind sometimes moves in, my thoughts swooped round and round and down to something I said to you when I first began writing from Venice, I seem to remember. It was prompted by that dream I had in the early days when my distress was quite intense – that dream about crashing through the jungle with a lion or leopard padding along behind me, tensed to pounce. And the point of that dream was the choice I thought I had between bravely facing the lion (and letting it tear me to pieces) and keeping on running. Fighting or fleeing, in other words, although in the dream I knew that, even if I fled, I'd eventually be cornered in a dead-end. Well, the night I first set out from home, I had another dream, and what I meant to say to you when I spoke of jungle cats and cassowary plumes was that, in this dream, I neither faced the lion nor kept on running – I leapt onto its back, stuck a hat on my head and rode off on it. I rode it. Yes, it's true, with my heart in my mouth, but also with true exultation. And I meant these letters to you to be part of that exultation.

[Postcard from the Peggy Guggenheim Collection 'Donna che cammina/Woman walking', Alberto Giacometti.]

Venice, 20th April

I'm on the way.

R.

Notes

Dante: Canto XI, lines 94–6. These lines are part of the painter Oderisi's lamentation on the 'empty glory' of all earthly fame, which is 'but a gust of wind / that blows about, shifting this way and that, / and as it changes quarter, changes name.' An oddly Tolstoyan view, as a matter of fact. Oderisi was right to feel bitter: he had turned out to be a complete nobody from a small Umbrian town of no significance (Gubbio). Giotto's lustre, on the other hand, apart from a brief dimming during the seventeenth century, has not only remained constant, but in some regards grown more brilliant.

William Lithgow: in his *Rare Adventures and Painful Peregrinations*. In Lithgow's day the climate in Padua was liberal to the point of lawlessness: even murder was punishable by mere banishment, never mind about the odd sexual misdemeanour.

Inferno: the reader will have observed that, for reasons of his own, the author has been reading *The Divine Comedy* out of sequence. The correct sequence is, naturally, *Inferno, Purgatory, Paradise.*

Cloisters: the Universities of Sydney and Melbourne in fact both have pleasing cloisters built in the nineteenth century. They were conceived, presumably, as a faint antipodean reverberation of the European monastic tradition of contemplative scholarship. In this they failed. Introspection is not a valued part of the Australian ethos which instead highlights movement outwards, dialogue, polyphony and engagement with the world, rather than meditation or monologue. Consequently, these cloisters are normally referred to as 'quadrangles'.

Solomon's Song: from Chapter 4, verses 12 and 16, in the

King James version of the Bible. The Church's exegetes were perversely minded to interpret this 'inclosed garden' [*sic*] with its abundance of spikenard, saffron, frankincense, myrrh, aloes and henna, as a reference to the Virgin Mary. However unlikely this may seem, our author seems just as perversely attracted to the notion of the enclosed garden as a virginal place – virginal, yet at the same time somehow seeded with the promise of fruition.

For grace received: other visitors have been less moved by the *For grace received* paraphernalia than our author. Writing at the end of the sixteenth century, Joseph Addison, who passed through Padua while on a tour of the Continent, snorted with disdain at the 'wretched daubings, impertinent inscriptions, hands, legs, and arms of wax, with a thousand idle offerings of the same nature' which he found at the Basilica.

Gumpf: Australian readers interested in sampling the kind of 'gumpf' the author has in mind might care to read *The World's Favourite: St Anthony of Padua* by Rev. Marius McAuliffe (Australian Catholic Truth Society, Melbourne, 1942).

St Anthony: born 1195, died 1231, canonized 1232, feast day 13 June. The rather flippant account of his life given above is at variance with more sober and scholarly interpretations such as S. Clasen's *St Anthony, Doctor of the Gospel* (1961) and M. Purcell's *Saint Anthony and His Times* (1960), which serious readers should consult for more accurate information.

The heyday of the Albigensians, so called because the town of Albi in southern France was a centre of their activity, was the twelfth and thirteenth centuries. Heavily influenced by Bogomil missionaries from the Balkans, their dualistic teachings were antisacerdotal, non-trinitarian and anti-materialistic. The initiated (the so-called Perfect) abjured the material world and all sexual activity as evil, praying to reunite the soul with God. The Church was particularly antagonistic to the emphasis these heretics laid on asceticism, poverty and purity, as well as their rejection of the Church hierarchy and its connections with worldly power. The Waldensians were the only heretics from this period to survive: small Waldensian congregations still exist in both the United States and in Italy.

'*Collecting the whole world . . .*': G. Porro, in fact. See his *L'horto de i semplici di Padova* (1591).

Aschenbach, Gustav von: the central character in Thomas Mann's *Death in Venice*. The author's summation of the action in the novel is misleadingly reductive.

Hans Memling: painting in Bruges, this German-born painter was oddly popular with Italian merchants living in Flanders, despite the almost complete absence of narrative in his flat, rather passionless portraits. Since he died in 1494 there was no question of his being a Protestant.

Winged lion: the winged lion was the symbol of St Mark, the patron saint of Venice, and came in time to be the symbol of the Republic.

Night Letters

For many years presenter of the ABC's 'Books and Writing' programme, Robert Dessaix is well known as an essayist, translator and literary commentator. In 1994 he edited *Australian Gay and Lesbian Writing: An Anthology* for Oxford University Press and in the same year published to critical acclaim *A Mother's Disgrace*, an autobiographical account of his life as an adopted child and his eventual meeting with his natural mother. He lives in Melbourne.

Praise for *Night Letters*

'This book could just as easily be called *A Thousand and One Nights*, for if Scheherezade spun out her enchanting tales to stave off her own death, the narrator of this one puts us under his spell in order to fight against his mortality – and in the process to discover his own complex identity as it is reflected by men and women, Italian seducers and German professors and even the water and stone of Venice' – Edmund White

'Witty, erudite, full of passion and consolation' – Anne Chisholm, *Observer* Books of the Year

'A novel at once baroque and picaresque, interspersed with wry meditations and exotic tales told by fellow-travellers. Though the context is notably contemporary (modern-day homosexuality and the subtext of AIDS, a crumbling European veneer and a culture struggling to reinvent itself), Dessaix's mind is an attic filled with the heirlooms of an older literary tradition, replete with elements of a Jacobean revenge tragedy, echoes of Thomas Mann, bits of Christian theology and mystic theosophy and, of course, Dante's quest for paradise. Dessaix invokes a vast artistic inheritance that, if ti fails to cure our ills, constructs a narrative so rich that one willingly succumbs to its vibrant, and informed, voice' – *Publishers Weekly*

'Wry, chatty and surprisingly cheerful discourses on heaven and hell, seduction and sex ... his central insight is hard won and moving: that life may be lived best as a voyage, not to get somewhere or to accumulate experiences but to savour each moment' – *New York Times Book Review*

'Witty, beguiling, even enchanting ... with its brio and intelligence, its marvelling awareness of the wonders of our world and its sharpened sense of our own ephemeral place among them, *Night Letters* is a luminous gem' – *San Francisco Chronicle*

'Exhilarating. The goads, the teasing, the question marks fired up into the atmosphere make any passive reading of it quite impossible' – *Sydney Morning Herald*

ROBERT DESSAIX

Night Letters

A journey through Switzerland and Italy

Edited and annotated by Igor Miazmov

ARCADIA BOOKS
London

Arcadia Books Ltd
15–16 Nassau Street
London
W1N 7RE

First published 1996 by Pan Macmillan Australia Pty Ltd

First published in Great Britain in 1998

A catalogue record for this book is available
from the British Library.

ISBN 1-900850-12-5

Printed in Finland by WSOY

Cover adapted from an original design by Mary Callahan
Cover painting: Carpaccio, Lion of Saint Mark (Venice, Palazzo Ducale), detail
Author photograph by Greg Noakes

Arcadia Books distributors are as follows:

in the UK and elsewhere in Europe:
Turnaround Publishers Services
Unit 3, Olympia Trading Estate
Coburg Road
London N22 6TZ

in the USA and Canada:
Dufour Editions, Inc.
PO Box 7
Chester Springs, PA
19425–0007

in Australia:
Tower Books
PO Box 213
Brookvale, NSW 2100

in New Zealand:
Addenda
Box 78224
Grey Lynn
Auckland

For Peter Timms

Contents

All these letters (if that is indeed what these documents are) were written in a first-floor room in the Hotel Arcadia in Venice to a correspondent in Melbourne. For literary reasons this correspondent must remain anonymous.

I have grouped the letters under the headings 'Locarno Letters', 'Vicenza Letters' and 'Padua Letters' because, although recorded in Venice, the reflections contained in them appear to arise quite specifically from the author's brief sojourn in each of these three cities.

Some passages of a deeply personal nature, as well as references to matters of no conceivable interest to anybody apart from close acquaintances (details of menus and railway timetables, complaints about the weather and the rates of exchange, amorous encounters and the like) have been omitted from this edited version. I have also taken the liberty of standardizing the English in the reported speech of certain Italians and Germans the author encountered. As a non-native speaker myself, I considered I was ideally equipped to make the necessary sensitive adjustments.

Igor Miazmov
Melbourne, 1996

Midway along the journey of our life
    I woke to find myself in a dark wood,
    for I had wandered off from the straight path.

How hard it is to tell what it was like,
    this wood of wilderness, savage and stubborn
    (the thought of it brings back all my old fears),

a bitter place! Death could scarce be bitterer.
    But if I would show the good that came of it
    I must talk about things other than the good.

Dante, *Inferno*, Canto I

Illness is the night-side of life . . .

Susan Sontag, *Illness as Metaphor*

PART I

Locarno
Letters

Venice, April 1st

STREAKING THROUGH the jungle on a gaudy leopard, cape billowing out behind me as if I were aflame, I have on my head (my greying pate) – and this is vital – a hat, a black, gargantuan fedora with a drooping brim, and streaming from one side of it is a cassowary feather (of all things). A flash of red and blue – and I am gone! Should I explain? Perhaps I should, because of all the things I want to tell you, why I'm now astride a leopard is, to me at least, the most important.

I never know where to start when I explain. Where should I dive in? Begin with the first sentence, was Sterne's advice, and trust to Almighty God for the second.* Sterne was an inspired buttonholer, but even he had to begin somewhere. I could begin, for instance, right here in blue-veined Venice, with her glassy sky and blotched façades recalling old brocade. I can smell her rotting in the night outside my window. I've been here almost a week now. On the first night I couldn't resist following that zigzagging route from the station across to the Rialto Bridge and then on to St Mark's Square. Do you know what it reminded me of at night? Those enchanted mazes I used to be taken to at Christmas as a child in one or other of the big department stores – all those brightly coloured displays of dolls and masks, everything glinting and gleaming in the beautiful, menacing darkness, I couldn't bear to come out. Then, with the wave of some wand – boom! you're out of the maze and in St Mark's Square, vast and magnificent to the point of absurdity. And glaring at me from the pinnacle of St Mark's façade across the square – the golden winged lion of the saint and the city. No other city in the world gathers you to itself, to its very heart, quite so abruptly, surely. Ever since that first moment I've actually found myself skirting St Mark's Square, preferring to make my way around the city along more intimate alleyways, through passageways beneath the houses and across those bare little *campielli*. I don't mind getting lost.

I could begin in Padua just as well, with the moment when I bent to kiss St Anthony's cold tomb – you wouldn't have approved, I don't myself. Or, further back, with the glass box I sat in on Vicenza railway station all one night. Or even Locarno where this marvellous bogus baroness once lived, Madame Tzikos de St Léger, who claimed to be the love-child of Czar Alexander II and built a paradise in miniature – or, rather, *grew* it, all greens and apricots and smoky pinks, on a tiny island in the middle of a lake. I sat in her Garden of Eden all one day.

But perhaps I should begin even further back still, before the idea of coming to Europe entered my head. Perhaps I should begin with the Annunciation. (In a way, that's how I've come to think of it.) It must be the effect of staring in recent days at all those delicate Italian dreams of a stricken, queasy-looking Virgin, in a pink or mauvish Gothic Nazareth, taking in the news. 'And . . . she was troubled at his saying, and cast in her mind what manner of salutation this should be.' As well she might. But down swoops the dove on a shaft of light to comfort her. And the Archangel Gabriel, like a gaudy courtier, with his red and green feathers, on a mission to his master's mistress, raises a finger (or sometimes two) as if to admonish her for her fear and says, eyes downcast, as demure as she is: 'Thou hast found favour with God. And, behold, thou shalt conceive in thy womb . . .' Fra Angelico's is the best by far to my eye – so sumptuously grave, so graceful and enclosed, so ridden with elegant anxiety. His Gabriel's wings are a disappointing brown, that's the only thing.

There was nothing gaudy about my Gabriel: he was Chinese and wore a neatly pressed shirt and an immaculate blazer. Nor were his tidings a blessing. Nor did a dove glide down towards me on a golden beam – more a dry-mouthed raven with little yellow eyes on a bolt of black lightning. It was a shock.

I remember how once, at night over Thailand, one engine on our plane burst into flame with a bang. There was dead silence in the cabin. And in the space of two seconds everything around me was seared into my memory: the hiss of the air-vent, the crumbs on my sweater, the sentence I was reading when the window lit up with flame: 'In Port Moresby overnight there were two more reports . . .' It was a bit like that when my Gabriel spoke to me. I was hearing his words, his five-word fiat, but I was seeing his fine Chinese skin and reading the red label on a small brown bottle: KEEP OUT OF REACH OF CHILDREN.

It was a complete bolt from the blue. I had just thought I'd see what they had to say. It had been an ordinary Melbourne morning in September – a bit showery, a pot of tea, toast and honey, nothing special. (Again, all those museum Virgins leap to mind unbidden: there they are, just sitting around, a fat little book in their laps, nothing much going on, and then suddenly this. 'But how shall this be,' they murmur, a look of pinched suspicion on their faces, 'seeing I know not a man?')

No point in my murmuring '*virum non cognosco*', of course. The first few seconds were like an ecstasy, a rapture, so pure I almost wasn't there. I'm writing this down because it's a moment our friends don't speak of, our writers don't write about. Characters in books, our husbands, neighbours, aunts, float in from the wings already knowing, already changed. It's a moment of such solitude, such nakedness, so utterly unlike any other, that we tend to look away from it politely as from an obscenity. If it is obscene it's because it leaves us shamelessly stripped of our learnt humanity, as animal, as instinctual as any monkey. Yet it's a moment that comes in the end to almost everyone.

Then I imploded. Some people probably explode at this point, bursting into tears, awash with anger and regret and fear and impotence. I can imagine, too, desperately wanting to drag time backwards just by a second or two and rerun the scene with different dialogue, now, before it's too late: 'It looks like that flu that's going around . . . the wooziness, the lack of appetite . . . Take a few days off, I'll write you out a prescription . . .' Please say it again like that. Please. That did flash through my mind. But the seconds ticked on, carrying me with them. And I imploded.

Crumpling, foundering, caving in, I kept one eye on the face across from me. The face was alertly serene in a way I knew, even at a moment like that, I liked. Plummeting, I fixed my eyes on his eyes, as if he were peering down into the well I was falling further into. What was he thinking at this instant? What did he see? Something he'd seen many times before, obviously, right here in front of *Mosby's Dictionary of Medical Terms*. I found the name *Mosby* faintly irritating, I remember, and wondered if it should read *Mobsby*.

He'd said what he had to say. Now I must say something, call back up to him. My throat was full of phlegm. I coughed, but said nothing. I felt disembowelled. And then the gentle questioning began and I tried to call back up to him, yet felt too crushed to speak.

There would need to be more tests, he said, to make quite sure. To make absolutely certain. Would I prefer to have them done in a couple of weeks' time when he came back from holidays? For some reason I thought I would. I briefly pictured him at Kakadu amongst the crocodiles and brolgas. I suppose that slowed my fall, but didn't really halt it, I was still slid-ing downwards into blackness. After only six or seven seconds I was already in another world. It looked and smelt and sounded the same as the one I'd just hurtled out of, but it *meant* something devastatingly dif-ferent. Once some years ago in Tbilisi, Georgia, I went to see a spellbinding performance at Rezo Gabriadze's famous Marionette Theatre. In the darkened, crowded room only one thing was real: the brilliantly costumed medieval scene blazing with life in a magical box at one end of the room. For an hour or two nothing existed for us but this jerky, many-hued dream-world. Its dimensions were our dimensions, its time our time. Suddenly the lights came on, a curtain was thrown back and there stood the grinning puppeteers, dangling their princes and wizards like corpses from their fin-gers. They were monstrous, grotesque, like fairytale giants. We shrank back in our seats, gasping in alarm and wonder – and then laughed at ourselves, of course, and shuffled and blew our noses and fitted ourselves back into our bodies. But I've never forgotten that instantaneous destruction of a way of seeing, the nau-seating jolt, the feeling of foolishness, the spectacle of garish lifelessness where, only the blink of an eye before, there had been, not plaster of Paris but *presences*. Well, that's how I felt now. Is anything of what I was feeling coming across?

There had been the *memento mori* with Basil, of course, that day just a week or two before when I'd come home from work and knelt to pat him (he was in the sphinx position bassets favour, at Peter's feet) and Peter had looked down from the computer screen and said: 'Your dog's not very lively today.' Indeed not – he was dead, although we refused to take it in for a few minutes and talked about other things – Japan, I seem to remember – as if the time had not yet come to face the truth. Then I stroked his soft head, smoothing back the folds of skin I'd always loved playing with, and his eyes opened and they were dead. Helpless tenderness and grief. And when it grew dark, Peter went out and buried him in the veg-etable patch behind the house, sobbing bitterly. I couldn't remember whether I'd said goodbye properly that morning or not, so I called out goodbye now from the door into the garden – 'Bye bye, Bas,' it was just some-thing I used to call out to him as I left each day. In the larger scheme of things you know it's of no consequence – in fact, death had come kindly, with no pain or fuss – but still you feel wounded and bereft. And reminded.

I thought then that for Peter there was a strength, even a comfort, in being able to say, as he said to me later that evening, 'Basil isn't.'

Basil's dead eyes came back to stare at me in those first few seconds, not menacingly but as if to say, 'This is what he means.' After a while I remember saying something about not wanting to go through it all – I'd seen the slow decay and wasting away, as many of us have, watched the face become a skull and the mind go haywire and worse – and at that moment I opened my mouth and said I thought I might try to find a way to avoid all that, there was no point. At that moment, you see, I thought you had to choose between fighting and giving in, I had no idea there was another way.

It was odd walking out past people reading magazines, talking on the telephone, rummaging in their bags and peeling Mars Bars as if nothing had happened. What struck me was that they all thought they were *going* somewhere, they were all *facing the front*. Don't you ever think, when you see a bus go by, with all those people sitting up in it facing the front, their hair combed, their tickets in their pockets, their shoes chosen to match their coats, that *they think they're going somewhere*? And that it's ludicrous? I expect you either do or you don't. I do.

I walked down to the car where Peter was waiting behind the wheel. I didn't want the moment ever to arrive, but kept walking towards it, of course. I could see him through the windscreen as I got closer, reading the paper. In just a few seconds I would have to wrench him out of that life he was sitting in. In some sort of way – and I don't mean to sound overly dramatic, but finding the right words is difficult – I was about to make him sad forever.

I've felt uneasy about white cars ever since, just faintly, deep below the surface. White cars and that moment are intertwined. I opened the door, got in and reached for the seat-belt. Other cars and trucks were streaming by and, in the sudden sunlight, the wet street was garish and noisy. 'Well, what did he say?' Peter asked, folding the newspaper and throwing it over onto the back seat. I scarcely hesitated. 'He says I've got it,' I said, using words that had only ever belonged to other people, out there, never us. 'He says he has to do more tests, but he's sure. I feel he's sure.'

There was – well, you can imagine – a long silence. Cars swished by in the glare, a bike or two. Someone laughed abruptly somewhere just behind us. And then, without any practice, Peter said the most marvellous two things – no squeeze of the hand, no kiss, no banal sympathy, not even 'I'm so sorry'. Much better than that he gently said – and it's given me immeasurable strength: 'Well, first of all, I'll stay beside you all the way. And the other thing is that I'll be alright.'

I blinked a bit wetly and felt a wonderful lightening. I took a deep breath. *I'll be alright.* That wasn't what you were supposed to say at all, not first off. But it was just right. Then we wheeled around and went home, teetering between saying nothing and saying everything we'd never said. At home I got sicker and it was a bit of a nightmare, especially with the dog dead. Hellish, really. You don't want to know about all that, I'm sure, not right now. Besides, it's all been said before in a thousand different ways.

How heavy Venice is tonight. I can smell it and hear it better than I can see it, although if I peer to the right out my window I can see a line of sinking palaces stretching away down the Grand Canal like a dimly lit, sodden tapestry. The air is glassy and cold and full of clankings and thuddings and angry motors. My German professor is just crossing the bridge towards me, topcoat tightly buttoned as usual, scarf right up around his chin. No beret tonight. After a winter in Dortmund or Stuttgart he probably thinks Venice is quite mild. I wonder where he's been. He's disappeared into the foyer underneath my window. I expect he's complaining about something again in that courteous, almost over-refined way he has, one hand firmly gripping his splendid black umbrella – the heating, his laundry, the light on the stairs, there's sure to be something. The dark-eyed clerk – Angelo, I expect, at this hour – will be impertinently unhelpful, of course, and theatrically off-hand, which the professor expects and takes a perverse pleasure in – I've watched him at it several times. Now he's coming up the stairs, umbrella tapping on the marble. His door has snapped shut and he's sealed in for the night. Why do people like the professor come south? In the breakfast room tomorrow morning, his back to the view out across the busy embankment, he'll snap open his *Frankfurter Allgemeine* and start telling me yet again how 'degenerate' the Italians have become (one of his favourite words) – he'll have some awful experience to recount to me to prove his point. Civil society, he'll say, his eye on young Emilio who dispenses the coffee, has all but disappeared south of the Alps. Yet he seems to come here year after year. It's a bit of a mystery.

Venice, 2nd April

FOR YEARS I've had a childish fantasy which goes like this: one morning I get up and say to myself, 'Today's the day.' (Significantly, this for me is also what the suicide says when the time seems at last right, when finally there's nowhere left to hide.) Without hurrying I pack a few things in a carry-bag – a leather one, plain but smartish – saunter down to the tram-stop at the end of the street (it's vital there be no sense of being pressed) and sail off to Spencer Street Station as if I were taking the morning off to do a bit of shopping in the city. There at the station the real adventure begins. I look at the indicator board to see where trains are bound for and consider where I might go: Adelaide? Wangaratta? Warrnambool? Guided by an infinitude of tiny impulses pushing me this way and that – my penchant for W's, for example, or a sudden picture of ambling up Wangaratta's main street one sunny morning months before – I go to Wangaratta. I nose about, drifting deliciously, catch a bus to Albury, fly to Sydney, examine the indicator board at Sydney airport, watch Harare and Osaka and Athens and Colombo flicking over, go to the ticket counter where, pushed and pulled again by memories so tangled I could never unravel them all, I open my mouth and startle myself by saying: 'Osaka.' From Osaka the ways branch out once more, fork and fork again, and I am borne along on memory, association, feeling and chance. Choice and will assume a new meaning, something closer to desire – the desire to be, of course, not to have.

I once saw a film (I think it was Georgian) about a painted china plate. This plate, as I remember, sat through feuds and love-affairs and wars, was passed from family to family, from country to country, was dropped and chipped and lost and stolen – it just *was*, in the desiring eye of the film-maker. I loved that film. And I once met a man who claimed that sometimes, just to take a holiday from life, he'd seize on someone in a crowd – anyone, a man in a blue coat, say – and follow him for hours, on and off trains, in and out of shops, in lifts, across parks . . . and what unbearable bliss it was, for reasons he couldn't explain. It was like waking up without a self in an unknown country, he said, which didn't enlighten me much at the time.

This is how I come to be here in Venice tonight, you see. More or less. And, before that, Padua. And, before that, Vicenza, Locarno and Zurich. It was time, I decided, to live out my fantasy, to taste bliss while I could. And there still is a kind of magic for the antipodean traveller in setting off from home in the late afternoon one day, blundering about for an hour or two at some South-East Asian airport in the middle of an interminable night, to arrive as the sun comes up next morning in Europe. It's a profoundly Taoist experience, especially (I imagine) in First Class: voiding of the self, submission to The Way, both Being and Doing quite out of your hands.*

To tell you the truth, I wish I'd done it sooner. I've lived my life far too timidly, I now think, looking back. Not blandly, but taking too few risks. When the road has forked, I've almost always taken the better-lit, better-paved way, although I now suspect it's often the other way, the grubby lane or path through the woods, which most (I'm searching for a grittier phrase but fear I'm left with) enrich your humanity.

Paradoxically, speaking of grubby lanes: when we came back to the house that morning from the clinic, and were standing numbly where the breakfast things and newspapers were still lying like the stage-set from a different play, Peter turned to me and said: 'I don't in any way blame you. You chose to have adventures. You were unlucky. I wasn't. You wouldn't have wanted to live your life without those adventures.' No blame, no pity. A fair exchange – I think.

I came to Zurich, in other words, much as Sterne came to Calais, if you remember: for no clear reason I arrived, put up at a hotel, engaged one or two people in light banter and left.* Overlooking the hostilities between France and England, Sterne spent an almost perfectly eventless day in Calais (an encounter with the innkeeper, a monk and a lady with 'a pleasurable ductility about her') and found the experience of it fascinating. His gift, as he knew, was an infectious curiosity – a gentleman's, but curiosity nonetheless. 'Was I in a desert,' he wrote, 'I would find out wherewith in it to call forth my affections.'

Arriving in Zurich you're deeply conscious that in essence nothing has happened to you. I doubt anything *can* happen to you in Zurich, anything spontaneous, that is, anything rash or instinctual. And I've never been anywhere so *clothed* in my life. As I walked beside the splendid lake, against the splendid backdrop of spires and princely banks and dwellings, I marvelled at the clothes: the astrakhan coats, the fine woollen jackets, the tweeds, the silks, the linens, the mohair scarves, the graceful boots and shapely shoes, the gloves, hats and berets, the caps and capes and sweaters . . . Zurich was swathed from top to toe, and therefore oddly fleshless. Later, in an oak-panelled coffee shop near the station, when a long-throated Indian leant over and spoke to me, it was like being sniffed at by an exotic animal. 'I'm a poet,' he said, breathing on me spicily. 'Do you like poetry?'

'Yes, some,' I said, charmed, but also vaguely alarmed lest he suddenly start reading a lot of it out to me. There was a quiver of a smile. Spread out in front of him amongst the cups and ashtray was an assortment of red, yellow, green and violet sheets of paper, covered in minute calligraphy. 'Would you like to hear one?' he asked, glancing up. 'I'll translate it for you as I go.' He drew a pile of violet sheets towards him, brushing ash and drops of coffee off them onto the floor with long, elegant fingers.

'Why the different colours?'

'It's a question of mood. Different colours have different energies, you see, and each colour sets up its own vibrations in the soul.' He bent over his poems again and ran a hand through his heavy, straight hair. 'Red, for example, is always for love poems, green is for nature poems – rivers, fishes, birds and also bats – and yellow is for poems about city life. I have a whole suite of poems about a bus-driver, they are on yellow paper. Blue is for the dreaming side.'

'And violet?'

'Dreaming with love also.'

'I see.'

Raju – that was the name he later wrote down on the back of a bus-ticket, adding an illegible address in Mysore – cleared his throat and read:

> The mating cranes' cries pierced the hunter.
> His bow-string drawn taut, he let fly his swift arrow.
> With poisoned delight, as his shaft found its target,
> He dreamt of his love, pale breast heaving,
> Bleeding on silk, faithless arms round her lover,
> Twice pierced.

'That sounds more to me like a red poem,' I said, a little ungraciously. Raju ignored my remark and picked up another violet sheet. 'Listen, please.'

> Do not think that behind your fluttering ivory fan,
> Beneath your saffron and sandal paste, your swishing silks
> And your bangles clucking at me like pigeons,
> I cannot see your breasts like bowls of beaten gold,
> Your eager, amber thighs, nor hear your lilting cries,
> Nor smell your stickiness, nor that I don't yearn
> To nudge your fan aside and make my trembling way
> Inside your soft frenzy.

'Oh, certainly more red than blue, that one,' I said.

'Of course, to appreciate my poems you really have to be familiar with Sanskrit poetry. Are you?'

'Not familiar, no.'

'Haven't you even read *The Bhagavadgita?*'

'No, I'm afraid I haven't.'

'A pity. I have read the Bible.'

'Did you enjoy it?'

'Parts of it are very good.' It was on the tip of my tongue to ask which parts, because the answer is always so revealing: the moment of betrayal, Calvary, the raising of Lazarus, the pool at Bethesda – it's very telling. But I thought better of it and fiddled with the sugar. Then he talked a little about Mysore, which he missed, and I remembered sitting at night once in the sweet, fetid air in a square in Mysore, drinking syrupy tea in the inky blackness and listening to water trickling from a tap in the wall behind me and bats squeaking querulously in the gigantic banyan filling the square.

Gook-gook, something kept calling from the labyrinth of branches overhead, *gook-gook, gook-gook*. Whitish figures moved about in the darkness, bicycle bells rang, a radio crackled quietly. I could have sat there till dawn.

'Did you like Mysore?' Raju asked.

'Yes, I did. It had a special kind of atmosphere.' I couldn't think how to explain what it was about Mysore that had cast a particular spell on me. 'In its way,' I said, still playing with the sugar, 'I found it quite erotic. Do you know what I mean?'

'Erotic? Sexy?'

'No, not really. Almost the opposite.'

Raju looked surprised. 'What is the difference?'

'Well, the erotic, it seems to me, is always at one remove. Or two removes or even three.'

'From what?'

'Well, I suppose from the sexual act. Like dancing or hands or a certain way of talking. Or smoking a cigarette.'

Raju was quite unfazed. 'But perhaps the sexual act is also at one remove – or two or three – from something else?'

'From what?'

'For the answer to that,' he said, smoke trickling from his nostrils, 'you'd need to hear more of my poetry.'

'The red?'

'Red or violet.'

On my way back to the hotel through the late-night Zurich streets with their quiet trams and purring cars and softly lit windows, I stopped outside a stationer's shop. Ever since childhood stationers' shops have filled me with warm feelings. I often wander in just to smell the dry, papery smells, pick up pads and notebooks and eye the graded rows of inks. People's lives are poured out onto all this, new beginnings in the air. This shop glowed. It gleamed. From the exquisitely sharpened pencils and leather-bound diaries in the window to the trays of coloured cardboard and reams of snowy paper at the back, every inch of this shop spoke of ordered prosperity and well-oiled wheels, of lives lived comfortably, timetables observed and slender gold nibs pressing into thick bond. It attracted me, but not seriously. Something was missing. It looked embalmed, no pulse. Then all of a sudden a drunk lurched into me – quite well-dressed, moustachio'd – mumbled something and sat down heavily. And I thought of something Raju had said back in the coffee-house, while lecturing me on the evils of meat-eating and 'wine-bibbing', as he called it: 'Where is their passion?' And here he'd embraced the whole of Switzerland in a sweeping gesture around the room. 'Instead of passion they get drunk and even crow about it. They only have passion for banknotes, and even that's not passion, it's lust.' He himself, of course, some might say, was in Zurich for the money. Still, remembering his words, I felt I knew what was missing from the stationer's shop. And I began to feel that it would very shortly be time to head further south.

Speaking of which, Professor Eschenbaum* was

oddly distracted at breakfast this morning, I thought, his colour rather hectic and his movements strangely untethered (if that's the right word) – he's usually so composed. Of course, his luggage is still missing, which must be terribly unsettling, and he grumbles about it constantly. All the same, he had a full programme mapped out for himself for the day: the Ghetto, which was apparently the first ghetto in Europe – sealed off at dusk, the drawbridges closed, the gates locked from the outside, even the windows shut – 'the original pro- phylactic space', the Professor called it; then the Doges' Palace – he has a particular interest in the prison cells called the Leads on the far side of the Bridge of Sighs, the ones Casanova miraculously escaped from – he seems very knowledgeable about the Casanova legend; and, finally, the Tintorettos at the Scuola di San Rocco. I had to admit I had no real plans for the day at all. I could see he thought this was some kind of moral fail- ing in me. I was tempted to try to explain why I've lost interest in schedules and itineraries, but I didn't feel we'd really reached the level of intimacy where I could say the things I'd need to say. It's been very noticeable, though: now that time seems severely lim- ited, I've lost interest in ticking things off, in accumulating credit, in 'laying up treasures' of any kind. Funnily enough, I'd have thought the opposite. But no, time now is for beguiling, not for spending profitably.

Venice, 3rd April

I WAS IN that small local train that chugs up the valley from Locarno to Intragna, such a dour,
stony-looking valley after the lushness of the lakeside
at Locarno – the palms, the magnolias, the myrtles and
gardenias, the damp, warm air. I'd decided to go and
see Patricia Highsmith* who lives at Tegna, hardly a
quarter of an hour up the line. I thought she might
have interesting things to say about death, having
described it from every conceivable angle. Sitting
opposite me was a smartly dressed woman in her six-
ties or seventies with soft, grey hair and a red and white
silk scarf at her throat. I hardly glanced at her, to tell
the truth, Switzerland being full of reserved, smartly
attired older women, as you know. I did notice her take
a copy of Highsmith's *Little Tales of Misogyny* out of her
bag, but that kind of coincidence dots all my days, especially when I travel, and I gave it little thought. Then
the bizarrest thing caught my eye: pinned to the lapel
of her well-cut white linen jacket was a tiny gold

brooch. It struck me as rather Indian in its design and I looked across at it more carefully: it was a hugely endowed male copulating with a large-limbed female, all in exquisitely fine detail – every bead in the bracelets, every toe picked out. It was glinting in the sun.

'*Lei sta guardando il mio amuleto,*' she said with a smile. '*E bello, vero?*'

'Very striking,' I said. 'Is it Indian?'

'Almost certainly, but possibly not,' she said, still smiling in an undisturbed, amused sort of way. 'It belonged to *la baronessa*, so it's hard to say exactly.'

'Which baroness would that be?' I asked, still startled by the refined obscenity of the amulet adorning the ladylike, not to say prim figure seated opposite me.

She laughed. 'Which baroness? You can't have been here very long. Here there is only one *baronessa*.' For a moment she studied me and seemed disinclined to go on. 'Haven't you heard of the Baroness de St Léger?'

I said no, I hadn't.

'She lived on the Brissago Islands near Ascona. Haven't you been there yet? Paradise. And she created it all herself. You should go.'

I agreed, paradise being something that interests me.

'She was the daughter of a czar, you know. Or so they say.'

'What czar?' I asked.

'A Russian czar, naturally. Alexander II, to be precise.'

'It sounds unlikely.'

'Everything about the Baroness was unlikely. Do you

believe in ghosts, for example? On the night before Christmas every year she duelled with her husbands' ghosts – she had many husbands, you see, not all of them dead, but enough to make it a long-drawn-out evening. One was Albanian.'

'You speak wonderful English.'

'I *am* English.'

'How did you come by the amulet?'

'Oh, that's a very long story,' she said, smiling her well-bred smile again. We were beginning to slow down and she peered out the window. 'Ponte Brolla. This is my station.' She stood and turned to me. 'Do go to the islands. I really do think you should. It's the kind of place you should definitely see before you die.' And, very lightly, she was gone. What a peculiar thing to say – 'before you die'. But perhaps she'd meant nothing by it at all – just the usual flippant aside about needing to see this or that in order to have a sense of a complete life. But for some months now I'd felt free of any need to live out a complete life, I hardly knew what it meant any more, so perhaps I was just unprepared.

I stared at the granite cliffs rickety-racketing past. Tegna was the next stop. There was a ruined Celtic fortress up there amongst the gorges somewhere, I knew, and an old Roman bridge or two as well. It was up here somewhere not all that long ago that a mother had stabbed her son to death for not going to Mass. 'I'd rather see him dead than miss Mass,' she'd said. It looked a bit like that kind of place.

There's a wonderful moment of unreality, don't you

think, when you step off a train at an unknown station far from anywhere and the train clatters off round a bend into silence and you're left standing there, momentarily without a self. And then the sound of a motorbike or a bird or a car door slamming reaches you and you remember why you're there and compose yourself and walk towards the next thing. The next thing in Tegna was odd. 'Be under the clock in the main square at one,' Patricia Highsmith had said to me on the telephone in a kind of diffident drawl. And so I was. It was a small, unremarkable, greyish square, empty at that time in the afternoon except for the odd patron of the café on one corner.

The clock in the stumpy *campanile* above me chimed one. Nobody. The square was dead. Then after a few minutes I noticed a woman's head sticking out around the corner of a wall at one end of the square, staring at me. It vanished for a second and then the woman it belonged to reappeared and ducked into the post-office a few metres away. I hoped I hadn't proved a disappointment. I decided to waylay her at the post-office door.

I must have passed whatever test it was Patricia Highsmith was applying to me because I was quickly bundled into a small Volkswagen Beetle and we lurched off in the direction of her house just outside the village. As we got up speed she began to drive more and more erratically, careering around corners on the wrong side of the road and bouncing across a level-crossing without looking for trains. In fact, most of the time she seemed to have her quizzical eye on me. 'The locals drive like maniacs, of course,' she said to me, glaring at a small red van puttering up the hill towards us. 'It'll be a miracle if I'm not wiped off the road one day before I get home.' And she chuckled.

It was an oddly suburban sort of house in concrete brick, not at all the sort of house I'd thought Patricia Highsmith would choose to live in. It had nothing of the tasteful charm, for instance, of Tom Ripley's 'Belle Ombre' about it, although she must have been much wealthier than she'd made Ripley out to be.* Then again, her novels are often very suburban (in a sense), cluttered with the details of ordinary lives in ordinary settings. And she herself – what was my mother's phrase? – did not take much trouble with herself. Long, grey-brown hair, a brownish cardigan – the boutiques and salons of Locarno were clearly not her stamping-ground. Owlish is the word that comes to mind, perhaps because of the slightly hooded eyes. You never know what an owl has in mind until the very last moment.

In fact, we talked about the flatness in her novels for a little while, the piling up of humdrum detail, the sense of an eye, neither malevolent nor benevolent, registering *everything*. I recalled Ripley's banal telephone conversations with his wife, his lengthy travel arrangements when he was going to Morocco or Germany, the banalities of his postcards home ('and the forsythia needs watering *now*') – in short, the everydayness of her characters' lives.

'Well, I can only hope it isn't tedious to read,' she

said, her eyes fixed on me from the sofa. 'I think it builds up the character into a human being. I'm trying to make the character more real. Ripley knows it's absurd – writing about watering the forsythia and so on – but he just feels like writing it, so he does. But there's an *undertow*, I suppose you could say.'

I'm taken with the word 'undertow'. It describes exactly not only the way Highsmith's drifters drift into murder and revenge against their better judgment, almost innocently, but also how underneath our own everyday lives – the shopping and squabbles and weeding and trips to the vet – there's a sense of being dragged slowly off, not against our will but regardless of it. And fighting the undertow, as children are quick to learn, is not usually the best way of getting back to the beach. Floating along with it, on the other hand, can be fatal.

It's really the struggle, the argument with oneself, that interests this woman, which is why she's so drawn to Dostoevsky, and to *Crime and Punishment* in particular. 'I'm not at all interested in mysteries,' she said, 'or puzzles – books you read to see how clever you are. That doesn't happen to interest me at all.'

'I thought you liked Ruth Rendell, though.'

'I've read a couple of hers, yes. They were quite good.'

And now the telephone starts to ring in an adjoining room. It's almost always like this. When you're desired the way people like Patricia Highsmith are – or Vikram Seth or Paul Auster or George Steiner or Mario Vargas Llosa – someone is forever at you to agree to something, consider something, go somewhere.

Vikram Seth is by far the most entertaining in these exchanges. 'But I don't want to go to Frankfurt,' Patricia Highsmith is saying with a kind of drawling indifference. 'Why should I go? I don't like Frankfurt, I don't like book fairs . . . Well, that's just too bad.'

Ironically, Highsmith's life is not unlike the kind of life her Ripley began murdering for. Not as stylish, of course, but *civilized* in a way that attracted Ripley: the quick trips to Paris and London, the sculptures and paintings in the living-room (although Ripley was inclined to prefer the forged to the genuine), the tranquil *bienséance* just outside a busy, chic resort and the financial security, to put no finer point on it. There is even a hint of Ripley's sexual neutrality in Highsmith's plain manner, as well as of his mellow disconnectedness from other people's feelings. Actually, disconnectedness is not quite the right word. I find myself coming back to owlishness.

The handsome, amoral Ripley was greedy for the good life (for himself), whereas it seems to have landed in Patricia Highsmith's lap. For some reason this uncharismatic woman from Fort Worth, Texas, began talking at just the right moment about things a post-Christian world was fascinated by in a language it revelled in: questions of good and evil, guilt and innocence and moral action in a godless universe. 'Yes, it was greed and selfishness that made him murder Dickie Greenleaf as a young man,' Highsmith said. 'He envies Dickie's idle, wealthy lifestyle . . . he's impressed by what he sees as elegance, the right way of doing things, the nice clothes, the good leather suitcases, the money to enjoy leisure.' Once he's bludgeoned him to death in San Remo, however, and gets the leather suit-cases, the money and the nice clothes, he's caught in the undertow of more violence and lies – indeed, lying surfaces. Yet a civilized life is a matter of depth, surely, not surfaces. Otherwise it's just civility, expensive man-ners. We love all this in the late twentieth century.

We talked on for a while about this and that – her brilliant erotic writing in *Carol*, for example, something she'd found difficult – about religion, publishing, adop-tion, all sorts of things, but not about death. Death is just an event in other people's lives in her books. Highsmith is interested in guilt, not death, and the question of what sort of conscience finds everything permissible. For Ripley, after all, going shopping, water-ing the garden and killing all have much the same moral weight. No guilt or blame attaches to Ripley, and not much praise, either.

I got back to Locarno a little shaken and not just by the hair-raising dash to the station in the Volkswagen Beetle. *She* had rattled me, although I don't think she'd meant to. It was chilly down by the lake, but I went for a long walk along the shore in the dusk all the same, to let my thoughts settle. At first, starting at the wharf, you walk through landscaped gardens, then through a little quarter of walled villas, as silent as the grave, and then you find yourself on a tree-lined path with the lake lapping on the pebbles on your right and a line of old mansions in dank gardens on your left. The odd jogger, a dog or two, but apart from that

nobody. Then, just as it became dark, I came to the
gates of the Ca' di Ferro, a long, low, white building
with a large square stone tower at one end and a dainty
yellow chapel at the other. I was intrigued. A plaque
at the locked gates said it had been the barracks of a
captain from the canton of Uri (on the northern side
of the St Gotthard Pass). Apparently this was where he
quartered his men, all mercenaries ready to slaughter
for whoever could pay the right price. I could hear
raucous voices coming from the lighted first-floor
windows. They were shouting in English. Well-fed,
powerful voices. I leaned against the PRIVATE PROP-
ERTY sign for a few moments in the dark, staring at
the brightly lit, barred windows, then turned and wandered back the way I'd come.

Once it's dark in Locarno the massive, tawny flanks
of the mountains across the lake light up with thousands, tens of thousands of tiny lights, some of them
impossibly high up in the wilderness of escarpments
and snow-streaked ravines near the peaks. That night
they excited me, I think because of the sense of thousands of unthought-of possibilities hiding everywhere
in amongst the barrenness and the banality. Of course,
thinking like this about the lights was partly a way of
arming myself against the coming night, as is writing
these letters.

During those first days back in September I woke night
after night from chilling dreams about banging around

in a forest of hanged corpses. I'd stagger to my feet and walk in circles, wringing my hands. (People really do wring their hands.) I don't do that any more, but I do wake up feeling desperate to be companioned, to feel present with someone kind. Otherwise, in the night, any passing phantom can sink its teeth into your throat. In fact, I've been growing suspicious of the word 'solitude'. It's such an elegant word, so Latinate, it sounds somehow so elevated, but it seems to me to require a certain level of economic independence and social status to work. Otherwise it's called loneliness, abandonment or desertion. Perhaps it's a matter of balance. A few hours a week of solitude is enough for me, preferably during the day.

Venice, 4th April

PROFESSOR ESCHENBAUM came to breakfast this morning
with a crew-cut – all the grey bushiness has gone. I was
taken aback, but I must say it rather suits him. It highlights his splendid sunken eyes and even manages to
make him look a little more tautly *phallic* than he used
to. He's a cultural historian (or something like that),
so I expect he knows what he's doing. Emilio said something to him about it in Italian, which I couldn't catch,
but I could tell the Professor was pleased. He said he'd
been to the Vivaldi concert last night, the one at the
Scuola Grande di S. Giovanni Evangelista – a magnificent baroque hall with Tintorettos all over the ceiling
and walls. Vivaldi himself played in this very hall, as a
matter of fact. I was about to say that I'd been at the
concert myself and hadn't seen him in the audience,
but I am after all rather short-sighted, and he does look
very different with his severe crew-cut, and I didn't
want to sound as if I was trying to catch him out. So
I didn't mention it. He was actually off to Giudecca

Island this morning on the *vaporetto* to see the exhibition of medieval torture instruments. It's a wonderful day for it – glass-and-stone, hard-edged, transparent. There are racks, garottes, jaw-crushers, even an Iron Maiden, according to the hellish posters for it stuck up all over Venice.

Locarno, as you'll have gathered, was almost paradise. Not exactly Eden – at least, not innocent – nor the Holy City on the Hill ahead, but an earthly, human paradise, like the garden at the very top of Dante's Mount of Purgatory – Heaven's vestibule, so to speak, rather than the thing itself.* A little contrived, perhaps, as is Dante's: its sparkling streams run between municipally grassed banks, its leafy boughs are pruned and shaped, its sleek denizens a little too smug in their blessedness.

It comes upon you suddenly, too, when you take the train from Zurich: one moment you're in the North, with its doleful, tired cities and tamed farmlands, you slide through the fog into the St Gotthard tunnel, and when you emerge into the light on the other side you're in the South. It's like waking up on the other side of the looking-glass – you're still in Switzerland but everything has changed. You rattle off down a rocky gully towards the lakes, towards Italy, and you can *feel* yourself entering, not just a different latitude, but a different world with different coordinates. To the east now is the Ganges, not the Urals, and to the west the Gates of Hercules, not the Liverpool docks. And even the breezes (perhaps it's just your imagination) now seem to be laden with faint memories of Sicily and the Barbary Coast. Just before the point where the Italian frontier crosses Lake Maggiore, you find yourself winding along the lakeshore amongst old walled gardens, churches and villas and then you're pulling into Locarno.

It's overwhelmingly beautiful. Almost crushingly. I walked with my suitcase down the hill from the station to the lakeside, sat on the wall and gazed across the water at the honeycomb of minute houses (cream, pink, egg-yolk, even blue) clustered on the opposite shore where the mountains fall into the lake. Perhaps it was just the sun or the magnolia blossoms or the smell of warm soil again, but, whatever the reason, I felt I'd settled back into my body – not an entirely comfortable feeling in my case. I noticed appetite was on the boil again. In fact, I'm sure it's there they shoot those cigarette commercials where the ski-plane lands beneath the *palazzo* on the point – little hymns to appetite, to quenching it and then quenching it again.

One of the reasons, it struck me, that beauty on this scale can cause a kind of angst or ache is that it reminds you that your everyday expectations of life have been too narrow, too colourless. So, even while you're drinking in the abundant beauty, you feel a pang not unlike grief. I do, anyway, and I don't think I'm the only one.

But Locarno isn't paradise simply because it's beautiful. After all, the world is full of beautiful places. It's paradise because of the balance: in Locarno the North and the South meet and neither has quite yet got the upper hand because, for a few miles between the St Gotthard Pass and the Italian border, you're miraculously in both Switzerland and Italy at once. Here civilization seems tempered by Eros and Eros in turn is tautened and braced by contact with the Northern enemy. In other words, Arcadia with Swiss plumbing. (Speaking of which, I took a room at the Hotel Geranio, just opposite the spot where I sat on the lake wall – not a single geranium to be seen on the premises, of course. I suppose they think the name is evocative enough.)

At Monte Verità, just a mile or two away up on the hill behind Ascona, they used to describe this marrying of reason and deep feelings more poetically: 'Here oak and camellia come together – lime and mimosa, birch and olive.' Have you ever heard of Monte Verità? Probably not, yet this little wooded hill was a kind of psychic ganglion at the beginning of the century. People streamed to it from all over the world: Frieda Lawrence, D.H. himself, Hermann Hesse, Isadora Duncan, H.G. Wells, Jawlenski – not many other painters, as it happens, but hordes of writers, musicians, dancers, healers, mystics, seers, cranks and geniuses. Kafka was fascinated, Jung enthralled. Suddenly, on the second morning, after days of feeling a tourist, I decided to spend the day just nosing about and wandered up the hill to what was left of the old settlement on Monte Verità. Basically all that remains now is the museum in the old Casa Anatta (meaning 'Soul', of course – Hinduism was much in vogue here in the early decades of the century). For twenty years or so here they piped and danced naked in the moonlight, they drank herbs and underwent earth-cures, they devised phonetic spelling systems, they writhed and leapt and swirled to the beat of primitive drums, they worshipped the sun and voided the self and sang songs to the Great Mother. They let their sensual desires (although not the desire for roast beef or crispy pork, being rigidly vegetarian) bubble up freely and then indulged them with joy. They thumbed their noses at Father and danced around Mother. This was the Land of Cockaigne.*

It's all gone into the dustbin, of course. No one remembers. Civilized society won in the end. There are echoes of Monte Verità still in modern dance (so I'm told), and, of course, in the novels we still read from the beginning of the century. In fact, some would say the aesthetics of the Third Reich were influenced by Monte Verità in a distorted kind of way – the nature-worship, the cult of the body, folk-wisdom turned into the wisdom of the *Volk*. By and large, though, it's all blown away into nothingness. It was still quite wintry up amongst the firtrees the morning I was there – almost eerie, all rust-brown and black, no sound but the crunching of dead leaves. Down the hill in Ascona civilization was humming along quite nicely in the sun: smartly dressed families from Heidelberg and Munich were strolling along the quayside in flocks, setting out on scheduled launch-trips around the lake, consuming mass-produced food in chic cafés and swallowing powders and pills expensively packaged in factories further north. Down there the happiness industry was in full swing. In Ascona there's still even a functioning Christian church or two, anathema to the sun-worshippers on Monte Verità: the only aspect of Christianity they felt kindly towards was the local cult of the Virgin Mary, which they saw as a dim reflection of their own reverence for the Great Mother. On the whole, in other words, down the hill in Ascona both body and soul were still locked (by Father) in an iron cage and nature was still kept at bay – stared at through glass, perhaps, or the lens of a camera, but largely screened out.

I went into the creaking Casa Anatta (with its revolutionary flat roof or *Flachdach*) and began poking about amongst the old photographs on the walls: dancing truth-seekers, visitors from India, ritualized performances in flowing Grecian robes bringing to mind that ghastly play about the World Spirit in Act One of *The Seagull*. I was standing examining a map on the wall which showed that certain important magnetic fields meet right under Locarno (which is why, according to the misspelt label, the Locarno Pact, ushering in a new era of international peace and understanding, found itself being signed in Locarno rather than Gothenberg, say, or High Wycombe) when I heard a voice just behind me say: 'I wondered if you might turn up here.' I swivelled around and saw the small, gold amulet glinting at me in the half-dark. It was my English friend from the train.

Rachel Berg spent a morning a week, she told me,

helping out at the museum – talking to the visitors (in any of several languages), selling brochures, even dusting and sweeping sometimes, she was one of a team. Yet, with her expensive clothes, her fine-boned face and severe helmet of greying hair, she didn't really seem to belong to the slightly daft world of vagabond soul-dancers and psychic healers I was learning about. 'And are you, were you' – how should I put this? – 'are you interested in the ideas behind Monte Verità?' I asked. 'Theosophy and so on?'

'Theosophy and so on!' She laughed in an abrupt, English kind of way. 'I'm curious about many things, let's say, hopelessly curious,' she said after a pause. 'But no, it's not so much the philosophy that draws me, it's more the fact that my mother lived here during the First World War. A lot of English people, especially women, drifted in and out of Monte Verità in those years, you know, looking for . . . well, what *were* they looking for? Renewal of the spirit, I suppose you might say, some alternative to the culture of war and technology, all the things they felt were deadening the spirit. And the women, of course, were looking for somewhere . . .' She looked away for a moment, as if about to choose her words very carefully. 'The women were looking for a place where they could live more instinctively as women. In those days, you might remember, women usually had to choose between being sly and being servile – perhaps most women still do. Not here in Switzerland as a rule, I dare say, although there are villages just a few miles from this house where in that regard little has changed in a thousand years. But I'm making it all sound rather dreary, aren't I? And actually it was all sorts of things but never that. I think at Monte Verità they really believed they'd rediscovered paradise.'

By about 1920 it was apparently all over. Freud may have been right when he said that civilization was built upon 'renunciation of instinct' but the upshot of indulging instinct on the hill behind Ascona was jealousy, chaos and incredibly tangled blood-lines. Rachel's father, I gathered, was a German photographer who blew in for a month or two one summer and never left, although there were apparently other wispier father-figures in the wings (herbalists and dance-instructors, and, as I remember, a dashingly handsome Anglo-Indian from Dehra Dun who was translating the *Bhagavadgita* into modern English, or perhaps it was German). Rachel stayed with her mother, though, and when the community broke up moved back to England. She'd only come back to Locarno to live as a widow after the Second World War. I'm hazy about the details now – indeed, there weren't many.

My eye during the storytelling was mostly on the contorted gold amulet. It intrigued me. It seemed to depict a chubby female figure, with upturned face and minutely beaded anklets, acrobatically entwined with an eager male figure, grasping his jutting penis. 'Tell me more about the baroness you mentioned yesterday,' I said. 'How did she fit in?'

'She didn't, really. She almost never came here. This

wasn't her idea of paradise at all. She was too fond of what civilization had to offer. But you're wondering about my *amuleto*, aren't you? Where it comes from and why I wear it. It's very precious to me and it has a . . . well, a long story behind it.' She glanced down at it briefly and then asked me with a confident smile if it was a story I'd like to hear. I said it was.

'And have you been to the Brissago Islands yet? Do you remember? I told you I thought you should see them.' I said I hadn't yet, but did mean to.

'Then why don't we meet there tomorrow morning? And I'll tell you the story of the baroness and the amulet. Why not hear the story where it happened?' And so we agreed to meet in what she called the Herb Garden on the Isola Grande at eleven o'clock. 'You cross the island from the wharf, past all the stands of bamboo, the banana palms and a lot of Himalayan-looking plants, and you'll see it poking out into the lake. It's a tiny walled garden with a lovely square pond right in the middle of it, just the place to sit if it's sunny. And I've got a feeling it will be.' And it was, of course. It almost always is in paradise.

Speaking of which, Professor Eschenbaum says I absolutely must go and see the torture exhibition in the old church on Giudecca Island. He's terribly intrigued by the fact that Giudecca is actually the name of a region of Lower Hell – he thinks it's a great joke. If I'd ever known, I'd forgotten. 'It's where souls are punished for the Sins of the Leopard,' he said with a kind of fastidious relish, leaving me none the wiser.

'Sins of appetite committed with evil intent. Utter rubbish, of course, but as a symbolic structure . . . *sehr nett,
sehr pikant.*' I've just had coffee with him downstairs in
the bar, served with sullen grace by Emilio, who has
one of those astonishing Venetian faces – pale, refined,
drawn, pained. Almost like a mask, I said to the
Professor. Yes, he said, and it will drop off just as suddenly at the age of about twenty-six, if not earlier. He
seemed very frisky. He was actually wearing an *Istrumenti
di tortura* T-shirt – I've never seen him out of a silk tie
before, even at breakfast – emblazoned with whips and
a gruesome spike for impalement. 'You must see it to
remind you of how far we've come,' he said in that
slightly fussy way he has, 'of how unimaginably cruel
human beings were to each other not so long ago. And
why were they so eager to invent ever new ways of
inflicting excruciating pain on each other? What were
all these lead-tipped whips and spikes and spine-
crushers and racks and wheels for? For keeping power
where it was, for stopping change, for locking everyone and everything into place, forever.' I thought of
things I could say in reply, but sensed this was a performance rather than an exchange and so said very
little. Besides, I fancied his audience was perhaps more
Emilio than myself, although as far as I could gather
Emilio had no more than five or six words of English.
I stood up to go. 'Have you read Dante's *Inferno*?' he
asked, clearly still engrossed in thoughts of sin and
punishment. 'No? You should. Hogwash, of course,
from start to finish, philosophically speaking. And the

man was obviously a paranoid obsessive – all that Beatrice business, for example, the man was ill – but as a treatise on the Christian idea of free-will, as well as the suitable punishments for exercising it wrongly, it is quite fascinating.' I hadn't much enjoyed *Purgatory*, but agreed I should perhaps begin at the beginning. I said I'd look out for a good modern translation.

I'm now up in my room, listening to the *vaporetto* motors roaring, their hulls grinding up against the wharf-posts, the knots of tourists talking and laughing as they stroll home after dinner. And I can hear a piano high up in the house across the laneway – someone's playing Chopin (I think it is), it sounds like a nocturne, over and over again. I went over to the window to see where it was coming from and caught sight of the Professor slipping out on one of his midnight walks in the direction of the station. I taught him the word 'constitutional' tonight and he was extremely pleased with it.

Venice, 5th April

YOU CAN ALMOST SPIT into Italy from the southern tip of the Isola Grande. That's why for centuries there was always a nest or two of smugglers on these islands. And nuns as well, apparently. The Lombard Order of the Umiliate had a cloister here in the Middle Ages, until thrown out by a saint for degeneracy and a love of luxury.* Seclusion, obviously, even with a window to a wider world, is no proof against 'the vicious streak' (I mean the viper lurking in the undergrowth). After all, as some Jesuit once sourly remarked, the Terrestrial Paradise was not so much exempt from sin as the place where sin began. He was inveighing, I think, against an immoderate passion in Italy for grand gardens.

Rachel was waiting for me as she'd promised in the Herb Garden on a stone bench in the sun, swathed in blue wool. It's a small island (although the bigger of the two) and it hadn't taken me more than a few min-utes to find my way across it, up past the rather grand pink and grey Renaissance pavilion on the knoll and then down through the rhododendrons, the Burmese palms and figs to the walled garden jutting into the lake on the opposite side, just as she'd described. I'd paused to watch the pheasants picking amongst the shrubbery, their gold and black hoods sliding up and down against the teal and red of their necks. It all seemed flawlessly beautiful. I half expected to see moon-faced houris in blue silk flitting amongst the palms and roses.

The Herb Garden, a sunny *hortus conclusus* with stepped pool, rectangular beds and small ivy-draped openings onto the lake outside, was nothing less than Koranic. It was the raised garden within The Garden, the lush, shaded and well-watered garden of the Isola Grande. The Arabs, I expect, had their own good reasons for picturing Paradise as a walled domain of pomegranates and orange-trees, hyacinths and honey-suckle, crossed by rivers of milk, honey, water and (yes) wine. I don't live in a desert, but something about the Islamic vision appeals to me very strongly. On reflection, I don't think it's the date palms and roses that draw me so much, or the silver combs and burps smelling of musk, or the absence of children and semen, or even the presence of handsome serving youths (of whom there are several in the pavilion on the knoll, as it happens). No, it has more to do, I think, with the vision of interlocking enclosures, the cloistered, secluded design the Muslim vision entails – the *firdaus* or *djanna*, as Arabs call Paradise, is after all a *walled* garden. But what is it I want to keep out? Might it in my case be the city?

Yesterday, by the way (and this is *à propos*), I happened

to see Tintoretto's terrifying vision of Paradise in the Doges' Palace here in Venice. Supposedly the largest oil-painting in the world, it covers a whole wall behind the rostrum in the Great Council Hall. The righteous in Tintoretto's version are trapped inside what looks like the umpteenth rehearsal for an underfunded block-buster musical, with a herd of joyless, sexless, anxious little supernumeraries stampeding towards the two badly dressed stars – no props, appalling lighting, come-as-you-were costumes. Who on earth could desire this? And my mind went back to the Viana Palace* in Córdoba. (I love Córdoba – I'm one of those who secretly regret the Moors were ever thrown out of Spain.) There you wander in and out of the white-walled villa through a succession of courtyards, each one a gentle surprise: the aristocratic, arched Reception Courtyard (night-blooming jasmine, musk-rose and bougainvillaea climbing up the pillars); the tranquil Chapel Courtyard (for meditating under the Seville orange-trees); the many-cornered Well Courtyard with its Moorish water-buckets, watered by an underground stream; the Maze Courtyard with its circular fountain at the centre of the maze and its fragrant border of roses and arums; the Lady's Courtyard with its ring of cypresses and espaliered lemons; there's even a Courtyard of the Cats, its high walls adorned with dozens of pots of red and orange geraniums ... thirteen courtyards and gardens in all, going off at odd angles from each other, higher, lower, inside, outside, the gateways softened with Chinese wisteria, bergamot and climbing roses. But the best of all is the Grille Courtyard: here you can stand beside the pink marble fountain, as the marquises and their guests used to do in earlier times, and look out through wrought-iron grilles to the dirty jumble of concrete and brick beyond – the city. This was all infinitely more desirable to me than Tintoretto's vision. Yet even here an hour is quite enough.

Well, we may have had no silken cushions to sit on in our Herb Garden that morning, but we were both conscious, I think, Rachel and I, of how close to perfection our hidden meeting-place was. She began to tell me her story almost immediately. One of the advantages of being Australian is that you are a kind of blank to other people, I usually find, and so of little interest to them until they have written on you. I've never felt any hostility towards me on account of where I come from, just a refreshing absence of any idea of what it might mean and an indifference towards finding out. I did once meet a postmistress in Cornwall, I must say, who was mildly interested in Australia because she had a son living 'out there', but even she could find no hook to hang a conversation on. I rather hope we can keep it that way.

So Rachel began writing on me.

The Story of Antonietta,
Baroness de St Léger,
and the Golden Amulet

Long ago in a city in southern India – centuries ago, when this island was little more than a bramble-covered rock, ringed by squalid fishing villages, remote from the squabbles of dukes and popes and emperors – long, long ago not far from Mysore, right down near the very tip of India, a prince fell in love with an enchanting princess from a neighbouring court.

Now, the prince had been born ill-starred and ugly. His legs were bandy, his skin was too pale, his cheeks were pitted and, to boot, he lisped – just slightly, but distinctly, and the flaw gave rise to mocking smiles. In his favour he had a heart of softest gold. How could he win the attention, not to speak of the affections, of the princess he'd seen dallying with his sisters by the palace pond?

He thought first of archery. He was an excellent archer. Yet, however unerringly his arrows found their mark at tournaments and on royal hunts, the princess never seemed to be amongst the throng of spectators. He would search for her face amongst the crowd but never find it. He thought of guile as well. He thought of begging his sisters to suggest to the princess she spend a day and a night with them at the palace as their guest. But when all was said and done, he didn't trust them and feared their jibes.

Then he hit upon a plan. He would send her a token of his feelings, with despatch and in utmost secrecy. He had in mind no gaudy trinket – no common necklace strung from Coromandel pearls or anklet studded with Golconda diamonds – but the very impress, eloquent and graceful, of his longing. That night he dressed himself in simple merchant's garb, slipped out of the palace by a garden gate and made his way into the lanes where the city's silversmiths and goldsmiths lived. There by the light of a single oil-lamp, swearing him to secrecy, he struck a deal with the most skilful craftsman in the city. Using only the most lustrous gold, the old man would fashion a mithuna in exquisite detail – a Loving Couple, symbol of the Self that once was one and, from desiring, now was two, desiring oneness. In those far-off times in that far-off place this kind of message was as plain as the moon in a cloudless sky.

Seven nights later the prince went back to the goldsmith's shop, dressed in the same merchant's garb, and was astounded by the beauty of the amulet, glowing in the amber light of the oil-lamp. He rewarded the goldsmith handsomely, gave him a small camphor-wood box and told him to take the amulet in the box to the princess in the neighbouring city and tell her nothing but his name.

And so the very next morning the goldsmith set out on foot for the palace a day's journey away. What happened next is in dispute: some say he was waylaid by bandits and robbed of the amulet, some say he sold it to some merchants from the Malabar Coast, and some even say that as he lay admiring it by a stream a thieving raven flew off with it. The goldsmith wisely said nothing. The prince waited in vain for word from the princess, for some sign his arrow had found its mark. Receiving none, he began to pine, soon sickened and slowly faded away. The goldsmith, for his part, was struck blind all of a sudden, sat on a yellow scorpion and died.

Now, some years later a Jewish merchant on the Malabar Coast named Yehudi took up his pen and added the mithuna amulet to the list of goods he was sending to his brother in Yemen. The cargo of finest buckram, ginger, cinnamon and pearls arrived on the winter monsoon, eluding the swarms of corsairs, although Yehudi himself by then was long dead, bitten on the hand by a yellow-eyed viper nestling in a bale of cotton. The Yemenite brother, Abraham, knew of a number of wealthy men in the city who would take pleasure in the Loving Couple, but the matter was a delicate one at that time, given the reigning sultan's public piety. So Abraham judged it more prudent to hide away the amulet in its sweet-smelling camphor-wood box inside a stronger juniper box inside a cavity in the wall at the very top of his house in a lane behind the souk, at least until the times were more propitious.

But rumours spread like dammusa lizards in the sun, scurrying through the souk and up the rocky hill to the sultan's palace, which towered blue and white above the city. And the sultan, who was rich beyond all dreaming from the trade in stallions with the East, as well as from plundering caravans, sent a blue-black Abyssinian down into the city to summon the merchant to the palace. Tiring of his wives and catamites, the sultan had spent the winter* sick with lust for a Syrian dancing-girl, yet, dose himself as he might with Chinese herbs, infusions of bark and pastes and potions, and despite astrologers' mutterings and Bedouin spells and magic bangles, his member would not awake. The whisperings he'd heard of the power of the amulet pricked his interest and raised his hopes. Rumours of the sultan's lust and his attempts to whet it had, of course, long ago scuttled like skinks down the hill to the souk, so Abraham went up to the palace in the lively hope of striking a favourable bargain, the camphor box hidden deep in his robes.

The sultan was delighted by the Loving Couple. He examined it in the box, examined it on a silken cushion, examined it in his hand. He liked the ample lifted thigh, the breasts both full and taut, the promise of pleasure in the jutting member. He closed his firm fist on it, warming the gold, and thought about his smooth-limbed Syrian. Yes, there were stirrings, he was sure, he could feel a trickle of warmth seep through his body, a gentle beating slowly growing more fervid. 'I must have this amulet,' he said. But when the merchant tried to bargain with the sultan, he grew extremely angry. 'So you would try to sell me a graven image, a heathen charm?' he roared. 'Only to then boast about your price in the market and to your Jewish friends?' And he called the blue-black Abyssinian and had poor Abraham thrown from the palace wall down into the dry ravine below where jackals prowled at night and vultures hovered in the sun.

Now, the sultan's preparations for his secret night of love were very thorough: tapers filled the air with musk, pomegranates, figs and jujube berries lay piled in silver bowls on tiled tables, crushed ibex horn was sprinkled across the doorways, and two lutes could be heard through the trellis being plucked with subtle mellowness in the courtyard below. From the sultan's neck there hung the Hindu talisman on a silken thread. After sucking on juicy pomegranates and quaffing Persian wine, the couple lay back on the soft divan amongst the cushions, languorously alert and torpidly elated. After some time, when Aisha's lips began to tremble and her breath came sharply, they tried the Ostrich Tail, the Squatting Frog and even Archimedes' Screw, all to no avail. Slithering and flapping like a dying fish, the sultan tried the Fluttering Butterfly, the Wailing Monkey and finally, foolishly, the Galloping Charger. Red in the face, then mauve, then white, he fell back on his cushions wheezing, hiccoughed twice and lay stone dead.

Aisha, being of a practical cast of mind, more a falcon than a silly dove, however she might coo and undulate at certain ordained times, quickly pocketed the amulet, feasted on plums and slices of melon until the candles had burnt low, and then, with a sign to the Abyssinian to leave his master sleeping, she vanished down the hill to the maidan by the Covered Well from where, a few hours before sunrise, the caravans set out for the cities of the north.

The Abyssinian caught her, of course, and slit her with his scimitar from groin to scalp, but not before she'd sold the amulet to a camel-driver bound for Ta`izz and thence for Cairo. He had cheated her shamelessly, as it happened, but as it turned out that mattered very little.

It was not the camel-driver but his son who sold the amulet to a Jew in Cairo. The camel-driver had died of the plague in Mecca, choking on his vomit. The Jew, as Heaven wills these things, was none other than Abraham's and Yehudi's elder brother, Simon, the wiliest of the three, black-bearded, portly, pious, up to his ears in frankincense, nutmeg and gold. He thought of softening his mistress's heart with it, of selling it to some Turk or even a Greek from Alexandria, but at that time trade with Sicily was flourishing. Ever since Roger (the Great Count's son) had set up his kingdom there, ships had been sailing for Palermo heaped with costly goods from the Levant and even further to the East. And Simon's agent there was his nephew Aaron, sharp as a knife and growing richer by the month.

And so, like his brother Yehudi some years before on the distant Malabar Coast, Simon took up his pen and listed the amulet in his consignment to Palermo. And, as had befallen Yehudi, news of its safe arrival (Saracen pirates notwithstanding) never reached him because, on his way to the synagogue of Ben Ezra the following sabbath, he was kicked in the head by a shying horse and his neck was broken. Aaron, however, was well-pleased with the glinting charm and took to carrying it with him in his pocket both in Palermo and on his trips around the island. He would finger it there sometimes, strolling in the Saracen gardens or standing on his terrace above the sea, tracing with a kind of unaccustomed tenderness the sturdy arms and legs and upturned faces. It seemed to promise him something, something almost unbearably sweet, something at the same time faint and vigorous.

A year or so after the amulet came into his possession, Aaron went to Messina, having business in the port there with some Jews from Naples. The cold was wolfish, the town forsaken, so one evening when the winds off the frozen spine of Italy were biting into his very bones, Aaron turned in at a small establishment in a lane near the fish-market, seeking warmth and solace. La Conchiglia, as it was known, was as rosy and snug inside as the conch-shell hanging outside promised. La mammana herself was rosy and plump on her Moorish divan, a dish of sticky confections beside her, although her girls appealed to a diversity of tastes: there was a slender, coal-black Ethiope, a German, solid as a statue (fetching in the candle-glow), a sullen Greek, and a prancing Neapolitan or two with rotten teeth, but Aaron decided on the Turk, who won him over with her ravishing blend of brazenness and modesty. He liked the way she moved across the room, her fat, warm body and a spicy smell. She proved, in fact, a little indolent in her efforts on the grubby couch, but Aaron went out by the sign of the conch-shell feeling not displeased, and in some measure even warmed and soothed. It was only when he was dressing the next morning at his inn to leave for home that he found he was without his amulet. He was, like the far-off (now dead) Indian prince, at something of a loss: he couldn't show he'd ever had the piece with him and couldn't take steps to retrieve it without covering himself in shame. To bargain with la mammana was clearly futile. Although it was still early morning, the amulet would doubtless be by now in very different hands.

So Aaron set out from Messina much dispirited (for home, he thought, but actually for a ravine near the sanctuary of the Black Virgin where bandits cut his throat). Meanwhile, la mammana, noticeably less rosy in the morning light, had sold the Loving Couple to a customer she knew well from Naples, a 'princeling' (as she was fond of calling him) of the Church, an exceedingly learned man, especially in all things Mohammedan – the art, the music and the doctrines as well, which he held up to ridicule in the most scathing and convincing way when roused, which he easily was, even at La Conchiglia and particularly in his cups. A few days later this erudite princeling carried his trophy off to Naples (escaping, by God's grace, the earthquake which that very afternoon flattened the fish-market, the church he'd prayed in and La Conchiglia, crushing the life out of la mammana, the Turk, the Ethiope and the German, but not the Neapolitans who – grazie alla Santa Maria Vergine! – were casting their nets down by the docks out in the open at the time). He was as well-read in the errors of the Hindus as in the heresies of the Mohammedans, having heard tales of the lascivious adornments in their temples along the Ganges (halfway between Jerusalem and the Mount of Purgatory, as he knew) and prized the piece for many years as precious evidence of the foulness in the souls of idol-worshippers, unredeemed and headed for the pit of Hell.

One morning in an excellent temper, as he was passing Egg Castle, which as everyone knows the Angevins (at that time lords of Naples) had taken it into their heads to rebuild (and where Virgil's magic egg lies hidden to this day)*, he clambered up onto a shaky scaffold to get a better view of how the work was proceeding, slipped and tumbled into a vat of pitch. His books and jewels and paintings were seized that very afternoon in an unseemly mêlée in his less than monkish quarters. Men of the cloth and brothers and nieces and one or two ladies of Naples (having hastily thrown on black) all scrambled for mementoes of their revered friend. But no one thought to open up the wall where, in a dusty cavity, one or two objects lay hidden which, in a city distrustful of the Evil Eye and the power of unholy things, even our enlightened prelate judged it wise to keep well out of sight: a hair from the Caliph Ali's head (the husband of Mahomet's daughter), a Persian book of lessons in the art of love and the small, gold amulet from India. And there they all stayed, believe it or not, for nigh on six hundred years.

'And that,' said Rachel, sounding now more her English self, 'is when things started to get quite interesting.'

'But do you believe any of it?' I asked after a moment's silence. 'I mean, the hair from Ali's head, those Jewish brothers, the crushed ibex horn, that mooning prince with bandy legs . . .'

'Believe it?' Rachel looked amused. 'All I've done is tell you the story. I'm not sure I know what it would mean to say I *believed* it or didn't. Do you remember what Kant once said about ghosts?' I didn't, of course, have the faintest idea what Kant had once said about ghosts. 'He said that while he was unconvinced by a single ghost-story, somehow or other he was still convinced by the idea of ghosts as a whole.' I was not sure quite how far this got us.*

'For the next part, though, the Italian part, I think we should sit looking into Italy, don't you?' So we left the Herb Garden and walked around by the avenue of date-palms along the water's edge to a second raised garden, sitting squarely this time on the southernmost point of the Isola Grande, with seats affording a spectacular view down the lake into Italy where the mountains are almost always a soothing milky blue.

Venice, 6th April

IT'S SO EASY to believe in magic here in Venice. When you first see the city from the train it's like a mirage, like a vision of wild splendour some sorcerer has conjured up far out to sea.* But it's magical in less obvious and banal ways, too. Earlier tonight, for example, I went roaming around the lanes and alleys across the Grand Canal from the station, not far from the hotel. You cross that bridge jammed with tourists and pedlars and the Africans selling belts and bags and mechanical pandas and so on, you turn a corner and immediately you're plunged into a maze of stony chasms, echoing to a myriad of tiny sounds – heels clicking, dogs yapping, old men coughing – and at one corner, lost, I stood and listened to a sonata floating down from a window high up in the house across from me, and I looked back the way I'd come and the inky canal I'd been walking beside seemed at that moment to stretch out like a flute-note towards the moon – I was bewitched. By day, of course, it's just a raucous, tawdry sham, like a stage-set when the house-lights come up, but at night it casts a spell on you. You lose your reason.

I have to confess that I was prowling around the darkened alleyways of Venice because I thought, just for fun, I might tail the Professor and see where it is he scurries off to night after night on his supposed 'constitutional'. I saw him set off up the lane as I was leaning on the windowsill thinking about nothing at all. I almost didn't recognize him, to tell you the truth, because, of all things, he was wearing a leather-jacket and a black peaked cap! Bought, no doubt, in one of those stylish boutiques behind St Mark's Square, but all the same it was quite a transformation. Barely stopping to think, I dashed down the stairs and up the laneway after him. I was intrigued. I could still see his cap jogging along ahead of me on the San Simeon Piccolo embankment, and I caught sight of him jostling his way through the throng on the bridge in front of the station, but by the time I'd got up and over the bridge myself he'd gone – whether up into the station to the left or down the Lista di Spagna to the right where the crowds were still milling around the restaurants, I couldn't tell. It didn't matter, it was just a rather childish fantasy I'd had – following someone, going where I was led, unearthing a secret or two. It was silly, really, so I made my way back across the bridge and went for a walk alone.

But I was telling you Rachel's story of the baroness and the amulet. Well, we settled down into our chairs on the little terrace jutting out from the south-western end of the Isola Grande like the prow of a ship and gazed for a while at Italy. The ivy on the walls, twisting in and out of white-flowering clematis, droops right down to brush the lapping water. In August, Rachel told me, the huge old cotoneaster just behind us was always covered in a cloud of bright red berries – well worth walking all the way down to the terrace just to see. 'But you have to be sure to get here before the blackbirds eat them all.'

'Now, in the spring of 1872,' she said, after a thoughtful pause, her eyes fixed on some point in the blue haze to the south, 'a young schoolgirl from St Petersburg arrived with her governess in Messina. According to the governess, they were hoping the Italian sun and Mediterranean air would cure the girl's lungs – at least, that's what she told everybody. She was well educated (for a sixteen-year-old girl). Indeed, she'd been studying at the Smolny Institute in St Petersburg, which in those days was a school for young ladies of noble birth – it was specified in the Institute's full title. Have you heard of it? I was terribly impressed the first time I saw it. It's a massive, symmetrical, Italianate building – there's a touch of the Palladian about it, as a matter of fact – next to the old Smolny Nunnery.* Lenin, of course, made it the seat of the Soviet Government after the Revolution, it was where they plotted the October uprising, something the Baroness was always careful to point out in later life. She hadn't the slightest sympathy with the Bolsheviks, but she prized any kind of connection with . . . well, with people of significance – not so much power, I would say, as significance. In fact, she used to claim the Soviet met in the very room she'd studied in, but that may have been a heightening of the truth.

'"Beautiful" to me seems not quite the right word to describe Antonietta Bayer, which is the name she arrived in Sicily with. I've no doubt the Italians called her "*bella*" and the Germans "*schön*" and so on, but, looking now at her portrait as a young woman, I wonder if "beautiful" quite captures what it was about her that drew people to her. And people were certainly drawn to her. I know what she looked like when she was young – there are portraits by Ranzoni* from that period, rather impressionistic and dreamy, but not so blurred you can't see what was striking about her. The painting I know best shows her at an angle to the artist, turning her head slightly to look straight at us. She's wearing a high, ruffled collar – lace, I suppose – which her loose, dark hair just reaches at the back. Her face is thin and quite pointed with large, heavy-lidded, brown eyes. It's one of those disturbing faces which seems to be saying, "I'm here with you, yes, but I don't belong here." There's a well-brought-up gracefulness to her figure, of course, as you'd expect in a young lady from Smolny, but also a hint of something more hoydenish just below the surface, something capricious and impulsive. She was what you call *interesting* – you know, with that special kind of stress on the first syllable.

'She and her governess found lodgings in Messina

in the house of a Neapolitan, a certain Giulio Jaeger. Goodness knows what he made of them – the sickly little Russian aristocrat with the German name and her prim companion with her head in French novels. Day after windy day they seemed to have nothing much to do except stroll in the sun and turn the heads of Messina's idler citizens. Apart from anything else, there was the question of who Antonietta Bayer really was. I'm sure Signor Jaeger tried to find out – with sensitivity, of course, being after all (did I mention this?) the American Consul in Naples and, if anything, too diplomatic for his own good – but in the end he was left to mull over the same sketchy versions of her life all her other husbands were later offered. As far as we know, not one of them ever quite got to the bottom of it all.

'We do know, however, that the more bizarre rumours started right away, in 1872 in Messina, over that first summer. It was the hairbrush, fairly clearly, which started it all. Antonietta's hairbrush was engraved with a gold crown and the letter A, and one morning when she was sitting on the terrace brushing her hair in long, slow strokes (something Jaeger apparently found quite bewitching), he asked her what the crown meant. Exactly how she answered him is not recorded, but the impression was left that she was not just of aristocratic blood (the daughter of some noble Baltic nobody called Bayer), but of royal blood. And indeed, she later recorded her father's name with the Swiss authorities as "Alexander" – no surname (in the royal manner), no family details. Her mother's name she gave as "Wilhelmine" – again, no surname, no other information.

'Well, the rumour spread through Messina – and eventually to Naples, Rome and Switzerland, reaching you here this morning over 120 years later – that the enchanting Antonietta Bayer was in fact the illegitimate daughter of Czar Alexander II and a Prussian mistress. Certainly never during her long life did Antonietta utter a single syllable to contradict the rumour. Nor by the same token did she offer a jot of evidence to support it. The intriguing thing is that it's perfectly possible. Alexander is now remembered for freeing the serfs and building railways all over Russia. At the time, though, he was notorious for his numerous affairs with captivating young women, some long-lasting and scandalous, some of no consequence at all. Whether the Wilhelmine who caught the royal eye in September, 1855, was one of his more permanent liaisons or merely a servant to be taken advantage of, say, or some nobleman's niece up from the Baltic provinces for a month, I dare say we'll never know – I rather hope not.

'Whatever really happened, it's easy to imagine arrangements being discreetly made for the young Antonietta to be educated at the Smolny Institute with other young women of blood – Alexander was, after all, a man of some culture, tutored by the great poet Zhukovsky himself, and he'd have thought of Smolny, I'm sure, as a gentlemanly gesture on his part.

'By the early 1870s, though, when Antonietta was fifteen or sixteen, Alexander couldn't afford to behave in quite as cavalier a fashion as he had when newly on the throne. A student had tried to blow him up some years earlier – in 1866, I think it was – and ever since then he'd led a more cautious, reined-in sort of life, relying heavily for advice on matters of state on the head of the Secret Police. And there was trouble brewing with the Turks, as well. I think he thought if he put one foot wrong he might fall and break his neck. At the same time he was in the middle of a tumultuous affair with a very young woman – Catherine someone, I think it was. It had been going on for years and was getting out of hand.'

In my mind by this time I was deep inside the Winter Palace in St Petersburg. The tang of the waxed parquet flooring was pinching at my nostrils. I had been seduced. Rachel, however, to my surprise, was busy fitting a cigarette into a small amber holder with a gold band at one end. 'Do you smoke? I find it relieves the flatness at about this time in the afternoon.' I must say smoking suited her.

'Of course,' she went on, 'it's almost impossible for us – what shall I call us? Northerners, perhaps, the English, the Dutch, the Germans, the children of Northern Protestants – almost impossible for us to understand how these things were viewed a century ago in upper-class circles in Russia. Do you know your Tolstoy? One can't be sure these days. Well, you might remember that electrifying scene in *Anna Karenina* where Anna, a fallen woman, goes to the opera and speaks openly with her lover, Vronsky, in her box. St Petersburg is scandalized to the very marrow of its bones. The divine Patti is forgotten, completely upstaged – the theatre is a sea of opera-glasses trained on the outrage taking place in the Karenin box. I love that scene. Well, I adore the whole novel, actually.'

'Why *Anna Karenina* in particular?'

'Because it's about all the things that are important – still, over a century later. It's about different kinds of people trying to be happy and, on the whole, failing. The entire novel, it strikes me, is a brilliant attack on the notion of happiness, which your society and mine are, of course, still devoted to. The younger generation, I sometimes think, even feels affronted when happiness eludes it – it thinks it has a right to it, for some curious reason, it thinks happiness can be legislated for. Bliss, now, is a very different thing. But we'll come to that.

'The scandalous thing about the scene at the opera, you see, was not the fact of Anna's adultery – society couldn't function without adultery, after all, because it's the only thing that allows people to be true to their feelings and keep the institution of marriage functioning. Without adultery half the population would go mad and shoot itself. Absolutely vital to maintaining law and order, adultery. No, it wasn't the fact of adultery that caused the opera-glasses to swivel, it was Anna's failure to observe the proprieties – to lead a decent double life, in other words. It was the threat to public order. A night at the opera was a kind of ritual public display of your allegiance to all those things which kept society functioning smoothly and to your advantage, especially marriage. Perhaps it still is – I haven't been for years. Sexual passion, the antithesis of married love, belonged on the stage or in your lover's bedroom, it had no business flaunting itself in a box at the opera. Are you married, by the way? I'm very much in favour of it myself, always have been. It's often a bit on the dull side, but it gave me a toe-hold against all those law-givers – bureaucrats, governments, the Church, other people – it was a little space belonging just to me. Without it I feel blown about, I must say, and put upon. I can see you're not convinced.

'Anyway, at the time we're talking about, Alexander was showing definite signs of "going to the opera", so to speak, just when public order (from the point of view of the Head of the Secret Police) needed to be strengthened – against the bomb-throwing nihilists, the volatile peasants, the Turks, the free-thinkers – there were enemies everywhere, it seemed. And so it may well have seemed the ideal moment to pack a capricious illegitimate daughter off to Sicily, to declare her consumptive and in need of sea air and hot sun. The consumption, by the way, seems to have disappeared almost instantly, although she used to have 'lung troubles', as she called them vaguely, from time to time throughout her life. People did. And, curiously, Jaeger seems to have been convinced soon after Antonietta and her governess took up residence with him that the question of his guests returning to Russia would simply never arise. Nor did he seem surprised that none of her presumably wealthy family ever seemed moved to visit her. He seemed assured very early on that this was in the order of things.

'Equally well, of course, Antonietta Bayer may have been just Antonietta Bayer, daughter of some Baltic German of means, sent to Italy for her health and left to her own (very adequate) devices. I do hope no one ever manages to find out which version is the true one.

'When Giulio Jaeger went back at the end of the summer to his post in Naples – not a little smitten, I might add, with the exotic bird which had flown into his cage – with her wilfulness and ladylike manners and elegant German – Antonietta dismissed her governess and stayed on in Jaeger's house alone with a cook and a servant. This was not quite seemly, possibly, but Jaeger had left her under the watchful eye of his friend Federico Stolte, who was renting a house a little further up the hill. Stolte was a wealthy Neapolitan *homme d'affaires* with a finger in several quite lucrative pies, and, although he was a little dandified, perhaps, he was by no means dull-witted. Now, one of his great passions, ever since he'd been a boy and gone to Venice with his father, had been Marco Polo and his incredible voyage to Tartary. There was something about the sheer happenstance of it all, the astounding extent of it in time and across space, as well as the hobnobbing with khans and princes, the Shangri-las and the death-defying adventures, which captivated him completely and had him reading and rereading Marco Polo's accounts in their various versions until he almost felt he'd been at the court of the

Great Khan with him six hundred years ago himself.

'On the way home from China, of course, the Polo brothers stopped off in India, where they travelled for some months around the very towns and villages our mysterious lovelorn prince knew so well near Mysore. (I hope you haven't already forgotten about him, have you?) In fact, although it's hard to put a date to all those tales I told you this morning, working back from the Angevins at Egg Castle, the Polos must have been in those parts not so very long after the mithuna amulet was crafted. Perhaps – who knows? – our prince even lived long enough to see the Polos riding stiffly by one day, or dined with them on one of their forays into the countryside. It does happen, you know, that sort of thing – rarely, of course, but it happens.

'So, having delved into every aspect of the Polos' story with the dilettante's passion (and there's none purer) – the Arab trade with India, all the tall tales about gigantic pearls and tarantula spiders and holy men – have you ever read them? – as well as the art that had dazzled them in the temples and palaces – Federico knew what he was gazing at when he first found the amulet in the cavity in the wall of his father's house in Naples, exactly where the prelate had left it six hundred years earlier. The hair he overlooked, naturally enough, and the Persian book on the art of love was indecipherable, but the small, gold amulet was something he recognized immediately. The house the Stoltes lived in had, of course, been rebuilt many times, but one wall, the one with the cavity, had survived from earlier centuries more or less as it was. Federico had decided to have the worm-eaten panelling overlaying it torn out and replaced and, while the walls were bare, had discovered the loose stone, which had shifted a little in various earthquakes over the years. Nudging and pushing at it, he chanced upon the cavity behind it.'

Rachel paused. 'You know, sitting here with the world going about its business right in front of our eyes like this, it's oddly more difficult to talk about the amulet than it was this morning, cloistered, so to speak, in the Herb Garden, hardly able to see out. What I mean to say is that for the first time in its journey, if we're to believe the story as it's been spun, someone had come into possession of the amulet in innocence – at least, that's how I've always understood it, and so, I think, did the Baroness. No one until then had taken it and valued it for what it really was. Innocently – or as innocently as the prince – Federico gave the amulet to Antonietta that summer in Messina, and just as innocently she took it, and, indeed, it seems at last, after all those centuries, to have found its mark and woven its spell.

'It's hard to know quite whom to believe, but Antonietta seems to have been like a rose eager to leave the hothouse and put down roots in the world outside, and Federico appears to have been just the man to transplant her. At this distance it's all too easy, knowing what we now know about Antonietta, to suspect ulterior motives in her hasty attachment to him. By "ulterior", of course, we nowadays mean perfectly *sound* motives, such as the desire for social position, property and a life of ease, but not love – whatever that might be.

'They declared themselves to have fallen in love, naturally. And I have no doubt they had, according to their lights. Antonietta, as I've said, had that exciting, about-to-bloom quality men find so beguiling, the almost unbearably thrilling aura of consumption and a mind aquiver with interest in the world. In a word, she was what the French would call *fatale* – in fact, the Russians say something similar, I understand, but I don't imagine you speak Russian, it's as useless as French and far less chic. At that time, you have to remember, the Russians were much taken with the idea of the *femme fatale* – well, you've read your Dostoevsky, I expect, perhaps even your Turgenev, although he's wildly out of favour nowadays, I know. So part of Antonietta's *fatalité* was doubtless a game she'd learnt to play as a forward young thing in the salons of St Petersburg.

'There seem to be no photographs or portraits of Federico, but by all accounts he was young, fair-haired, and had a fine profile, so important in a gentleman. Like many men attracted to *femmes fatales*, though, there was something weak about him – "weak" was how they used to think of it in those days. What they meant, I suppose, was that need in some men to invite humiliation, even cruelty, and to take a kind of erotic pleasure in it when it came. In the company of other men they could be perfectly self-assured and self-possessed, but with women, for some reason, they seemed to hunger to be betrayed and wounded. I think that's what aroused Federico – the hint of humiliation in the wings.' She looked at me briefly as if considering if it might also be what aroused me.

'Messina in those days, needless to say, was a dreary, corrupt little town – well, it still is a dreary, corrupt little town – with spectacular views across the strait to Calabria. Antonietta, as you can imagine, was impatient to move to Naples, consumption or no consumption. There Federico owned the rather splendid villa on the bay I was telling you about, and after a rather hastily arranged marriage ceremony Antonietta Bayer became its youthful but enchanting mistress. Here at last was a garden Antonietta could come into bloom in, and bloom she did. There were sailing parties to Capri, excursions to Pompeii, sojourns at Sorrento and Ravello on the Amalfi Coast, candlelit dinners at the villa in Naples, and all around her a crowd of culti-vated, well-travelled men and women eager to feed her curiosity about the world with all the latest ideas from London, Vienna, Paris and Berlin. And circling about her like a faithful swain all this time, at the theatre and on outings to villages in the mountains, was Giulio Jaeger, the American Consul.

'The couple quickly had a daughter – Maria Grazia Vera, a nice mixture of the Italian and the Russian – and soon afterwards, in 1875, a son. But something about the Stolte ménage was not quite right. Antonietta took to travelling farther and farther afield without her compliant husband, fetching up in Rome or in one of the fashionable resorts along the coast in the company of often rather shadowy young gallants who were every bit as *interesting* as she was. Eventually, on a trip to San Remo with her baby daughter, she simply failed to go home.

'In a sense, you must admit, it was an elegant solution – no ugly scenes, no shouting or threats, just a slow unfurling of a more brightly coloured self. But Federico was not denied the satisfaction of one last humiliation. Two days before her birthday – it was in mid-June this happened, you see, a heady moment in San Remo, because everyone had just arrived for the season, but no one had yet made their first move – Antonietta sent a telegramme to Federico begging, indeed imploring him to come. She couldn't bear to spend her birthday all alone, she said, in that dramatic vein she was inclined to cultivate, in a town where she knew no one. And so Federico, aroused, perhaps, by the prospect of an annihilating scene, left immediately for San Remo – a long and exhausting journey, I might add; it's up on the Riviera near the French border, it took him two days and two nights to get there. But by nine on the morning of his wife's birthday there he was, a little dishevelled (but no doubt appealingly) and a little overwrought with red-rimmed eyes, presenting himself at the desk of the slightly down-at-heel Hôtel des Bains, asking to see Signora Stolte.

' "The *signora* has asked me to give you this note, *signore*," the desk-clerk said, with the air of somebody who has been waiting all morning for just this moment.

'Federico opened the note, too tired to sense that anything was wrong. Antonietta was probably just finishing breakfast, or perhaps she'd gone to the station but had missed him in the crowd. He *had* been a little downcast, to be honest, when he failed to find her waiting for him on the platform. He'd been picturing her standing waving in her English jacket and boots.

'"*Federico, I have changed my mind,*" the note read, "*I can no longer see you and would be grateful if you would leave San Remo immediately. Antonietta.*"

'Federico felt at first that he didn't exist. From upstairs he could hear the vague clinking of coffee-cups and a woman's voice talking loudly in German, but it was like sounds from another world. Then he heard himself say numbly: "Thank you, but I must speak to Signora Stolte. Can someone please show me to her room?" The vile clerk, who was immaculately dressed in a maroon jacket and freshly pressed white shirt, could barely suppress his glee. He knew. Obviously he knew everything. "I'm sorry, *signore*, but the *signora* has given strict instructions that she not be disturbed today." What else did this sleek, smirking youth know? Who *was* allowed to disturb the *signora*? Federico was dimly aware of a right to say, "But I am her husband, I demand that you show me to my wife's room," but all of a sudden he felt so crushed, so finally broken and discarded, that he knew these were words he would never say. He stared at the marble floor for a moment, felt grief begin to claw at his throat, picked up his valise, turned on his heel and left. As it happened, he never saw his wife again. And after their little son drowned – drowned stupidly at a swimming carnival in the bay near their home – he lost all taste for life and became a mysterious recluse.

'There was, as it happened, one visitor that June morning that the obnoxious clerk *had* been instructed to show up. He knew him well. He was a tall, quite imposing-looking young man, fair-skinned, impeccably turned out according to the weather, whom the clerk referred to as *la zucca pelata* because, although fine-featured, he was as bald as a coot. When he got to Antonietta's room, he found her unusually distraught. She'd been weeping, obviously, and was still in her Chinese morning gown, whose greenish sheen lent her face a disagreeable hue. She would neither allow herself to be comforted nor explain the source of her distress. Baby Maria had been annoying her with her crying and whining for a week or more, it was true, and she'd been having trouble sleeping, but she seemed disinclined to hire a nanny – perhaps that's all it was, he thought, the constant irritation of the fretful child.

'In fact, Antonietta had been trying to decide for a month or more whether or not to divorce Federico and marry Guido Mozzi. On the one hand Guido was wealthy, with interests in South America and New York, kindly and good-natured with a lively mind, while on the other hand . . . well, he was quite simply terribly bald. Not balding, or with thinning hair on the crown, or with only a monkish fringe circling his scalp, but

completely, one hundred percent, dinner-plate bald –
not a whisker in sight. It was not that Antonietta did
not find Guido attractive (she did, almost overwhelmingly), it was just that baldness on this scale
overshadowed any other qualities he might have had
– it was a question of balance and taste.

'In the end she sent off another telegramme, this
time to her faithful friend Giulio Jaeger in Naples. Like
Federico, he also immediately left for San Remo and
arrived at the Hôtel des Bains during breakfast. This
time the clerk had instructions to show him up immediately. Antonietta poured her heart out to her old
friend – she'd read so many novels detailing this scene
that she didn't get a word wrong – and the consul took
a comforting stance, patient with her tears and vacil-
lations, sensitive to her desperation, insistent that good
could come out of the muddle she was in. On the one
hand Federico was an honourable man who would
provide for her well, and the father of her son, whom
she scarcely missed but was attached to; on the other
hand she was passionately in love with Guido Mozzi,
who was just as honourable and able to provide, but
also . . . well, she obviously *desired* Guido in a way she'd
never desired Federico. But he was startlingly bald.

'The solution to Antonietta's dilemma proved
utterly simple: she went back to Naples with Giulio
Jaeger and married him. The widower and his exotic
young wife made a brilliant couple and over the next
few years they seem to have led a glittering life in
Naples and Rome. At the spa in Albano they met Franz

Liszt, for example, who quickly became an intimate friend and Antonietta's music teacher – he even dedicated a small work to her, as a matter of fact, kindly calling her his "best pupil". Liszt was clearly fascinated by Antonietta – that febrile, questing, volatile quality she had, together with all the social graces and an infinitely curious mind – it was like watching a song-bird fluttering in its gilded cage, longing to be let out. How Liszt, I imagine, would have loved to ease the little door open. He used to visit the Jaegers all the time on the pretext of giving their son Giulio Antonio English lessons.

'After surprisingly few years – Antonietta was still only in her mid-twenties – the wandering started again: staying on in Rome alone, trips to Florence that grew longer and longer, extended stays with friends in Tuscany, until one day Antonietta was in fact living in Milan with her daughter, while her husbands were living with their sons in Naples. At least there was no scandal. Then one night at the opera (and this is partly what the opera was for, I know) Antonietta had one of those meetings she came more and more to believe were "fated" – I see you smiling, you probably find the whole notion quaint, but you have to remember that in . . . what was it? 1880 or thereabouts in certain circles it was taken for granted that our lives were shaped by all sorts of thrilling unseen forces – spirit-forces, the stars, magnetic waves, quite a heady brew. In St Petersburg, for instance, when Antonietta was a girl, there was an absolute epidemic of ectoplasm, table-turning and voices from the beyond. No soirée was complete without a foreign medium or two among the guests and levitation was routine.

'Anyway, Antonietta was always inclined to see patterns in her life she hadn't willed, and she loved to tell the story of how she'd been going up the stairs at the opera-house as the Baron had been slowly coming down and how their eyes had met and she'd simply known. If you asked her what it was she'd known, she'd just laugh and give a flick of her hand. It wasn't, she said, the officer's uniform that had aroused her, and it wasn't the abundant black hair and trim beard, it was the *tread*, she always said, on the carpeted stairs, the light, stalking tread and the *eyes*. They were eyes, she always said, which seemed to have known her for a thousand years – that's the sort of thing she said. Then a few days later (and the number of days always depended on her mood when she told the story) he got into her compartment in the train to Bologna. Not a word passed between them, apparently, but again she felt elated by his light, long-limbed presence and felt his eyes brush over her from time to time as he turned the pages of his newspaper. Refined animality is always so seductive. And when, after an hour or so of silence, he suddenly stood up and was gone with nothing more than the faintest of nods, she felt (she used to say) as you do when a cat gets up from beside you in an empty house and silently vanishes – again, that's the sort of thing she said, you see, and in a way you know what she meant. When a cat leaves you like that, it's suddenly *everywhere*, if you see what I mean. I can see you don't. At any rate, the pale, black-haired officer was Antonietta's black cat.

'Their third meeting was in a *pasticceria* and much less tense, and Antonietta always spoke of it as if it was a mere formality which had to be gone through for the sake of social decorum. This time they spoke politely, establishing friends in common, and I gather she allowed him to carry some parcels for her to her door. Just a year after the night at the opera – "And I never *went* to the opera, that's the thing," she used to say, "I hated the opera, I can't think why I was there" – Antonietta married her Irish baron, Richard Flemyng of St Leger, and came at last, as it were, into her estate. There was something almost Hindu, something Brahmin about the way she saw the world, I some-times think, as if she believed she was *born*, not so much to rule in some kingdom of her own, as to be high priestess, to hold sway – that was her destiny, her proper place. Liszt had called her "*la reine des îles de Brissago*" and the locals here called her all sorts of things – *la principessa, die Märchenkönigin*, as well as witch, of course. Back in St Petersburg something had obviously gone awry, something had got out of kilter, but now, thanks to her Irish baron, an adjustment had been made and she could be herself.

'Like a true Brahmin, Antonietta was never inter-ested in wealth as such. Wealth to her was more like air or water, it was just something she had a right to and only of interest if it was in short supply. With

Richard it was never in short supply. The St Legers, as perhaps you know, had houses all over Ireland – Dublin, Cork, Tipperary, as many as fifty in Dublin alone, I've heard. Richard was the distant descendant of Sir Anthony Saint Leger – no one remembers who he was nowadays, but he was Viceroy of Ireland, it was he who persuaded the Irish Parliament to bestow on Henry VIII the title of King of Ireland, and rewarded the Irish chieftains for renouncing the Pope by giving them land and titles. Mary Tudor got rid of him very smartly, needless to say. It all looks rather grubby to us, I suppose, but Antonietta felt she'd entered a fairytale. After they were married they lived for a while in Ireland, as well as in Italy and Switzerland, and always in great style. They had a son they called James, and Maria, of course, Federico's daughter, was still with them.

'It must have been while they were staying with the Princes Trubetzkoi* at the Villa Ada on Lake Maggiore here that they first saw these islands. I can imagine how they must have appealed to Antonietta. She was nearing thirty, she had her prince, now all she needed was a realm – a kingdom and a castle. Travelling up and down the lake to Locarno, as they did from time to time, I can imagine how she must have looked across at these two small islands, covered in brambles and low bushes, with the old Lombard nunnery half-hidden by ivy and holm-oaks at one end of the larger one. She must have thought to herself: "I could take possession of those islands and turn them into paradise."

'Travelling on was what she did throughout her life, she was always travelling on. Even on her deathbed at ninety-one, you know, she was busy learning Greek, forging onwards into some unknown world. But at twenty-nine, married for the third time, she decided to cast anchor, as it were, right here where we're sitting. She bought the islands in 1885 and soon after moved into the nunnery with Richard and the two children. She called herself Baroness – such an intriguingly vague title, almost meaningless in this part of the world – and renamed the islands St Léger, pronounced in the French fashion.

'You know, I envy Antonietta that moment when she first arrived on the island – she must have been rowed over in one of those flat-bottomed boats the fishermen here fished from, terribly dangerous, actually, they capsized in the slightest wind. I can see her stepping out of the boat and walking up to the house ... How often does any of us have a moment like that in our lives? Of complete renewal, a moment when everything has a new beginning. It's an illusion, naturally – it's what they thought they could do over there in Ascona, on Monte Verità – throw out father, throw out science, throw out civilization, and begin again as if it were the dawn of time. Yes, it's a complete illusion, every beginning is just another kind of ending, but it's an illusion I'd love to be inside, if only once.'

Italy was clouding over in the south. Rachel fell comfortably silent and gazed across the choppy lake at the mountains hemming in the southern reaches of the lake. Occasionally there'd be a flash of sunlight off the window of a car winding swiftly up the road cut into the cliffs above the water. Somewhere a motor would suddenly splutter into life, someone would shout something into the wind.

'Why don't we go up to the house? It's getting chilly,' Rachel said. 'We'll order coffee and some *pasticcini* – the tea's not worth drinking – and I'll tell you the rest of Antonietta's story. And the amulet's, if you've haven't forgotten all about it.' And so we set off along the main *allée* towards the house. The glimpse of striped awnings through the trees was quite inviting.

Sitting here now in my hotel-room in Venice, where it's suddenly piercingly cold and moonless, I'm feeling oddly stilled by my memories of the stories Rachel told me. I can't help remembering those first few days of raw anguish (there's really no other word – it wasn't depression, it was anguish and dread) when words like 'renewal' and 'beginning' lost all their sense. In fact, I actually remember thinking how pointless buying a new shirt or scarf would be, how shopping for new clothes or a new teapot or carpet would be something I could forget about forever, like doing the Asian cooking course or polishing up my German. There could be no renewal, just growing decrepitude, rottenness and death. The first time I left the house and went with Peter to sit for a while in a café on Brunswick Street, it was crushingly painful to listen to all those *soigné* young men and women with their shining skin and shining hair and shining eyes talking in clear, assertive voices about what they'd be doing next week, next month or next year, about the holidays coming up in Bali and the new job Fiona or Ben or Jason had just got for himself. I felt like a scaly bag of filth about to split and ooze all over the terra-cotta tiles. I thought they must be able to sniff me rotting, I felt like an affront to them and wondered why they hadn't asked for me to be removed. They were all *going somewhere*, you see, and that's what I couldn't bear to look at.

It was particularly difficult for the first few weeks because my Chinese Gabriel was going on a fortnight's holiday (to Kakadu, as a matter of fact, where I'd always meant to go some time) and so couldn't both do the necessary tests and give me the results himself, and for some obscure reason I can't fully explain I felt strongly that, when the day came, I wanted to hear the news from him and no one else. Waiting like that is indescribable. I suppose it's like waiting for a grenade someone's tossed you to go off in your hand – and it ends up taking three weeks. Of course, paradoxically, you've never felt more alive in your life – to every sound, every flicker of movement, every skerrick of meaning in every word you hear said.

The other thing that was difficult was the illusion that you must either fight or flee – now. That's the choice. You must take up arms, do battle, refuse to surrender, fight it, conquer it, go down fighting, marshal your resources, go on the attack . . . the metaphors are endless. Or else flee – ignore it, meditate, take up bush-walking, yoga, live a normal life, commit suicide . . .

I had a hellish dream one night at about this time of running through the jungle ahead of a prowling cat of some kind – now a leopard, now a lion – and it had its yellow eye on me. Whenever I tried to run faster it would pad up closer behind me, playing with me but carelessly deadly in its intent. It stank of dead flesh. I thought of just dropping to the ground and letting it tear me apart and swallow me. Why try to escape? Why prolong the agony? Any attempt to fight the animal was obviously doomed – admirable in some old-fashioned way, perhaps, but pointless. I was no match. Then I saw opening up not far ahead of me a kind of tunnel in the jungle, not unlike a railway tunnel, but with no light at the other end. I had to decide now whether to turn and face the leopard or whether to run into the darkness of the tunnel and hope I might give him the slip. More likely, of course, he'd slink in after me, smell me out and tear me limb from bloody limb . . .

I haven't been dreaming that dream in recent months because I don't think I see my choices any more in quite that light – at least, not during my better moments.

Venice, 7th April

ISLANDS AREN'T just islands, are they. I mean, they're not just bits of land surrounded by water, they also stand for something less tangible, always half-desired. When you look across the water and see an island, part of you always wants to go there, don't you find? I can't help thinking it's got something to do with sudden resolution. There you are floundering in the middle of all that eddying, featureless water, with unseen horrors you can only guess at prowling beneath the surface, when suddenly an island appears on the horizon: such a blessedly fixed point, a place of longed-for release from anxiety about disorder and aimlessness, not to mention the lurking monsters of the subconscious. So any island, even the flattest or rockiest or most barren, seems beautiful. It's the self we'd like to be. Dante, of course, if you recall, says that Purgatory is an island – Hell is deep in the earth and Heaven beyond time and space, but Purgatory, the realm of those who have not wilfully sinned, is an island. There reason still has some hope of becoming vision.

Certainly for Antonietta, Baroness de St Léger, these islands were her soul made flesh, they were the incarnation of who she thought she was – and of her longing for ordered peace at last. 'My small bit of earthly paradise' she used to call it in English.

In many ways the Baroness was a 'troubled soul', as Rachel put it once we were sitting comfortably again at a table on the terrace in the pavilion that had been the Baroness's home. 'Yes, she'd married well at last, she was unimaginably wealthy and she was the mistress of her own domain, two of the loveliest islands in the most magnificent lake in the middle of what many would think of as the Garden of Eden. Yet she was troubled. There was the death of her son by Federico, of course, and then the sudden death of her son by Richard, little James. I think she always lived with the sense of people slipping away from her into nothing – all the people from her childhood, as well as Federico, Guido, Giulio, her sons – and yes, you could have said to her: "Well, you've steered your boat erratically, no wonder almost everyone's fallen overboard." But that would only have made it worse. Her sense of rudderlessness and loss was overwhelming.

'And so she set about ordering her little paradise on the Isola Grande here. She hired gardeners and started clearing the island of the brambles choking every nook and cranny and killing off the vipers slithering everywhere – there are actually still some left: did you see the notice warning people to watch out for them by that pond down there at the bottom of the steps? She also started making the old nunnery habitable – whitewashing the walls, putting on a strong roof, ordering strong new doors and windows – you actually need them in winter here when the winds off the alps can almost sweep you off your feet. She repaired the old harbour and bought some new rowing-boats and a small yacht. In just two months the family was able to move in.

'So in all sorts of ways this was a very good time for Antonietta. Her joy was a little "soured", as she used to put it, by arguments and difficulties with the gardeners she took on, but then Antonietta had arguments and difficulties with everyone, there was nothing unusual about that. She laid out the pathways that criss-cross the island, the promenade with its thick stone walls around the island's circumference and the central walk we just came along linking the house with the terrace at the end. Then she had soil in vast quantities brought over from the mainland and, with the aid of books and gardening magazines she ordered from as far away as London, she began to direct the planting of her Eden.

'Whatever her penchant for the occult and mystical, Antonietta de St Léger was also a child of her times in other, more rational ways, so the garden she designed balanced fantasy with a vision of usefulness. There's nothing especially playful about the garden, no paths that wind around just for the sake of winding. It's in fact a miniature botanical garden, planted out with specimens from all five continents. The relatively mild climate here allows for that, you see. Because it's neither cold nor hot, it's not like anywhere and so a little bit like everywhere. So the gardens were a place to learn in as much as to take your ease in. Oh, she called them her "pleasure grounds", it's true, and had a terrible time convincing the gardeners she hired locally that a garden did not have to be an orchard, did not have to produce fruit and vegetables, but could equally as usefully "feed the soul" instead. (That was her phrase.) Still, the idea of rational use was always there at the back of her mind, counterbalancing any notion of unearned delight or letting nature off the leash.

'A daughter, Joan, was born about a year after they moved to the island, and for the next few years, at least on the surface, the Baron and Baroness de St Léger must have seemed to many in the villages on the lakeshore to be living an idyllic life. The tunnel under the St Gotthard Pass was now open, so it was easy to visit Locarno from the north as well as from the south, and the "hermitage", as the Baroness called her home on the island, was constantly full of guests from all over Europe, and even further afield.

'It's hard to say exactly when everything went awry again, but it did. Antonietta used to say she felt cursed, trapped in one of the outer circles of Hell. She wanted so much, of course, and she wanted it so passionately. In 1893 her daughter Maria Grazia Vera died, the daughter who'd gone to San Remo with her, and then to Milan – her first child. She died of a bronchial condition here on this island at just nineteen years of age.

This death, more than any other, seemed to break Antonietta's spirit ... no, those are not the right words.' Rachel was looking away from me, across the shallows to where the Herb Garden we'd sat in earlier poked out from behind some giant figs. I could see it was important to her for some reason to find the right words. 'No, it wasn't so much that her spirit was broken ... Her spirit was soured, she became ... well, you won't like this word, but she became soul-sick. It's not the kind of word we feel comfortable with today, is it? But none of the modern words seems quite right – "depressed" (she wasn't depressed), "anguished", "disturbed", "unbalanced" – none of them quite captures her state of mind after Maria died.

'She had Maria buried in the wall of the house – this house, whose terrace we're sitting on – and when that became known in the villages round about ... well, as you can imagine, the priests, the fishermen's wives, the children, the shopkeepers, everyone began to speak of her as a sorceress, and tales began to spread of every kind of occult orgy taking place in the seclusion of the old nunnery. Then it was discovered that the body of her young son James had been removed from the cemetery and also sealed up inside one of the walls and the whole lakeshore was up in arms. The gardeners and servants would go back to their villages at night with stories of candle-lit pagan masks appearing on the walls, mysterious dark-skinned visitors speaking strange languages coming to stay, crockery falling off the shelves of its own accord, rituals by firelight, séances . . . the Queen of the Isles was gradually turning into necromancer, siren and witch, all rolled into one.

'And when one day the Baron left for Naples, never to return, the fairytales became even more extravagant. Of course, from one point of view there was something rather amusing about the way her three husbands and son were now all gathered forlornly in Naples – and the Baron actually found himself a position at the United States consulate there – while the Baroness and her surviving daughter Joan continued to live their bizarre fantasy life on their islands here on Lake Maggiore, surrounded by conspiring servants and guard-dogs. More and more guests came to stay, more and more often the house was thrown open to throngs of revellers and the Isola Grande would be swarming for days at a time with princes and playwrights and singers and musicians – and cooks and boatmen and valets and gardeners, who back in Brissago and Ascona and Locarno naturally told and retold ever more fantastic versions of what they had seen. Among the guests one summer about three years after the Baron had disappeared was an Albanian aristocrat called Perikles Tzikos, a tall, swarthy pasha of a man outfitted in London who brought his silver service with him, engraved, like Antonietta's hairbrush, with a royal crown and his own initials. This was the kind of refined exoticism that appealed to the Baroness and she married him almost immediately. After a decent interval she added Tzikos to her title: the Baroness Tzikos de St

Léger. It undoubtedly had a certain ring to it, didn't it? That's about all it did have, though.

'In 1903, on one of those windy winter nights when the trees are all tossing and the waves are crashing against the sea-walls and it's hard to make out anything in the gloom, there were sudden gun-shots and hysterical screaming and Joan disappeared from the island. There were police reports and even a court case, but what exactly happened is still not completely clear. Presumably the Baron had abducted his daughter with help from one or more of the gardeners – rescued her from her mad, necromancing mother, as he'd have thought of her. Antonietta never saw her daughter again.

'Not so very long after that her Albanian prince died. He was buried on the mainland according to Orthodox rites, with an icon of the Virgin in his arms and one or two ornaments around his neck encrusted with precious stones. Some time later the grave was dug up and the icon and ornaments were removed. The local villagers were naturally in no doubt about who had robbed the grave.

'And so the fairytale was over. Oh, the gardeners kept gardening for another twenty years or so, the magnolias and myrtles and hydrangeas kept blooming, the copse Antonietta had planted just down there beyond the lawn thickened and became a forest in miniature – did you walk through it? It's eerie, isn't it? You feel as if you could get lost in it, but it's hardly a minute's walk away from all these people sitting drinking cappuccinos. Yes, the pretence of an earthly paradise was maintained, and the house became even more of a *palazzo* than it had been – Venetian glass everywhere (vases, goblets, lampshades), Etruscan beakers, glazed tiles from Bassano on all the downstairs floors, lots of milky green celadon from China, frescoes on the walls, religious paintings from France and Italy – she had a wonderful Madonna from Padua with a golden nimbus, fourteenth-century, so she said – and lots of mirrors and tapestries and paintings brought over from Ireland. And in the library there were rare editions of all sorts of books: a sixteenth-century cookbook used by the Pope's cook in the Vatican, for example, and an ancient miniature edition of Dante's *Divine Comedy*. My mother told me how she'd been shown through the house once by the Baroness, two baskets full of keys in her hands, and as they came to each door she'd carefully unlock it and then lock it again behind them. It was her castle and for twenty years after Perikles died she lived there as if under siege.

'Just before Christmas every year a certain climbing rose called Maréchal Niel used to flower just near the main door – a miracle, really, almost as if the seasons didn't exist in her kingdom. Antonietta saw it as some kind of sign. "The marshal has arrived," she'd say, and after that she'd scarcely leave the house until after Christmas. The legend is that on Christmas Eve she'd order the table set sumptuously for eight and dismiss her staff as soon as evening fell. I can almost believe it really was like that, it accords so perfectly with her whimsical nature and taste for the theatrical. And although no one ever seemed either to row over to the island or to leave, the windows would blaze all night with light, there'd be music, the occasional sound of raised voices, shadowy shapes outlined against the blinds . . . Well, here I begin to wonder, but who am I to say? I wasn't there. The rumour grew that on the night before Christmas every year she summoned the shades of her Seven Husbands – she actually only had four, not all of them dead, and I wonder, should there be any truth behind the legend, if she had the table set for her four husbands and three dead children – it's not impossible. The rumours were soon embellished wondrously, needless to say: it was said, for example, that each husband had to bring with him some precious object – a necklace or a bejewelled charm, a silver brooch, perhaps – and give it to her, and when one year the Baron came empty-handed she challenged him to a duel and beheaded him with the Abyssinian sword, and a thousand miles away in Naples the unfortunate Baron died. Which he did, I must say.'

Rachel smiled in a suddenly quite warm way and looked straight at me. 'But you're wondering what became of the amulet, aren't you. You're wondering how the amulet fits in. Well, I can tell you now, you'll understand. One summer the Baroness joined a party of hikers and picnickers setting out for the hidden lake right up near the peak of that mountain just round to the right – if you lean forward a bit, you can just see it. No? It doesn't matter – believe me, it's there. She usually had nothing to do with the Monte Verità crowd – to her they were too much of a rabble, living in caves and huts they'd built themselves and despising all the trappings of civilization she herself craved. Meanwhile, to them she appeared little more than the batty, degenerate face of the patriarchal civilization they were all trying to escape. Yet they in fact had quite a lot in common: lives lived out with passion and strong feelings, an unending celebration of the erotic and seductive, an interest in philosophies the Christian church poured anathema on, a love of nature rather than cities – quite a lot. Anyway, on this particular morning, my father and the Baroness found themselves in the same party – the Baroness on a mule, of course, and my father on foot. It took about five hours to reach the lake – even today it's a day's outing there and back – and I suppose Antonietta was expecting some sort of elegant *déjeuner sur l'herbe*, something just faintly disreputable, given the presence of the contingent from Monte Verità, yet stylish, and so she was wearing her Indian amulet. In fact there was no *herbe* at the lake at all – it just nestles there, ultramarine and sparkling, amongst the barren rocks.

'Walking beside her at one point, my father noticed the amulet and, being much taken up at the time with the Monte Verità philosophy of seeking paradise through the senses and Tantric yoga and so on, he asked the Baroness to tell him about it, curious to hear what the mysterious *principessa* might allow herself to say. Well, in the grip of I don't know what mood on that day, what mixture of devilment, despair and defiance, she began to tell him the story I have told you – the Indian prince, the Yemenite Jew, the sultan, the synagogue, the brothel in Messina, Vergil's Egg, everything. And as they made their way higher and higher up the mountain, my father fell more and more under the spell of the lady on the mule and the amulet on her breast. Eventually, of course, they came to the hidden lake, the Baroness dismounted and, having finished her tale, went down to the edge of the lake, which lies quite still, as if made of glass, in even the highest winds, and unpinned the amulet. Then, to my father's astonishment, she threw it out into the lake.'

Rachel fitted another cigarette into its amber holder but didn't light it. 'We're really at the end of the story – and just as well, perhaps, because the last ferry will be leaving soon and we must be on it.'

'Why do you think she threw it into the lake?'

'I think she thought that it was time to step off the treadmill, time to break the circle of desire and disappointment. I'm not sure if she really believed she needed to get rid of the amulet to do that – probably not, in her heart of hearts, but there are times, aren't there, when a little ritual helps. Whatever the case, it worked, in a sense. She gardened quietly for a few years, and then after the war she sold the islands and slowly slid into poverty, mostly because of legal battles she lost – she was even reduced to begging for money for cigarettes. Eventually she had nothing left at all, apart from a few odds and ends: a ring or two, several odd glasses, part of a necklace, and the Queen of Rumania's blouse – she refused to give that up. In November 1940 she arrived one night at a hospital in Intragna – that's just a little past where you got off the train the other day at Tegna – and that's where she stayed, in a room facing north, for eight years until she died. They tried to put her in rooms facing in other directions, but she insisted on due north. She had an old Portuguese compass she pulled out as they showed her each room, so she knew the right room when she came to it. Hardly anyone even knew she was there. Her remains were reburied here on the island some years ago, but still no one knows she's here.'*

'It's rather a sad ending,' I said.

'Oh, do you really think so?' Rachel tapped out her cigarette and looked at me very directly, which she'd scarcely done at all while telling me her story. 'Endings, I suppose, are always "sad" in some conventional sense, but I don't think the ending to Antonietta's story is *particularly* sad. Would it have been "happier" if she'd died, say, twenty years earlier? Or forty, when she lost Perikles? Or surrounded by a chorus of children and husbands? Antonietta Bayer was a troubled soul craving bliss. She thought she could *create* paradise – buy it, build it, marry it, make it happen – but all she got was intermittent happiness. Happiness has nothing to do with bliss. I'll have this last cigarette, shall I? And then we'll go.' I like watching women of a certain age smoke, especially (for some reason) in a hat, alone.

'I had a Sufic phase once,' she said, her eyes on the smoke curling up from the smouldering tip. 'My

Asconan roots, you see – we were always looking for ways to thumb our noses at Christianity. Well, there was a Sufic saying I read somewhere which stayed with me: "O God, if I worship you in fear of Hell, burn me there; and if I worship you in hope of Paradise, shut its gates against me."* You don't have to believe in Heaven or Hell to see what the Sufis were getting at.' I made a mental note to give this further thought, although I doubt I'm a natural Sufi.

'But what about the amulet?' I said. It was niggling away at me. 'It clearly didn't stay in the lake.'

'Well, no, obviously not. Of course, the closer you get to us here today, the less certain everything becomes – have you noticed that? Thirteenth-century Naples, on the other hand, is not a problem, everything's as clearly etched and coloured-in as in a Botticelli. What my father said happened is this – but he was a Jungian, you must remember, as almost everyone was at Monte Verità, mostly in a rather sloppy kind of way.* What he said happened was that he started to have a recurring dream that the amulet . . . don't smile in that superior way, even stranger things will happen to you if you let them . . . that the amulet was calling to him from the lake, asking to be brought back down the mountain into the world again – it wanted, he said, to get on with its journey.'

'Where was it going?'

Rachel smiled. 'What can I say? Home, I suppose.'

'To India?'

'Why be so literal? No, not necessarily to India. India is beside the point.'

'Well, what is the point?'

'My father would have said that the point was understanding desire.' This seemed incredibly wishy-washy and vague to me. 'He would've said that the point is to desire to be, not to have. And that the amulet would not deliver its blessing until this point had been understood.'

'It could be a long journey. So your father fished it out of the lake?'

'Yes, he did. He went back up the mountain one day – he says he went three times, but I suspect he may just have been entering into the spirit of the story – and swam around in the lake until he found it, wedged between two white stones. He came here to see me about a year before he died. It wasn't a maudlin occasion, as you might think, it wasn't overshadowed by any sense that this was to be our last meeting, although we both knew it was a significant meeting . . . and he gave me the amulet, and told me the story the Baroness had told him, and said that when I was ready to pass it on, I should do so.'

'But you've never felt moved to?'

'Oh, I've thought sometimes that the moment has come, yes,' she said, 'but either I still have something to learn or else I haven't yet met the right person. There's no hurry. But we really ought to be getting down to the wharf, my friend – that's the ferry you can hear now.'

Steaming back to Locarno in the fading light, we chatted about this and that – books, mostly – and I tried to see if Rachel was wearing the amulet today under her coat, but couldn't. Just as well, perhaps. I don't know if I'll ever see her again – these days I don't make long-term plans. In any case, I'm not at all sure we need to see each other again. Too often in my life, I think, I've tried to hold on to acquaintances and feelings which I should have allowed just to be what they first were – something to enjoy and move on from. When she left me to walk up the hill from the wharf to the railway-station, I actually felt a little surge of freedom and energy, as if I'd floated down to earth again after rather too long in the air. I'd had enough abracadabra for one day. I walked off quite briskly towards the main square looking for something to eat – it's always a joy nowadays to feel hungry, it's so rare – forgetting that in terms of restaurants I was now a tourist in Italy. Who on earth started the rumour that you can dine well in an Italian restaurant? Pasta, veal, fish, lettuce, fish, veal, pasta, dumped on the table with a surliness that takes your breath away. Had the trend-setters never eaten Japanese? Here in Venice I've at last found a Chinese restaurant where they know what dining means.

I think I know where the Professor goes at night, by the way, leaving his rimless gold spectacles behind. I expect he's there now as I write. But it's not the Professor I want to tell you about just at the moment – it's what happened to me after Rachel left. From the Garden of Eden I was swept down into hell.

Notes

Sterne's advice: Laurence Sterne in Tristram Shandy, a novel posing as autobiography.

Taoist experience: see Lao Tzu's Tao Te Ching (The Book of the Way and Its Power). Reference is being made here, presumably, to the concept of wu wei, on which the author seems to have a fairly shaky grasp.

Sterne in Calais: a rather sweeping oversimplification of Sterne's description of his short stay in Calais at the beginning of A Sentimental Journey through France and Italy (1768), a book sometimes seen as an example of post-modern travel-writing before its time and sometimes as a disguised meditation on God, given that Sterne died almost immediately after its publication. Certainly, Sterne does seem to be asking why we are here (or there). It is very little read nowadays.

Professor Eschenbaum: actually Dr Heinrich Eschenbaum, who has acquired a modest reputation for himself as an historian at the Westfälische Wilhelmsuniversität in Münster, Germany. His published works include Psychosexuelle Stereotypen der italienischen Kunst in der frühen Renaissance (Munich, 1972), Geschlechtsbezogene Aspekte der Magie im Europa des Mittelalters (Hamburg, 1975) and his renowned Gegen den Mystizismus: eine multifaktorielle, systemische Untersuchung der esoterisch-mystischen Pseudowissenschaft im Europa der Renaissance. More recently, his Pädagogik/Pädophilie (Berlin, 1992) understandably caused considerable controversy in certain circles. The journal Zeitschrift für europäische Soziologie described it as 'an . . . undeniable . . . contribution'.

Patricia Highsmith: the well-known American writer of murder mysteries, very popular with the post-modern set because, although there is almost always a murder, there is rarely any mystery. Her works, which are all about 'moral spaces', include *Strangers on a Train* (filmed by Alfred Hitchcock), the Ripley series and one lesbian novel *Carol*. The murder of Dickie Greenleaf at San Remo, mentioned later in the interview, is in the first Ripley novel, *The Talented Mr Ripley* (1955). *Little Tales of Misogyny* (1974) is a collection of stories about characters who get caught up in their own fictions and perish as a result. Gore Vidal thinks very highly of her work, as did Graham Greene. She lived for the last thirty years of her life in France and Switzerland. She died in 1995.

'*Belle Ombre*': the elegantly comfortable residence of her shady hero Tom Ripley in Villeperce, near Fontainebleau south of Paris. It incorporates all the trappings of gracious living (multiple bathrooms, original paintings, bowls of freshly cut flowers) as imagined by the middle classes.

Dante Alighieri: the reference is to the third and final part of *Purgatory*, Book II of his *Divine Comedy*, in which the Pilgrim reaches the Garden of Eden at the top of the Mount of Purgatory. If it had not been for Adam's breach of contract, humanity could have passed directly from here to Paradise proper. Since the breach few even make it this far. Everyone is 'happy' here (*beatitudinem huius vitae*), mostly in ways that would seem infinitely tedious to modern sensibilities, although no one here has yet been vouchsafed the bliss (*beatitudinem vitae aeternae*) that comes from seeing God. Interestingly, according to Dante's cosmography, the Mount of Purgatory, which sprang up in response to Lucifer's plunge into the earth's core, is situated in the 'watery hemisphere' opposite Jerusalem, which would place it east of New Zealand and south of Tahiti.

Land of Cockaigne : a mythic land of instant gratification of all desires. The Land of Cockaigne (or Cockayne) is not a utopia – it involves no structured social vision with supporting rituals, as does, for example, Dante's vision of Paradise or St Augustine's of the City of God. Monte Verità's connection with modern counterculture is well-documented in Martin Green's *Mountain of Truth: the counterculture begins – Ascona, 1900–1920* (Tufts University, 1968).

The Umiliate and the Jesuit: the Umiliate (the Humiliates) were expelled from the island by St Charles Borromeo (1538–84), renowned for his good works amongst the poor. In fact, the immensely wealthy and powerful Borromeo family, in the person of the delightfully named Lancellotto Borromeo, already owned Isola Bella and Isola di San Vittore (now Isola Madre) at the Italian end of the lake, the so-called Borromean Islands, which Ruskin called 'the Eden of Italy' and Stendhal, a little lamely, 'one of the most beautiful places in the world'. Turgenev was entranced beyond words, as well. Wordsworth's sister, on the other hand, called the gardens on the islands 'the peak of absurdity' and the English painter of alpine scenes William Brockedon wrote home that they exhibited 'the extravagance of a rich man with the taste of a confectioner'.

The Viana Palace: a fifteenth-century palace in the Santa Marina de Aguas Santas district owned by various noble Córdoba families, including the Fernández de Córdoba, the Figueroa and Saavedra families and now the property of the Córdoba Provincial Savings Bank. The Saavedra family motto was 'Suffer in order to live'.

Spent the winter sick with lust: the Sultan may have been following the advice of the Emir Kai-Ka`us ibn Iskander in his eleventh-century *Book of Counsel*: 'In summer devote thyself to boys, and in winter to women.' The climatic reasons for this curious advice are nowhere explained.

Egg Castle: presumably the Castel dell'Ovo at Naples, remodelled by the Angevins in 1274, in which the poet Virgil is said to have hidden a magic egg. If the egg is ever broken, the castle will be destroyed.

I was not quite sure how far this got us: not, in this commentator's view, very far at all. Rachel Berg's story is best construed as a sad mishmash of Orientalist stereotyping, primitive moralizing and mysticism of the most banal kind. On internal evidence (quarrelling popes, Roger II, the Yemeni trade with India, Egg Castle) the story purports to open in about 1210 or perhaps as late as 1215. While the basic 'facts' of the story as related by Rachel Berg (monsoons, pirates, buckram, Jewish traders, the Angevins and so on) are not inconsistent with known historical 'facts', there is no evidence whatsoever adduced here to verify that this was the history of this particular amulet. Indeed, under the circumstances, it is difficult to imagine how there could have been any.

Sorcerer has conjured up: hardly an original response: c.f. Byron's oft-quoted lines from *Childe Harold's Pilgrimage*, Canto IV:

> I saw from out the wave her structure rise
> As from the stroke of the enchanter's wand.

This now rather hackneyed Romantic reaction to Venice has been reinforced by Turner's dreamlike evocation of Venice in numerous paintings, sketches and watercolours. In fact, in the late twentieth century Venice appears to be precisely what it is: a messy conglomeration of dilapidated buildings and port facilities in the shadow of massive petrochemical installations.

Smolny Institute: this institute, set up by the Society for the Education of Young Ladies of Noble Birth, originally opened in the Nunnery itself, designed by Rastrelli and called the Tar or Pitch Nunnery in Russian because it was built on the site where pitch was distilled and stored for the St Petersburg shipyard. The building Antonietta Bayer claims to have studied in was designed by another Italian, Giacomo

Quarenghi, and opened as the Smolny Institute in 1809. The Petrograd Soviet of Workers' and Soldiers' Deputies moved there in August 1917. Lenin arrived on 25 October that year and Smolny remained the seat of government until the capital was moved to Moscow in March 1918.

Ranzoni: Daniele Ranzoni (1843–89), studied at the Art Academy in Cremona, lived in London and at Intra at the Italian end of Lake Maggiore, some 50 kilometres south of the Brissago Islands.

Princes Trubetzkoi: Pavel Petrovich (Paolo) and Pyotr Petrovich (Pietro), both born in Italy and both painters. Their Villa Ada at Intra at the Italian end of Lake Maggiore was curiously named, since in Russian the name can mean 'Villa of Hell'.

'*. . . still no one knows she's here*': in fact, the life of Antonietta Bayer is very well-known indeed, including the fact of her reburial. Many articles and even books have been written about both her and her islands. It is true, however, that facts are hard to distinguish from rumour and malicious untruths in the many retellings of her life, and whole areas of it remain clouded in mystery. Rachel Berg's version strikes me as no more reliable than any other.

Sufis: a paraphrase of a well-known precept of the eighth-century mystic Rabi`a al-`Adawiyya.

Carl Jung: Jung was deeply interested in Ascona and analyzed Otto Gross, one of the founders of Monte Verità, at Burghölzli in 1908. His thoughts on Gross and Monte Verità are recorded in his notes on Gross and in his correspondence with Freud, who became increasingly hostile to Gross and the Monte Verità movement.

PART II

Vicenza
Letters

Venice, 8th April

STRANGELY ENOUGH, the thing I remember most distinctly about that Thursday afternoon in Melbourne is standing in front of the fresh pasta shop in Lygon Street* staring at the amazing array of different pastas in the window: squiggly, green, curled, creamy, pillow-shaped, pinkish . . . It was five minutes to four and I was on my way to the clinic to hear the final verdict. I'm not at all fond of pasta but, knowing there was nothing at home for dinner that night, I thought I'd better concentrate and buy something now, because afterwards it might be difficult to put my mind to it.

It had been a tense but undramatic last week between the tests and the verdict. On the one hand you must stack the dishwasher, clean out the bird-bath and decide whether or not to watch *Seinfeld*, while on the other hand something inside you has shrunk, you care equally little about everything, except coming to terms with dying. Ironing, Rwanda, just missing the tram — they all meant as little as each other. Or as much.

There's little urgency to anything any more (oddly enough). It's not a *completely* unpleasant feeling.

In a funny way the week had begun on an off-key note. Our friends Harry and Jill (let's call them) came to dinner on the Sunday evening. At one point in the evening Harry started telling the story of Bruce Chatwin's slow decline. He'd apparently been a good friend of Chatwin's, who, even while he was dying, would often pick up the phone and call Harry in Australia. It was a long story – the illness in India, the two-hour struggles to get to the bathroom and back unaided, every tiny, ghastly detail. The consensus, of course, was that Chatwin had Aids, although the moment Harry mentioned the word on the telephone, the calls ceased. A taboo had been broken. Very English.

The striking thing about Bruce Chatwin stories (and Harry's was no exception) is how consistently the male tellers of these tales emphasise his physical beauty. It's a vital element in the story, part of its undeniable power. Chatwin was astoundingly beautiful, apparently, startlingly, even breathtakingly beautiful – not hand-some (that's not the word that springs to his friends' lips), but beautiful. Is there a difference? Men usually skirt around the topic of another man's physical beauty, of course, very often claiming they're oblivious to it, even unsure of what it could mean. Once a man is dead, however, and if his beauty somehow enhances the tragic narrative of his death, it may be mentioned. Indeed, there is almost a compulsion to make mention of it. In the case of diseases such as Chatwin's is rumoured to be, beauty becomes a flaw inviting infection. Or as Freud put it, Nature destroys us through the very things that occasioned our satisfaction.*

I fixed my eyes on Harry and listened to the story of mounting decay and disability, feeling as the minutes ticked by as if I were being slowly winched into the maws of some infernal machine and crushed. Peter couldn't stand it and went into the kitchen to stack plates. Then Jill followed him, and I was left facing Harry across the dining-room table, caught up in the toils of his tale of death. It was an idiotic situation: I felt I might make Harry feel awkward by interrupting, yet he, I presume, was unaware anything at all was amiss. Over time I learnt to handle this kind of situation more adroitly.

The next morning, still feeling a little scarified, I went back to work for the first time in several weeks. Why not? Even if time is limited, you have to do something, you can't sit at home just writing your memoirs and putting your affairs in order. (In fact, I refuse to put my affairs in order, to clean out the cupboard in the bedroom, get the side gate rehung, sort out my tax and generally tidy up. It's a temptation, but I refuse to start crafting a neat ending to my life, as if I were some minor short story. The more loose ends the better.) Besides, there was a lure: I actually had an interview with Salman Rushdie lined up for that first day back. How enlivening his scurrying wit was, his passion for spinning stories and running off in unexpected directions. He gathered me up and took flight with me in tow, and for nearly an hour I forgot about rotting and death. Well, to be honest, you never completely forget. It's wearying. Have you heard the sound a blackbird makes when it sees a cat slink into the yard? It's a ceaseless, low, slow twit ... twit ... twit ... almost murmured, if a bird can murmur. Sharp-clawed death is on the prowl. That's the kind of murmur I hear in my ear all the time.

Craving was one of the things we talked about that day. I suppose I remember that, rather than all the more important literary things we discussed, because it shone a light on something that was stirring in the darker reaches of my own mind at that time. All the stories in the book in front of me were about desire – for happiness, riches, home, power over others – and about how intoxicatingly easy it is to manipulate desire, to mould it into craving. What is the difference? Is there one, except in degree? (Had I too often craved?) Desiring to be is one thing (to know, to see), craving to have quite another. And the more you crave, the more you must force the complicity of others, the more warped your love for others, the more vulnerable you are to the loss of *everything*. Yet how quickened you feel when you crave, how galvanized, exhilarated, how close to ecstasy.

The wonderful thing about desire in Rushdie's stories is the way it destroys absurdity. The lover knows it, the saint in his cell knows it, even the housewife choosing a new toaster knows it. And Christopher Columbus knows it (in Rushdie's story): if Isabella, who eats like a horse and is devouring Spain city by city, will send him west 'beyond the Edge of Things' as he desires, give him ships that he might cast his glittering eye on the golden paradise he knows must lie there, then life is radiant with meaning. Otherwise he must retire from meaning and accept that the philosophers are right: life is absurd. And so he 'dogs her footsteps, hoping for the ecstasy of her glance', hoping for consummation, rapture.

'Absurdity and the need for meaning are things I've been writing about forever, really,' Rushdie said to me. 'On the first page of *Midnight's Children* the narrator says that more than anything else he fears absurdity and then he tells this huge, rambling "shaggy-dog story" as a way of inventing a meaning for his own life – a meaning which, even as he talks himself into it, he fears it may not actually have.' We all know the feeling. Talking to Rushdie was like an elixir.

By the Thursday, all the same, I was feeling a little scratchy. I was aching with the waiting, sighing a lot and making small 'oh' noises at odd times. I didn't tell Peter that this was the day – why have two of us feeling like this? At about three o'clock I left work and took the tram north to Lygon Street, wondering (how could you help it?) what sorts of meetings and conversations my fellow-passengers might be travelling towards. Arriving a little early, I sat for a few minutes at a table on the pavement, sipping a coffee and listening to a host of sentences form and fade in my head: *If the news were good, he'd have rung me this morning, so . . . His*

silence means nothing, he wouldn't tell me anything over the phone
. . . If he smiles too brightly when he first sees me in the waiting-
room, then . . . If it's good news, he'll tell me right there as soon as
I stand up to follow him . . . If he says nothing but my name and
smiles briefly, then . . . If it's good news, I'll levitate, I'll fly out the
window, I'll be home in two seconds and fling open the door and
we'll be so happy we'll burst, I can see it . . . And I could actually feel my heart-beat grow stronger with the
imagined joy of it all.

I crossed over to the fresh pasta shop, bought the
evening meal and made my way to the clinic. I usually like to flick through trashy popular magazines in
waiting-rooms – a surreptitious snuffle in the trough
of mindlessness and perfect bodies – but felt blank
today and sat staring straight ahead. Eventually he came
out, Chinese and immaculate, and said simply 'Robert'
with the briefest of smiles as he picked up my file and
ushered me into his room. I sat down beside his desk.
This was it. I looked up at him, scarcely trying to read
his face. I knew.

He sat down close to me. 'I have bad news, I'm sorry.
The tests are positive,' he said, gently.

I did crumple a bit then – I didn't cry, I think I felt
too crushed to cry, although later at the cinema I cried
at everything that happened and it wasn't even a particularly sad movie. Then I said the oddest thing – and
I remember the exact words because I caught myself
choosing them carefully. 'I'm sorry,' I said, 'that it fell
to you to tell me.' He looked a bit startled, but I meant
it: at that moment I was struck with how unbearable

it must be for him to sit beside people like this, week in and week out, and have to say what he'd just said to me. I'd wanted it to be him, though, if it had to be anybody.

'I'm sorry,' he said again, 'it's horrible news, I know.' And then (although I was spinning again, almost surprised to see my feet still on the ground) I heard his voice saying more things, quite graphic things I didn't want to hear, couldn't really bear to hear. You won't want to hear them, either. And then I was walking home again, barely connected to time and space, shrunken into the tiniest dot. I stopped at lights, crossed roads, passed blocks of flats, but I wasn't there. From wherever I was, I just kept an eye on the moving dot, like an ant at the bottom of a pit. This was a low point.

The lowest point came, though, when I got to the front door. Through the window to one side I could see Peter working at his computer. I would go in and quickly say what had to be said. Again. There was actually a small point of etiquette I had to negotiate here. Peter had to go out within minutes, at five o'clock, to give a lecture somewhere. The point was whether I should tell him when he got home or straight away. In either case, the next two hours would be harrowing for one of us. I found myself telling him. I told him in two or three words, staring at the point on the floor where Basil had lain quite dead not long before. There was a heavy silence. Sometimes you're drained to the point where nothing inside you moves.

Thinking back to that afternoon, I expect I senti-
mentalized the figure of the doctor. Doctors, after all,
are almost the only people we allow to talk directly
of death. It can't be pleasurable, but, like a small child,
a doctor is given leave to sit and talk to you in detail
about your dying, if not your being dead. In its way
it's quite refreshing. Everyone else, you soon discover,
whether sad, concerned, excited (and that does happen) or merely anxious that you go without leaving
a mess behind you, tends to talk to you about everything else except death. People regularly assure you
with relief how well you look, for instance, particularly seizing on a suntan (as if still functioning
pigments were some kind of miracle) as a sign that
everything is basically normal. Sometimes, feeling they
should at least acknowledge your situation, they tell
you stories from their own experience, frequently terrifying, occasionally adding an inquiry about practical
matters, a question about what treatments you might
be undertaking or contemplating . . . but not a word
about your dying or being dead. Not as a rule. No one
minds talking about death as a statistic in Bosnia, or
hospices for the terminally ill, or quoting a poet or two
('Because I could not stop for Death – /He kindly
stopped for me –' and so on)* or even Woody Allen,*
but no one much feels comfortable talking about *dying
and being dead*. In a country like Australia at the end of
the twentieth century death in these senses is a blank
for each to fill in in secret, as he or she sees fit.

I don't think there's any taboo on the subject, I just

don't think people quite know what to say. There's little the materialist or atheist *can* say, after all, apart from an expression of sorrow and support, yet to speak in terms other than the strictly materialist causes excruciating embarrassment in most circles, unless, of course, you're discussing Aboriginal beliefs, when everyone nods politely and tolerantly while thinking privately they sound even sillier than the Christian or Islamic varieties. To talk about dying and being dead makes us intolerably anxious, I think, not just about our own eventual fate, but about the pointlessness of our own present lives. Yet we're living them, briefly, and to spend too much time contemplating and preparing ourselves for the aeons when we won't be seems as futile as all the other things we do.

All the same, sometimes I do bring the subject up myself. After all, unless you consider it, how can you know how best to live now? Without thinking through what death means to you, aren't you walking backwards towards a precipice? Much better, surely, to walk facing what's ahead, stepping forwards with care, judging your footing and pace.

I think it's almost morning, I think I've written right through the night. *'The tender tint of orient sapphire, suffusing the still reaches of the sky . . .'* Isn't that beautiful?* And somehow very Venetian because the East does steal over you here. It used to come in ships laden with cottons, silks and spices, and it was from here Marco Polo sailed off to Cathay and India six hundred years ago on his visit to the court of Kubilai Khan. In fact, there are some wonderful jutting points in Venice where you can still stand on a squally day, squinting into the morning sun, convinced a fleet of galleys from Acre or Byzantium will hove into sight at any moment – just hold your breath and they'll come skimming home towards you, sails furled, two hundred oars striking the water, circling and striking again. Yesterday morning, after sitting for a while on a hot, empty square (all washed-out browns and whites) tucked in behind Santa Maria della Salute, I strolled out onto the embankment just along from Customs House Point. As I came closer and closer to the magnificent columned Customs House itself, crowned by that gigantic golden orb, right on the very point, at the entrance to the Grand Canal, my spirits were suddenly fired by a kind of mad exhilaration. Round St George's Island they must have come in those days, right to the point I was now standing on, gazing east. And the breeze must have been perfumed with nutmeg and cinnamon, saffron and pepper, and scores of strange languages must have swarmed in the air. And up by the Rialto Bridge the bags of gold and silver must have been dragged from the strongrooms, the money-lenders rubbing their hands, while the middlemen, victuallers, whores and pedlars readied themselves to ply their trade. Time simply crumpled. I have no idea how long I stood there – it hardly matters.

I can smell breakfast wafting up the stairs. In fact, I can smell hundreds of breakfasts wafting through my window from all the kitchens and cafés along the lanes and embankments round about. Unfortunately, at this time of the morning the aroma of fresh bread and coffee is always mixed with the sickly stink of garbage. In Elizabethan times an English traveller I dipped into wrote that the streets of Venice were so miraculously clean that 'one might walk about with nothing on one's feet but silk stockings and satin slippers.'* Well, she's become quite squalid in her old age.

I might avoid Professor Eschenbaum this morning by taking breakfast somewhere else. Something happened last night which has left me feeling awkward. At about ten o'clock as I was making my way back across the bridge in front of the station from my evening meal I noticed the Professor pass me in the crowd headed the other way. He had on his stylish new leather-jacket zipped up to the throat, charcoal jeans and his peaked cap. I didn't think he'd noticed me in the throng of pedlars, pickpockets and ambling tourists swarming this way and that across the bridge, and on the spur of the moment I decided to see where he was off to. Just for fun, as a caprice, an adventure. I'm sure that's all it was.

He strode along at a purposeful pace through the crowds towards the Rialto for quite some distance, but it was easy enough to keep my eye on him. It buoyed me up, it quickened my pulse – he so bent to his purpose while I, not without intent, was drawn along in his wake. He was the wrist, in a sense, while I was the whip, recoiling and flying in fitful arcs at his command. When he turned left off the Strada Nuova into quieter, darker laneways, the crowds thinned out abruptly. In an instant all the smaller sounds came back – keys dropping, a spoon on a plate, a sigh behind a shutter – and the air smelt suddenly dank again. I could see him ahead of me passing in and out of small shafts of light – the doorway of a backstreet hotel, a bakery window, a streetlight. He would vanish to the left into a narrower lane, and then vanish again to the right. I thought he might disappear into thin air, but then somewhere ahead of me I'd glimpse his leather-jacket gleaming briefly as he passed a window or door and quicken my pace. Where could he be going? I was just beginning to wonder how wise it had been to embark on this little adventure, and how long it would take me to find my way back through the maze of laneways and canals, when, turning a corner to the foot of a small bridge, I found him standing in front of me, hands in his jacket pockets, staring me straight in the eye. Maddeningly, he didn't utter a syllable. What he was supposed to say was 'Why are you following me?' or 'What is the meaning of this?' – there are several stock phrases – and then I would normally choose a stock response (feigning astonishment, asking him to mind his own business, admitting candidly and disarmingly to my idiotic prank – there are many). But he said absolutely nothing. He just stood there in the darkness and stared at me. I opened my mouth to say something but nothing came out. After a few seconds, utterly unnerved, I turned around and walked back the way I thought I'd come.

So you can see I'm not anxious to go down to breakfast this morning and meet his eyes again. I'm feeling sheepish. I still don't know what to say to him. Of course, I've been inventing all sorts of untrue and half-true things to say, some of them quite ingenious, but perhaps I should choose my moment and just tell him the truth. It's just that I'm not yet completely sure what it is.

Venice, 9th April

I CAN'T IMAGINE how things could have gone so wrong the day I left Locarno. There were no omens at all. It was another idyllic morning on Lake Maggiore – sun, ease, palm-trees, boats on the lake – and I made a very leisurely start. I knew it was time to drift on, I could feel it was the moment to experience something else, but I wasn't in the mood to map out an itinerary or set myself goals – not initially, not as I was packing to leave. I think I was in a vaguely Taoist mood that morning – you know, let the pattern appear, don't strive to craft it, gravity is the root of lightness and so on and so forth. On the other hand, you have to decide which train to catch and get on it.*

Perhaps, from the Chinese point of view, that's where I made my first mistake. For some reason I got Bologna on the brain. Waiting with my case at the station I was flicking through my Michelin guide to Italy and got stuck on Bologna: 'long, arcaded streets lined by sumptuous 14 to 17C palaces', squares of rare beauty, medieval towers . . . I'm partial to towers, I must say, and Bologna appeared to have two of the leaning kind. I'm not absolutely sure why I feel so drawn to towers. Professor Eschenbaum says (and I've discussed it with him, he's encyclopaedic) that it could, obviously, represent a public celebration of the phallus 'which you may find irresistible for reasons of your own' (as he put it) or, striking a more Freudian note, it could stand for the supremacy in civilized society of sight over the lower, more animal faculties, such as smell, whose domain is still in the street below – and, certainly, I was always faintly irked by Basil's indifference to the *view* on our afternoon walks, the splendid vistas afforded on every side by the Edinburgh or Fitzroy Gardens, for example, and the way he would focus instead on old pizza boxes and dried turds. The Professor on the whole, though, favoured Barthes' theory of the city tower:* it's the city-dweller's belvedere, turning the cityscape back into nature, allowing us to reinterpret our denatured surroundings as a kind of garden. Hmmm, I said. Or possibly, he said, for you it's an exciting amalgam of all three.

Anyway, I love climbing towers and I locked onto the Asinelli and Garisenda towers as two I must go up. I pictured them and then set off from Locarno determined to take myself to Bologna.

You glide through more mountains for a little while towards the Italian border. Very picturesque, very Swiss. Even the snow-drifts look strewn there by someone with taste. The man with the food trolley came

trundling up the aisle. That's when I had my first intimation that something had gone askew: he wouldn't
accept my Swiss francs. It was an Italian train, he said,
and it might be Switzerland outside, but inside it was
Italy. It was *lire* or nothing. I was a bit peckish – it was
early afternoon and I'd had nothing to eat or drink for
four or five hours – but I kept my sense of proportion
and decided it would do me no harm at all to wait
until I got to Bologna. Indeed, perhaps fasting before
Bologna was the thing to do – it was famous for being
what my Michelin guide called 'a sanctuary of good
fare'.

The moment you cross the border into Italy, you
realize something is deeply wrong. You coast down into
Como on your expensively upholstered seat and suddenly, through the tinted glass, you see the First Circle
of Hell. Crowded around the lake in a brownish haze
are scores of tower-blocks, pitted with tiny, box-like balconies like a pox. High up above the car-choked streets
you can see women leaning out from amongst their
washing, staring dismally down at the garish jumble of
concrete and glass hemming them in. Now and again,
as you descend lower and lower towards the lake, you
glimpse an old villa or two and a stand of straggly trees
amongst the sprawling car sales yards and factories and
road-side restaurants. To say I had the sensation of being
'upon the brink of grief's abysmal valley'* is probably
too melodramatic, but the line does come now into my
head – it's one I underlined last night, that's what paper-
backs are for – and I was definitely alive to the *forsaken*

air of the place we were going down into. I'm not sure what it seemed forsaken by exactly, but in my Dantesque mood this evening I'd probably say by hope. 'In this alone we suffer: cut off from hope, we live on in desire.' Little torment, just sightlessness in the broadest sense, and vague wellings of desire, very striking in such panoramic surroundings.

I think, like many people, going back centuries, I'd nurtured the illusion that here in the South, on this sunnier side of the ice-barrier, Nature in some blurred sense still took the upper hand. The Romans, I know, took the opposite view: north of the Alps was brute Nature's domain, a land of aurochs and elks and wild-haired Germans wearing nothing but pelts and bark, as if sprung from the very earth, marauding and plundering amongst their bogs and gloomy, haunted woods; south of the Alps, on the other hand, as the Romans would have it, the land was cleared and shaped, the lawless, Etruscan-infested forests had been turned into timber, stone cities had risen up, laws had been written, civilization had taken root and subtle minds wrote verse and philosophized. Silk, as Simon Schama has said, instead of fur, marble instead of wood, gold instead of iron, and 'elegant irony' instead of crude reality.*

That's not the myth any more, though, is it? Now it's the North, surely, which stands for civilization triumphant, for the regulation of human behaviour and the environment in such a way as to banish untamed nature from human experience entirely. In fact, you could live out a whole comfortable lifetime in Munich or Amsterdam and never suspect there was such a thing as Nature. Here in the South, on the other hand, people are at least supposed to be more in tune with their instincts and passions, letting them flower for good or evil, refining their animality but only to heighten the pleasure of being human, not to extinguish it. The cult of death, the obsession with food and the savouring of sexual passion – at least in these ways the South keeps the memory of Nature alive. However, in its more primal form you soon discover that Nature has virtually disappeared. As you roll on down towards Milan, an hour or so south of the border, the scene of devastation becomes almost overwhelming. It's not how we think of Italy, is it? Our heads swim with images of sublimely terraced gardens, mossy balustrades, domed churches, palaces, ornate fountains, streets of severe Palladian town-houses, sunny *piazze* . . . and all those things are there, of course, squeezed in amongst the industrial parks, the shabby forests of high-rise apartments, the abandoned wrecks, the dilapidated farmsteads and stinking, steel-grey rivers. Now and again you see a tiny copse of bedraggled trees awaiting the axe beside the railway line, and occasionally you catch sight of an ancient church or *campanile* amongst the giant neon signs and hideous human antheaps, but by and large this land has been macadamized and concreted over, ploughed and cropped, built on, sprayed, polluted and poisoned to the point where Nature has been entirely obliterated.

Animality may still be alive and well in the Italian psyche, but actual animals and birds are nowhere to be seen, apart from the odd lapdog and caged canary, which have as much to do with Nature as a Dutch tulip. You pull into Milano Centrale in a state of shock, or at least I did. Or was I just feeling ratty from not having eaten all day?

I was certainly feeling trapped. I hung over the lowered window in the corridor and stared out into the echoing gloom of the cavernous station. I was beginning to feel indiscriminately hungry – peanuts, half a chicken, a bar of chocolate, anything would do. But it was simply too risky to dash up the platform to change money and buy a roll or bottled drink. Up at the far end of the platform I could see people milling around the kiosks and bars. Loud-speakers were booming, wheels were screeching, people were hurrying, struggling with packages and suitcases. A watchful anxiety was in the air. But I'm a coward when it comes to leaving waiting trains. I can never forget hopping off a train once around midnight in deepest Bulgaria to buy a quick snack in the station buffet – I was only gone for two minutes, but when I got back the platform was empty. Just the infinite night, two dying fluorescent lights and me. The very word 'Bulgaria' still makes me feel obscurely alarmed.

With no warning (as far as I could tell) we started to slide out of Milano Centrale into the orange glow outside. The scabby, blighted buildings creaked past as we picked up speed, all bathed in a hellish red–

yellow glare that seemed to leave no shadows. I turned from the window and looked back into my compartment. Good shoes, silk blouses, suave jackets. Smartly coiffed heads in magazines with no text. No one seemed to notice me come back in. Two hours of hunger until Bologna. My mind was firmly fixed on Bologna. The woman in the spotless linen suit was eating Smarties.

The livid-looking sun set quickly in its sky of fiery chemicals and the world went dark. I was feeling a bit homesick. Partly it was the sense that every inch of the landscape I was travelling across was known – trodden on, measured out, marched across, fought over, built on, ploughed up, transformed, disciplined. This is wearying, it grinds you down. Quite untypically for me, images started to cross my mind of bushland outside Melbourne – thickly wooded hills scarcely stepped on in millennia, escarpments gazed at but never climbed, views out across valleys with no house or road in sight, cockatoos squawking somewhere up behind you in the trees. Walk off up a gully and you can hear small, unseen animals scuttling off amongst the ferns and fallen branches. Turn the other way and you can almost make out the skyscrapers glinting in the haze down by the bay. I was getting irrational and maudlin.

Partly, though, I was feeling ground down by the sudden, obvious pointlessness of what I was doing. When life stretches out without a foreseeable end to it, you don't mind doing things you know are ultimately pointless – reading yet another detective novel, watching yet another episode of some television serial, having dinner with people you're not much interested in, spending a day vegetating on the beach. You can *give* these things point, if it really worries you, by linking them to other things whose point you haven't got around to questioning yet: puzzling over who the murderer is relieves your anxiety about social chaos; at dinner with Julie and Ken you at least get to hear about the Persian carpet sale next weekend in St Kilda; and a day at the beach sends you back to work with renewed energy. Why in their turn any of *these* things matter is something you can keep pushing further into the future: you need the Persian carpet to make the living-room look friendlier, you need to work to pay the bills and feel fulfilled . . . and so on.

When an end to life is perfectly foreseeable, everything's telescoped. At least, in my case it is. There's simply not much left to push meaning onto any more. (Except another dimension – the future, God, that kind of thing – very tempting.) In the first few days after that dismal Thursday, meaning stopped right where I stood. I remember thinking (with relief) that I didn't care a scrap about whether or not I wrote another book, got the new bathroom cupboards built, ever really understood poststructuralism, ever travelled again, even (and this may surprise you) whether or not I ever saw a whole lot of people I loved again. I'd thought quite the opposite. I'd thought, if it ever happened to me, I'd do what all those courageous men and women I'd read about in biographies and newspaper articles did and write on in agony until the last line was finally down, jet off around the world to quickly say goodbye to people and places that had meant a lot to me, make myself read a list of great books, make every precious moment of consciousness count. Well, it wasn't like that at all. Urgency, in fact, was the first thing to drop away. It had gone within hours and has never really come back. I don't even run for the tram any more. I walk much more slowly. I feel much more like a point in space than a body going somewhere. So it's the moment I'm living through I must invest with mean- ing – waiting for the next tram, watching pigeons pecking for breadcrumbs, looking at someone's face. It changes the experience of time. It has to do with an awkward concept: good.

Cooped up in that railway compartment, gliding through the darkness towards Bologna, grubby and ratty and gnawed at by hunger, it was hard to feel high- minded. It just felt uncomfortable and pointless. Would I really lie on my death-bed thinking: 'Well, at least I saw Bologna'? What, out of interest, would I lie on my death-bed thinking? Would I have a million-volt vision of eternity, like Tolstoy's Ivan Ilyich and a Coventry cleaning-lady I once saw on television? If I'd been on a Russian train, I could just conceivably have brought the matter up with my companions in the compart- ment. My Italian fellow-travellers, to be frank, looked impervious to any intrusion, even violent death on the carpet at their feet. What was wrong with them? I thought Italians were supposed to live life like one long carnival, brimming over with heartfelt song and animal passions. And where was Bologna?

We arrived eventually, of course. Another vast booming cavern. I walked off down the platform quite smartly, anticipating a transformation: money, a room in a characterful hotel, good food, a stroll off the leash. As it turned out, it was here things began to go seriously awry.

The exchange booth was shut. *Chiuso*. I stared at the notice hanging on the glass door, took a deep breath and headed off for the Left Luggage. It was open (spurt of optimism), but you had to pay a fee in advance (deepest dejection). I surveyed the raucous bedlam around me and decided I had no choice: I would have to lug my suitcase into the city and look for lodgings street by street.

I've never felt such an outsider as I did in Bologna that night. This was *Bologna la Grassa* – the fleshy city, the plump and fleshly city, the city of goose-fat and greasy juices, of fatty cheeses and sausages stuffed into pigs' trotters. Trudging along the rose-coloured arcades, I stared at the smart crowds in the cafés and *trattorie*, laughing, talking, smoking and gobbling down their *tagliatelle*, their *tortellini* with chicken brains, their eels, their tarts and their chocolate meringues. The smell of roasted meats and coffee and fried bread was thick in the air. A patch of semi-darkness and then another splash of golden light: I'd rest the suitcase and gaze with vague resentment at the refined abundance on display behind the glass, the dedication to appetite. People more perfect than paintings made their way around me.

Then snap! Right outside a butcher's shop the handle on my suitcase broke. Two feet from my nose, hanging by the door, was a whole dead deer. I watched two ancient, black-clad widows poking around like a pair of bloated flies amongst the piles of dead flesh – the forest of salami, feathered ducks and pheasants, boars' heads, capons, sides of bacon, turkeys (plucked, obscenely white), the trays of leaking brains, the slabs of veal . . . I stood there stock-still for a very long time.

Dragging and pulling at the suitcase, I spent the next hour or more plodding and stumbling around the streets of Bologna looking for a hotel – a *pensione*, a rooming-house, a five-star palace, anything – that would take me in for the night. Nothing. The clerks behind their polished desks barely bothered to raise their eyes to look at me. I was beginning to stagger. Someone asked me if I was Polish. In the end an old man standing smoking by the door of a back-street hotel told me I was wasting my time. '*C'è la fiera,*' he said, 'there's a fair on. There are no rooms in Bologna – *non trovi nulla.* Go back to the station and take the train to another town – Modena, Ferrara, Faenza, Florence, anywhere. You'll find nothing here. *Niente, capito?*' It was a long trek back to the station with the broken suitcase. My spirits were badly battered. And there was something in the air back at the station I didn't like, as well: a feeling of vacant menace, of men prowling, hands in pockets, sharp-eyed. I got onto the first train

I saw. It was going to Verona. I went to Verona.

We trundled through nothingness for about two hours (I now realize, looking back) but at the time I felt so disconnected from who and where I was that I didn't experience it as a two-hour trip. It was infinite. Strange amber lights jerked across the window's black square. I watched back-to-front people come and go the wrong way in the glass. The dimly lit carriage was almost empty. A man whose breath smelt of violets spoke to me for a while, but I could barely make out what he was talking about – something about Lucrezia Borgia's perfect navel and how *tortellini* got their name, or perhaps it was about someone else's navel, *tagliatelle* and Lucrezia Borgia's hair.* A cheerful woman in a brilliant floral dress handed out religious tracts. Someone behind me was speaking Japanese. We all sat there, fish-eyed, not even waiting to arrive. But we did.

I felt a little surge of hope as I scrambled down from the train at Verona. I had sudden memories of throwing back shutters years ago to look down on a sunlit market square, with boxes of fruit of every colour stacked under striped awnings. Plates of spinach and nutmeg, *risotto* with clams. Something about Ostrogoths. Verona would do. Downstairs in the grubby, yellow station vestibule, however, it took on another aspect.

Stalking, padding, prowling, slinking, strutting all around me was a bizarre collection of highly painted whores, almost all of them in thigh-length leather boots and vividly clashing colours – yellows, cherry pinks, blacks and oranges. How tall they were, too, how at home in their flesh. Circling amongst them and loitering by the doors were clutches of unsmiling men – swarthy men, black men, North Africans, smoking and watching. Everyone gleamed. Someone's tinny radio was playing trashy music with a heavy beat. Outside I could see there were smudges of fog around the street-lights. Conscious that I had been noted, I kicked and pushed my suitcase over to the doorway and peered out. Of course – I had forgotten: the station was some way from the town itself. Between me and the town there was a gulf of dark parklands. The roadway linking us was completely empty. I looked round at the garish, restless crowd in the vestibule, sniffing the sourness in the air. They looked at me and drew on their cigarettes, and I knew I'd never make it. I was beginning to feel I'd careered right off the rails.

Back I went, pushing and dragging the hateful, lumpish suitcase, past the mocking eyes and muttering lips, up the stairs the way I'd come. I felt hollow and choked all at once. A train pulled in. I struggled aboard. We slid out of the station, across a river and into the darkness again, into that timeless, rocking clickety-clack. The carriage was all but empty. It was getting quite late. Nobody spoke.

When we finally clattered into the light again and drew screeching to a halt, I climbed out. I would stay here. The sign said VICENZA. It meant next to nothing to me that first grey moment on the empty platform. By sunrise, believe me, it meant a good deal.

Venice, 10th April

I'VE HAD a wonderful day here in Venice today, just nosing about. There are nooks and corners here, quite forsaken by the tourists, well away from the grubby remains of grandeur on the main canals, which are perfect for the ambler in a pensive mood. I've stood thinking today on several of those little vaulted bridges on obscure canals, watching splashes of light from the water below opening and closing like fans on the stone walls of the houses. I sat thinking with a roll and coffee for over an hour on a silent, yellowish square, watching a little terrier dart in and out of its doorway every few minutes to see what might be going on, if anything. Nothing was going on. Not so much as a cat stirring. There's a paradox which I've been mulling over. What struck me was this: on the one hand Venice sent Marco Polo to Cathay and Sumatra, inspiring Columbus to sail west and discover the Americas; traded with India, Egypt and England; was home to multitudes of Germans, Dalmatians, Armenians, Turks and Persians; yet on the other hand it was a closed society, riddled with spies and double-agents, which locked up its foreigners at night for fear of contamination. Venice even policed how its citizens dressed, forbidding lace and other vanities, decreeing that men's shirts be closed at the throat, lest even a glimpse of intimate flesh and hair inflame the passions.

It hits you in the eye, of course, at the Doges' Palace: Gothic arches, Classical sculptures, Byzantine roofs, Egyptian obelisks, Renaissance façades – 'all civilizations have their culmination here,' you're being told, 'this is the centre of the civilized world.' Yet sunk deep in the heart of this centre of the world is a prison, the Pozzi (the Wells), and next door, reached by the Bridge of Sighs, is a vast complex of dank, cramped cells called the New Prison, with the dreaded Piombi (the Leads) on the top floor under the leaded roof. However many Norwegian tourists in primary colours tramp through them, the smell of death and hopelessness will never be eradicated. Casanova was imprisoned here on the charge of being a magician. Not that anyone bothered to tell him that, apparently: forty policemen were sent to seize him, he was marched in past the garrotting machine and locked up in solitary confinement for ninety-seven days, without being told what the charge was. It was only when the Lisbon earthquake made the ceiling beams in his cell warp and turn that he began to hope that one day somehow a way to escape would present itself.*

Professor Eschenbaum was telling me about all this

in some detail just this afternoon in the hotel bar. We seem to have patched up our little misunderstanding – or at least he seems to be acting as if nothing happened. Emilio had a scorch mark from the iron on his otherwise spotless shirt. It made him look quite fetching. A minor imperfection is always so seductive, especially if it hints at a story – the faint trace of a scar, the most discreet of limps. The flawless tea-bowl is less beautiful, after all, according to the Japanese, than the tea-bowl with a slight distortion to its roundness, just as a full moon is less beautiful than a half-moon glimpsed through cloud, a cherry-tree in full bloom less beautiful than cherry-trees about to blossom, pristinely raked pebbles less beautiful than pebbles strewn with faded flowers.* Emilio may well have less appealing imperfections (less accidental ones – that is, more willed) but in the bar in the late afternoon light as he came towards us with his tray of sparkling glasses the mishap with the iron was working to his advantage.

When I mentioned to the Professor my thoughts about opening and closing, expansion and contraction, as contradictory impulses in Venetian life, he got quite animated, as I'd rather thought he might – he seems partial to abstractions. He was provoked into talking to me for quite a while about the Venetian Ghetto, the old foundry not far from the present railway station. Once the Jews were all back inside at dusk, he said, the drawbridges were raised, the gates locked and the shutters on the outer windows closed. Police patrols circled all night. The streets around the Roman ghetto were gated shut as well, but in Rome Jewishness could quite easily leak out in the city – without canals defilement of the Christian body could not be completely prevented. In Venice at night the ghetto was a sealed-off island. Christians were safe from the polluting sensuality of the Jew. And the Jew, it must be said, was safe from the violence of the marauding Christian mobs.*

'But it wasn't just Jews who were locked up at night,' the Professor said, tapping the table. 'The Germans fared even worse. They were shut up every evening in the Fondaco Tedesco down near the Rialto – same thing: doors locked, shutters closed, security patrols – but they also had spies placed inside the building. At least the Jews were left to their own devices within their prison. All foreigners, in fact – the Armenians, the Turks, the Albanians – were segregated like lepers. At night.'

He was waiting, I could tell, for me to ask an intelligent question about why. 'Why?' I asked. No doubt the answer would involve the Other, and possibly Transgression.

'The key,' he said (I knew there'd be a key), 'is seduction.' Emilio put a bowl of nuts on the table. His hand was still quite delicate, not yet a paw. 'Venice was haunted for centuries by the desire to be seduced – and the fear of being polluted. She's fallen, of course – she fell centuries ago, the ghettos were no help at all. Now, there are two kinds of seduction. Venice was long accustomed to the first kind – all those ritualized displays of licentiousness, the carnival, the respectable courtesans in their *palazzi*, the naked youths floating in gondolas on the canal. These things may be a threat to virginity, but Venice, while not a whore, was by no means a virgin. In fact, I would say that this sort of sport confirmed Venice in her ultimate virtue. These games of seduction were always just games, keeping marriage intact, power where it belonged and good-ness in the hands of the Church. Of course, eventually laws had to be passed to make sure virtuous Venetian women could not be confused with those merely pro-viding a temporary service. So prostitutes, for example, were forbidden to wear silk, pearl necklaces, gold or silver. Did you know that? In fact, like Jewish women, they were made quite early to wear yellow scarves in public, not so much to stigmatize them, as to warn all the players.

'But there's another, much more dangerous kind of seduction. That's the kind where, for the pleasure, much stands to be lost. It's the kind of seduction that takes a hold on the affections and leads to betrayal. This is the sort that Venice was on constant guard against. With the desire for spices and silks and gold came a sense of the seductiveness of what lay behind those things – the cul-tures, the religions, the secrets, the ways of living. And it was all covered in a cloak of erotic pleasure because, at root, Venice knew she was trembling on the brink of ravishment. Mustn't touch! To touch could be fatal! And so the priests thundered and the Church called lewd anything that was not Catholic – Jews were lascivious and ridden with syphilis, Turks were fornicators and rapists, Orientals practised monstrous sexual rites and so on. The outsider is *always* in the final analysis a sexual threat *because he is so desirable.* Not Eskimos, of course, or Finns, because there is no heat in them, but just about anybody else. Casanova is another prime example.'

'I don't know much about him. I don't think I even saw the movie.'

'Brilliant man! Dangerously brilliant! Dangerous *because* he was so brilliant – composer, poet, writer, diplomat, inventor, confidant of cardinals and princes. He was a theorist of the occult, a free-thinker, a mason and a linguist – he was a wit in half the languages of Europe, even Russian and whatnot. Yet what do we hear of him? That he was a philanderer, that he made love to hundreds of women, seduced nuns and virgins, cuckolded dukes – that he was a sexual threat and irresistible seducer. But this is not why he was a danger, this is not why he was interesting. He cuckolded the Church – that's why he was interesting. He was incarcerated for heresy, not for adultery. Yes, his sin was one of Eros, but we in our vulgar way make his sin sexual. Sometimes I think we human beings will never get the point.'

'What is the point?' I thought the question was a nice mixture of naïve affability and mock profundity. The Professor reached out and chose a nut. I caught the glint of the sun on the soft gold of his bracelet.

'The point?' he asked after chewing on it for a

moment or two. 'Come with me. I'll show you something and then tell you a story.'

I'm warming to the Professor. He's got more sides
to him than at first appears. That clenched quality you
notice when you first meet him is by no means the
whole story. He tips Emilio outrageously. He took me
outside, along the embankment, then right, then left,
across a bridge or two, through a *sotto-portego*, up a
laneway . . . All those *campi* and *calli* and *corti* and *saliz-
zade*, it was dizzying, I felt as if I'd been spun round and
round a thousand times and then told to open my eyes.
'There!' said the Professor, pointing across the canal
we'd emerged beside to a slender, four-storeyed *palazzo*
in the Renaissance style. The three upper floors each
had a row of three high windows on the left in arched
embrasures, then a square of blank wall, still smudged
with earlier decorations, and then in the right-hand
corner a single identical window. Pleasingly symmetrical and out of kilter all at once. At water level was a
grim, rotting wooden gate, greenish-black, flanked by
two narrow barred windows. I waited to hear what
would come next. A faint plashing broke the silence.
It was like leaves brushing against glass.

'That was the house of Camilla Scamozzi,' said the
Professor, '*la ninfa*, as she was known – the nymph. Let
me tell you about her and about this house.'

So we sat down on the lower steps of the small
bridge arching over the canal and in the fading light
the Professor told me, with a wealth of detail I may
have difficulty recalling, the story of

The Disappearing Courtesan

Imagine to yourself a May night in Venice when dwellings like this one were stylishly new and the Grand Canal was 'the most splendid street in the world', as the French Ambassador once put it (with unaccustomed generosity), aflame with sumptuously painted, gold-encrusted palaces, aswarm with gleaming dolphin-tailed gondolas in every colour — red, blue, yellow, turquoise, even black — their upholstery edged in the finest bonelace. Even so, despite the curving vistas of flamboyant Gothic palazzi, the floating markets, the fleets of galleys and the vast domed churches, on this particular night Venice was no longer at her most resplendent. Indeed, ever since the Turks had seized Constantinople almost a century before, she had felt her power and wealth decline. Vasco da Gama had only made things worse by discovering a route to the East around Africa.* The world was no longer quite her oyster — a delicious moment in any city's history, don't you agree?

It's a May night, as I mentioned, and down near the fish-market, not exactly amongst the stews but not, by the same token, on one of the more fashionable calli, either — no nightingales hung up in their cages outside the shops to sweeten the air, you understand, and few wigged ladies strolling with their maids through these streets — on this May night down by the fish-market a simply dressed woman fetched up with her young daughter at the door of a modest inn. They had just arrived from Vicenza and had been directed to the inn by a tout on the quay. There was nothing particularly remarkable about them at first glance, not that anyone much would have paid them particular attention — Venice, after all, was awash then as it is now with day visitors and tourists and traders from towns as close as Padua, just over the horizon, and as far as Bruges and Isfahan. There were guided tours to see Constantine's thumb and St Catherine's arm, there were package tours to the Orient. Panders and touts on every corner were ready to sell you the Holy Land or a night in an inn or change your money or find you a strumpet. If you were a man of quality with a fat enough purse, they might offer you an evening with a lady of refinement, adept at both Petrarch's sonnets and Turkish politics, as well as at simulating passion. They might even produce a printed catalogue for your perusal, with services and charges all boldly listed and portraits inserted here and there of the most fashionable ladies to whet your appetite.

So Donna Scamozzi (as she styled herself) and her tender daughter would have passed almost unnoticed in the streets of Venice, had it not been, perhaps, for the striking comeliness of young Camilla's face. Her skin was pale, if not alabaster-white, her long hair was fairish and prettily dressed, her dark eyes were bold but not insolent and she carried herself, even at her young age, with an erectness and ease which must have caught more than one passing eye. As Donna Scamozzi raised her fist to rap on the inn door, she can hardly have foreseen just how far and for how many years the knocking would echo.*

When the innkeeper's wife saw Donna Scamozzi and her daughter at the door, before a single word had been spoken, she knew instantly what kind of guests they would be: they would require a second-floor room with large, shuttered windows overlooking the street. The innkeeper's wife had had guests like these before. They were profitable, but as often as not more trouble than they were worth, to put it mildly. Yet there was something about this pair that the innkeeper's wife rather took to. The two women talked frankly for a while in the dingy parlour while Camilla sat stock-still and silent, watching them. Then they climbed the creaking stairs, candle held aloft, to inspect the room giving onto the street. Once the shutters had been flung back it was remarkably light and spacious, if bare. A colourful rug, something Mohammedan, would make a nice touch, Donna Scamozzi thought, and, of course, a bedspread – something special, something chaste but warming . . . roses, perhaps, red roses and violets. The pillow-cases could wait, but the bedspread was vital. Downstairs in the parlour again, after speaking even more frankly, Donna Scamozzi took the room.

Since her looks had faded abruptly in her thirty-third year, Donna Scamozzi had worked in a Vicenza bakery, but it was a struggle. Occasionally, at a fair or market, she might make a few scudi plying her old trade,* but something in her resisted 'opening her quiver to every arrow', as it was thought of then. She hankered after a way of life that offered her a little more dignity. When Camilla turned twelve and her young body showed some signs of promise, Donna Scamozzi's thoughts rose above fairgrounds and bakeries. When she turned thirteen and her breasts became rounder and firmer, her hair stayed fair and the skin on her cheekbones grew taut, Donna Scamozzi's thoughts became even airier and she watched her daughter like a hawk. When she turned fourteen and her thighs had grown plumper and her breasts had attained the perfect balance of softness and firmness – inviting but not brazen – Donna Scamozzi knew steps must be taken without delay. The best prospects were undoubtedly offered by Rome, not simply because, like armies, the clergy made abundant and avid use of harlots, but because of the quality of the churchmen in Rome, their wealth, their immense power, their willingness to reward a woman not just handsomely, but magnificently, with houses, retinues, villas, vineyards, dowries, pearls, diamonds, silks and extravagant furnishings. At awkward times they would even reward them with convenient murders.* Rome knew the meaning of the word cortigiana.*

There were drawbacks to Rome, however. The journey there was long and dangerous, the city itself had not long ago been sacked and was still half in ruins, and the competition for men of means was, if anything, too fierce. Venice was much closer, much larger, a much more splendid, gracious city, and it was crowded all the year round with foreigners, seafarers, adventurers and men it was easy to take advantage of. Straight after Holy Week, which they observed with a particular passion that year, Donna Scamozzi and her daughter set off for Venice.

The innkeeper's wife and Donna Scamozzi wasted no time. The rug and the bedspread were bought the next morning, the sheets were scented with lavender and Camilla herself was dressed in a long, high-breasted cotton gown. Her hair was braided and coiled on her head and her skin was washed with lemon water. Then, as evening drew on, the three women took up position behind the drawn shutters and peered with close attention at the traffic in the street below. Donna Scamozzi said very little, while Camilla said nothing at all, but the innkeeper's wife buzzed like a bee. 'That's Carlo Strozzi — pay no attention to the satin doublet and gold chains, he's ruined, not a ducat to his name . . . Ah! Wait a minute . . . here's Giulio Montecchio, can't be more than twenty-two, his father's in silk, his brother's a . . . no, I think he's just passing . . . Bruno Gualdo, the Cardinal's preno-tary, what's he doing here, unless a little bird told him? . . . Sshh! he's looking up . . . you could do a lot worse . . . and a lot better, if the truth be known. Now this pair looks likely, I'm trying to place the one on the left, the tall, dark-haired one . . . I'm sure we've had dealings before . . . dressed like a prince, all that velvet and crushed satin . . . still, that doesn't mean much . . . they're looking up, hold your breath . . . sturdy figure, strong jaw, I wouldn't mind being bedded by that one myself . . .'

And so, until the light faded and the figures in the street became just shadows, the women stood peering down through the slats at the sauntering men — the peacocks, the blades, the old men with dyed hair, the young bloods jostling and displaying their jaunty feathers. Some were just out roaming restlessly, but others had already heard rumours about the beauty behind the shutters. The innkeeper's wife had told the laundress, the baker's boy, the butcher and the wine-seller, who in turn had told the maids and stewards in a dozen or so of the grander houses, who in turn had told the chamberlains and majordomos, who in turn . . . well, suffice it to say that, long before the afternoon grew cooler and clouded over, all Venice (in other words, three or four score men of substance, taste and whetted appetite) was aware that a virgin of outstanding quality and refinement was presently at such-and-such an inn in such-and-such a street care-fully considering her prospects. Well before sunset the street was aquiver with men eyeing the shuttered windows of the inn and, with an edgy sensuality, each other. On that first afternoon, however, there was no reason to open the shutters.

The innkeeper's wife, who was not unpractised in these rituals, advised her two guests to take their time and choose with utmost care. The first man was the trickiest, the most perilous, the most vital of all. He must be exactly right for their purposes. To be right, in the opinion of the innkeeper's wife, he should be young (and so vigor-ous) but not a stripling (and so under his father's thumb), he should be lithe and strong (to defend her against other cocks on the walk) but not brutishly robust (and so dangerous to cross), rich (to pro-vide her with comfortable apartments) but not beyond all measure (and so difficult to tie down), unattached (except to a wife or much older lady) but susceptible to strong feelings. He should also be honourable, respected and well-connected. A man such as this would make an excellent beginning.

It was on the third afternoon that the innkeeper's wife saw Lorenzo Cordellini stroll elegantly to a spot directly in front of the shuttered window, turn his fine, youthful head to gaze up towards them and then stroll slowly on out of sight. 'The fish, my dears, has swum into our net', she said, putting a hand out to touch Camilla's bare shoulder. 'If that one comes back, we should fling the shutters wide'. Five minutes ticked past. Across the street a group of garishly dressed youths pushed and grabbed at each other and egged each other on. A priest knocked at the door opposite and vanished inside. Then, just as the sky went from green to a deeper blue, Lorenzo Cordellini sauntered back up the street, stopped again right in front of the window and turned his whole body around to face the unseen women above.

'Now!' whispered the innkeeper's wife. The two women sank back on either side of the window and Camilla, her face serene but knowing, pushed at the shutters until she stood in a shaft of pale light from the street. In her hand was a book, not unlike the original Virgin's, and it was some minutes before she raised her eyes from its pages to look into the face of the man below her. She didn't smile, but he did, doffing his cap and nodding with a brisk mixture of good humour and complicity which made Camilla catch her breath. Neither spoke. He was all in black, except for the silver buckles on his shoes, and stood strangely, stockinged legs slightly apart, as if ready to spring. 'Read your book, girl!' the innkeeper's wife whispered hoarsely. 'Don't be so bold! Turn a page or two and then leave the window . . . slowly . . . that's right . . . Perfect! A little saucy for the first time, but . . . well, we'll see. Now we wait'. Donna Scamozzi closed the shutters without looking at Lorenzo, although she was dying to, and the women went downstairs to the parlour to wait. Camilla asked for a little wine.

The innkeeper's wife was quite flushed with excitement and kept speaking in a rasping whisper even though there was no need to at all. If (as she was sure he was) the young gallant at the window was one of the Cordellini brothers, then their three-day wait had been more than justified. Banking, pepper, cotton, two monsignors, a villa on the river Brenta . . . A wife? Of course. And two sons. He adored all three. Perfection. At nine o'clock there was a knock at the door. The innkeeper's wife walked with exaggerated dignity to open it.

All Donna Scamozzi could see in the blackness of the doorway was a long, pale face, hanging there like a misshapen moon. There was a murmuring, a smile — almost a grin — and then the face was gone. Camilla could see nothing. The innkeeper's wife came back to the parlour swollen with pleasure. 'Signor Cordellini would be pleased to make the acquaintance of my enchanting guests,' she said, affecting a slight Tuscan accent. 'And has agreed to dine with us here tomorrow evening . . . with that end in view.' And then the women laughed. Even Camilla smiled, but mainly at the accent.

When Lorenzo drew his gloves off at the door the next evening, Camilla was struck by the whiteness of his hands. Delicately long-fingered, they seemed to her to shine against the black velvet of his doublet and close-fitting breeches. She raised her eyes to his strong-jawed face, framed by dark hair brushed with silver. She was touched to see, in the papery-fine skin around his eyes, signs of faint embarrassment.

He'd brought two companions with him, not so much to give him courage as to guard against the manipulations of Camilla's mother and the mistress of the house. One was jolly and one wittily morose, inclined to quote Ariosto at some length. Camilla had been elaborately instructed: she was to laugh prettily at any jokes, never throwing back her head and squawking with hilarity; she was to hold her food daintily between thumb and third finger, never belching; she should offer no bawdy comments of her own, but smile demurely at others'; she should refrain from the slightest show of malice, but be amused by others' barbs; she should temper her virtue and modesty with gayness and a promising willingness to please. For the moment an appreciation of her gallant's skills in poetry would have to serve in place of an ability to quote moving sonnets without faltering. It was a lot to ask.

There was partridge roasted on coals of garlic and peaches in liqueur. After the peaches and another glass or two of a rather fruity wine, Camilla yawned coyly, covering her mouth. There was a brief moment of silence and then Lorenzo asked if he might 'light the young lady's way upstairs'. Donna Scamozzi said it would be much appreciated, the stairs being steep and so easy to slip on. And so Lorenzo took a candle in his fine, white hands and led the way into the darkness of the stairwell. Camilla noticed how soft his lips were, for all the hardness of his bluish jaw.

Only the swish and rustle of her gown broke the silence on the stairs. At the door of her room he reached out to turn the handle, still saying nothing, and gently pushed open the door. Little could be seen in the guttering light except the rose-covered mounds and hollows of the sumptuous bedspread, filling, seemingly, half the room. 'And might I spend a moment or two more with you, signorina? It would please me very much'. Camilla looked at the smooth fingers holding the candle — was it the flame that made them seem to tremble? — and looked at the corner of his lips where a teasing grin was just beginning, and said: 'No, you might not, signore.' 'Might I then steal just one kiss, do you suppose?' 'No, signore, you might not.' 'Ah!' Lorenzo said, and Camilla thought that it was quite the most enchanting and bewitching 'ah!' she'd ever heard come from a man's throat.

The next day the shutters were opened again, twice, and again next evening there was partridge roasted on cloves of garlic and peaches in liqueur. When Lorenzo knocked again at ten o'clock and came alone into the parlour, he was civil to his dashing rivals (a tall Flemish count with flaxen hair and a spruce young coxcomb from the ducal palace) but his smile was stiff and his hands stayed gloved. The women could sense the tension between the three male bodies. When the pert yawn came, it was the cocky young ducal notary who went upstairs with the candle. He came down again soon enough, though, his feathers slightly ruffled. Too boyish, surely, too impish. It was taunting.

The day after that the shutters opened just once more, and when Lorenzo came into the parlour to stand by the fireplace he found himself in the company not only of Camilla, her mother and the innkeeper's wife, the count from Antwerp and the palace cockerel, but of a gaunt English lord and his two rosy-cheeked nephews, both drunk by this time and beginning to paw. Only comfits and wine-bottles littered the table, but the smell of roast pork was still heavy in the air. Camilla's eyes were downcast. She gave him no sign. When the yawn came, though, something fired his blood and he said, with a slight tremor in his voice: 'Might I light your way to your room, signorina?' And this time Camilla spoke for herself. 'Please do, Signor Cordellini. Thank you.' And so once more he found himself reaching for the door-handle, once more pushing the door open onto the lush, red roses of the hilly bedspread and once more, with the merest catch in his voice this time, asking: 'And might I spend a few more moments with you tonight . . . before you fall asleep?' And tonight she said he might and took him by his long, pale hand and drew him into the sweet-smelling room with its dancing shadows. He kissed her lightly on the lips and then, without another word, stretched out two fingers towards the wick and pinched it.

Downstairs in the parlour the women's main task was to keep their guests hopeful that the evening's entertainment was not quite at an end, which in fact it largely was. In the room overlooking the street Camilla's main task was to show willingness in general together with unwillingness in the particulars. Lorenzo must go back down the stairs dissatisfied, but pleased with himself — which, after a time which was shorter than he'd hoped but longer than Donna Scamozzi thought prudent, he did. The English lord and his nephews, the Flemish count and the ducal coxcomb examined him in the firelight and, jiggling their knees and twirling their moustaches, laid bets with themselves about Lorenzo's success and their own immediate chances. Once Lorenzo had left, however, with (it must be said) a certain spring in his step, they were all turned out into the street.

The next evening passed much as the one before had, except that instead of the lord, the count and the coxcomb, Lorenzo found himself nodding to a prelate from Parma, a silk merchant he knew well and the coxcomb's elder brother, who was so overdressed he looked like an Englishman. And on this occasion he came much closer to his goal, tonguing and squeezing and caressing Camilla in hidden places he had to imagine because it was so dark, while teaching her gently to make him shudder and quiver, to undo first the pearl buttons on his shirt, to let her fingers linger for a moment, circling, on the lightly muscled skin . . . In fact, as the daughter of a fairground whore Camilla needed no lessons at all and only wondered at Lorenzo's reticence. And liked it and began to feel faint tremors of passion.

It was on the evening after that that things were to be brought to a head. When Lorenzo arrived at the inn, there was no fire in the parlour, no foreign counts or lords or barons, no Venetian merchants or bankers or ducal notaries, not even a bottle of wine or plate of sliced melon on the table. Lorenzo felt a twinge of apprehension. The innkeeper's wife with a strange, preoccupied air fetched Donna Scamozzi, who came down the stairs to greet him with a friendly but somewhat distant smile. 'I'm so sorry we can't receive you tonight, signore, but we must make an early start in the morning, you understand, and Camilla is already sleeping. It's been such a pleasure to . . .'

'You're leaving in the morning?' Lorenzo felt what he was later to call a shard of ice in his heart. His long, pale face and bluish jaws grew even paler and more bluish. Donna Scamozzi thought he looked devastatingly handsome at that moment. If it had not been such a delicate one she'd have tried to draw it out.

'Yes, before sunrise. It's such a long journey, it's . . .'

'Are you going back to Vicenza?'

'Well, not exactly, no. We've accepted an offer from . . . a gentle-man in Parma to . . .' Donna Scamozzi had practised all these phrases dozens of times but they still came out in a tangle. 'We've decided to avail ourselves of the kind offer of a gentleman from Parma to . . . avail ourselves, so to speak, of . . .'

So! thought Lorenzo, his blood up. 'Donna Scamozzi,' he said, almost without thinking, 'you mustn't go to Parma, I won't let you go to Parma — why Parma? You'll be stifled by the heat. I'll find a house for you here in Venice. I insist you stay.' And he had that deli-cious, foolish feeling of not having finished yet, of needing to finish, come what may, of having tasted and now needing to eat, even if it should poison him. A sudden memory of the aroma of lavender, hot wax and freshly laundered sheets pinched his nostrils.

'Well, perhaps we could delay our departure for a day or two while these arrangements are . . .' Donna Scamozzi was not accus-tomed to such nuanced bargaining.

'I'll come for you tomorrow night. You have my word.' And he turned to go.

'You're leaving so quickly? Would you not, perhaps, like to see Camilla before you go?'

Lorenzo looked her straight in the eye. 'No, if she's asleep, let her sleep. She will need her rest.' And with a slight bow he was gone.

Lorenzo Cordellini was true to his word. Just after sunset on the following day he sent two servants to accompany Donna Scamozzi and Camilla to their new apartments. Their gondola glided under this very bridge right up to those wooden gates which were drawn open and in the chilly shimmer of torchlight on water he took Camilla's hand and helped her onto the stone staircase. The gates creaked shut. Camilla shivered in the greenish blackness. They went upstairs.

That night they ate quail in a delicate sauce and drank Spanish malmsey, and to the sounds of a lute being gently plucked Camilla let her eyes wander over the tapestries and bookcases, the velvet-covered chairs, the vases of porphyry and serpentine on the cornices. And when he took her to their room and rolled geranium-pink silk stockings up her legs (since there were none to roll down), she laughed for the first time and felt impelled to plant him in herself quickly, however awkward and painful that might be, and she became his mistress.

That summer in this house we're looking at centuries later was like a voyage over the horizon, like an eventful journey to outlandish places she'd never dreamt existed, and when she sailed back into port, so to speak, at about the time of the Feast of the Virgin, in early September, she felt as if the girl who had stepped by torchlight into the watery darkness that May night and eaten quail to lute-notes belonged in another life, someone else's. By September she knew a dozen sonnets off by heart, went to church with two pages, could con-verse with scholars and well-travelled merchants (or at least gracefully let them converse with her) – in a word, she was becoming a lady. Patient work was still needed on her speech, of course, and Lorenzo engaged a young seminarian from Florence to school Vicenza out of her. It counted for nothing when she was angry or excited, but at suppers and in church she spoke now with a kind of eccentric elegance (when called upon to speak) which Lorenzo was not alone in finding utterly disarming.

In the arts of love Camilla became proficient, but was rarely ardent. She knew those hours she spent with Lorenzo were in some way the pivot on which everything else she enjoyed turned, but something rankled. It wasn't that Lorenzo was brutal or unfeeling – in fact, he was amazingly playful, given his serious mien, especially of an afternoon; nor did she find his body unappealing – he was lean and vigorous and when he was half-clothed (especially) amongst the quilts and pillows she often felt a frenzy to have him naked; nor was he ungenerous or overly demanding; nor did he apparently spy on her or enquire too persistently about how she spent her days . . . No, her lack of ardour, her slight detachment stemmed more from her conviction that this was not it – a feeling so vague it almost has no name, yet in a way so powerful it almost needs none. Barely out of childhood, she was left with nothing to desire. Her niche in the edifice of Venetian society was not only a gilded one, but revered and necessary. She stood in it like an exquisite alabaster statue. Sometimes she felt like toppling to the floor and smashing into ten thousand pieces.

Upstairs on the fourth floor, in her room backing onto the dingy campiello at the rear, Donna Scamozzi measured these changes in mood and temper and bided her time. By the Feast of the Virgin she knew the moment to act was about to arrive.

'And perhaps it's the moment for us to act as well,' said the Professor, smiling broadly, which was odd. It had in fact grown quite dark, I realized, looking around, and although it wasn't exactly cold, it was becoming too chilly to sit on a bridge. The Professor was trying to read the time on his watch, but it had a blank face, without numerals, and he was having to squint. 'Let's find somewhere cosy to eat,' he said, and we did, just a stone's throw away on the very *campiello* Donna Scamozzi had looked out on all those centuries ago.

The waiters were rude and sloppy and the food was some sort of peasant concoction Americans and Europeans (apart from the French) unaccountably take delight in – basically flour and water in a sauce – but I hardly noticed, I was spellbound by the Professor's story. Tomorrow night I'll go to the Chinese and eat properly.

Venice, 11th April

AS A CULTURAL historian, the Professor doesn't believe in truth, apparently, or doesn't believe it's knowable, or doesn't believe it's important – something along those lines, I gather – and that, he told me, is precisely why he likes to holiday in the South. 'Here,' he said, chewing on bits of leathery flour-and-water moistened with a tomato sauce, 'they have no doubts about truth at all and it's balm to my soul, in which I also don't believe. Here I'm off the leash, here I can be wicked. Here my laws do not apply. For two weeks. It's paradise. What do you know about the Assassins?'

'Which assassins?'

'The sect of the Assassins – Persia, twelfth century. Not much, I gather. When the reign of the founder, Hassan Sabbah, came to an end, a Redeemer appeared, to lift the yoke of harsh laws from the people. One morning in 1162, in the square in Alamut, a fortress town on a mountain peak and the Assassins' seat of power, this Redeemer, also called Hassan, stood up and declared the Law null and void because Paradise had now been attained, they had finally earned it, it was theirs, there in Alamut. In fact, not only was everything that had once been forbidden now allowed, but everything that had once been a duty – praying five times a day, for example, abstaining from wine – was now forbidden as a sign of doubt that this was now Paradise. That's why I come here for my holidays. My laws are all null and void, truth exists, the body is not a book to be written in, explained and argued over, but a self to be lived out, experienced. That's why I come here. It's my redemption.'

At that moment, though, I didn't want to hear about Assassins or redemption or why Germans holiday in Venice, I wanted to hear about what happened to Camilla. 'What about Lorenzo's wife?' I asked rather abruptly. 'What did she think of the arrangement?'

'Well, as far as we know, his wife, Isabella, spent that summer on the river Brenta outside Padua with her sons, who were just reaching a frisky age. Talk must have reached her, of course, of her husband's infatuation, the house on the canal, the clothes and necklaces and bracelets and so on ... doubtless, rumour reached her at her villa and, doubtless, she was less than overjoyed by what she heard. But you must remember that in Venice at this time this kind of arrangement was not only common, but almost *de rigueur* in powerful circles. Coming from Flanders, Isabella may have taken a different, less kindly view. Still, it was the kind of arrangement which kept marriage, in particular, stable and bearable, kept family alliances, and all the money that hung on them, firmly in place. It had the added advantage that it kept sin on the boil, officially speaking, which was pleasing to the Church. After all, without sin, like doctors without disease, the Church is reduced to social work and psychotherapy and there's precious little social power in that. It seems odd to us, but in those days the churches of Venice were always full of prostitutes and courtesans and their retinues. Simple parishioners at certain of the more fashionable Venetian churches could hardly squeeze through the door on Sunday mornings because of the crush of stately *cortigiane* in their silks and furs with their page-boys, maids and majordomos in tow, their crowds of admirers and favourites jostling to display themselves and win a promising smile or a bejewelled hand on the shoulder or elbow. No, Lorenzo's arrangement, although expensive, was the very cement of Venetian life, trussing up the Christian body as it aged and fell apart. This kind of arrangement channelled desire with the utmost decorum.'

But this was a lecture, not a story. I needed a story, probably because the story of my own life is in danger of petering out in a series of incomplete sentences, the main thread well and truly frayed. 'You seemed to be hinting that Donna Scamozzi was about to make a move,' I said, pushing aside the remnants of some tinned fruit from Australia.

'A move? Ah, yes,' the Professor said, settling back in his chair and studying the stale breadcrumbs . . .

By September Donna Scamozzi was ready to start playing a more complicated game. Needless to say, it was a more dangerous game because the penalties for losing could be more painful — being stabbed to death was not out of the question, for example, not to mention hideous disfigurement and a variety of other punishments — but the rewards for winning were so enticing: palazzi, villas, brilliant society, cardinals, ambassadors . . . they were rewards Donna Scamozzi believed it was worth taking risks for.

As the weather grew cooler, Camilla took to receiving certain guests in her salon, almost always gentlemen well-connected in the city who brought her gifts and made interesting proposals, and Camilla would entertain them, sitting on her green velvet sofa, with poetry, gossip, sweet confections and sometimes a musical interlude. Lorenzo was vaguely piqued, but also vaguely aroused by the atmosphere of courteous lust in the candlelit salon. At any event, he raised no definite objections to these more and more frequent gatherings. Camilla, out of the corner of her eye, would sometimes see his long, white fingers drumming on the table while some callow ambassador's secretary paid her court, but if she turned to him and whispered something tender in his ear, he would almost always smile and let his fingers rest.

By the time the first fogs of winter settled on the city, Camilla was offering certain guests rather more than a Petrarch sonnet or two and an apricot cooked in honey, especially in the early afternoon when she had the house more or less to herself. By the Feast of the Nativity she was ready to take the next step: when Lorenzo arrived at the door onto the campiello one night, he found it locked and barred with two strapping ruffians posted on each side. There were two more on the bridge over the canal. None of them spoke. He didn't lower himself to speak to them. A viola was playing behind a shuttered window. He strode off on his long legs into the bitter dark, and as he strode he began to burn, very slowly, with a faint hiss you could almost hear.

Upstairs in her green and gold salon Camilla hardly heard the viola. Nor could she really follow the story her companion for the evening was telling her, about his recent trip to Lyons. All she had the heart to do was listen for the arrival of Lorenzo. But she heard nothing.

Donna Scamozzi quickly cast her net wide, pulling in wealthy underwriters, cotton merchants, wool merchants, wine merchants and owners of transport and packing companies. They were mostly dull, but unstinting. The less generous amongst them were robbed in a gentlemanly way by the ruffians at the door.

It was asking for trouble, of course, to stay too much longer in the Cordellini house. Women were murdered for less. Although there was no lack of earnest admirers, they all seemed vexingly happy with arrangements as they stood – this one of a Monday, that one of a Tuesday, this one of a Wednesday, usually with friends. One liked a candlelit supper à deux of a Thursday, another a monstrously hearty table of a Friday evening, with whole boars and peacocks on maiolica dishes amongst jugs of snow-water and Spanish wine. Some liked to read poetry, some liked to dance, some liked to quiz priests, some liked to moon and eat chestnuts. Rodrigo Buffi, who was half-Spanish and came on Saturdays, liked almost everything. He was plumpish, subtly lame in one leg and had a red beard, and, like most plump, red-bearded men with just the hint of a limp, he was as light as a cloud in the wind on his feet. Camilla found him sweet as an orange. He called her his sugared almond and his beauteous nymph, being given to that sort of endearment. She called him in return her mandolin and ox-muzzle, which delighted him hugely.*

So, when one April night towards dawn the Scamozzi household erupted in murderous riot, it was to Rodrigo the half-Spaniard that Donna Scamozzi glided off down the canal to seek swift help from. What had happened was this: at midnight the ruffians had had instructions to let pass a certain young man called Guido, whose family had grown rich on weaving and dyeing, but not long before midnight another spirited young man called Donato, just back from Ferrara and inclined to be frolicsome, arrived at the door on the campiello and begged to be admitted. He thumped and sang and knelt and cried out with throaty extravagance until the door was unlocked and he was allowed to bound up the stairs. No sooner, however, had he bitten her neck and been pushed away like a playful, strong puppy, than there was more banging at the door downstairs: Guido had arrived a little early. Donato rushed to the window giving onto the campiello and roared abuse down at the caped figure by the doorway below. Guido, stung to the quick, roared a string of coarse threats back up at the wild-haired figure in the window and demanded he be admitted. Donato, reeling back from the torrent of foul language, recoiled, sprang to the window and spat down into Guido's upturned face. Guido gagged, clawed at his face and ran off into the darkness to gather support. Within minutes a crowd of raucous, jostling young men was banging and heaving at the door, weapons jangling. Camilla could hear Guido's staccato threats echoing around the square: 'I'll scar you, whore!* I'll slash you open! I'll slice off your lips! I'll . . .'. Donato he promised to impale and castrate. Donato's curses and imprecations from various windows became a little high-pitched, since he and the men of the household were outnumbered and virtually unarmed. Although he liked a good stoush and the smell of men bashing men, he knew this was a real arlasse he'd slid into, a Venetian stand-up or double-cross. Not only were harlots' faces ripped from ear to ear at moments like these, but good men such as himself were often garrotted and run through as well, blades were held to throbbing veins on necks . . . Foreseeing all this, unmiraculously, Donna Scamozzi, as I said, had long since glided off to hammer at the half-Spaniard's door.

While Guido and his deadly little band of friends were forcing their way up the stairs against the ruffians, Donato and one or two of the less faint-hearted servants, Rodrigo was handing Camilla into the care of his boatman, and by the time more men came bounding into the campiello and knives began to flash and drip, chests of fine dresses and jewels and carpets and silverware and earrings and silks and velvets and satins were being loaded creaking onto yet more gondolas, and by the time the curtains were torched and men started leaping into the canal, the Scamozzis were far away in another palazzo on an even wider waterway in a noticeably more elegant part of the city.

The spring months with Rodrigo were little short of blissful. In the high-ceilinged salon hung with Flemish tapestries there were nights spent dancing the pavane (Rodrigo's spirits soared when he danced), listening to madrigals (so beautiful they cut you to the heart), watching playlets and sketches, some da se solo (Rodrigo wept and roared with laughter), reading aloud from the best-loved poets, and arguing about the Turks and the Jews and whether or not the New World was paradise. The rooms in their new residence were abuzz with dozens of accents and tongues, alive with strange scents and exotically textured garments. Time took on a different shape.

When, at the height of summer, the Count first appeared at one of Rodrigo's musical evenings and let his gaze rest rather too insistently on Camilla's pale shoulders and coiled plaits, following the droop of her pearls to where they were rising and falling slowly on her taut, white breasts, Donna Scamozzi made a note. The Count was from one of the city's richest families, flamboyant in a restrained sort of way, not in his first youth but still handsome with strong, white teeth and a magnificent, gleaming aquiline nose. Well before the autumn drizzle began, after very little commotion – just enough to keep the city's interest pricked – Camilla and her mother, preceded by a caravan of truly Arabian proportions, were comfortably in residence in a splendid palazzo on the corner of two canals.

From the balcony overlooking the spacious campo behind, where Camilla sometimes rested her head on a gold-embroidered cushion to bleach her hair, she could gaze across at the magnificent white-domed church that towered above the square, watching the flower-sellers and the melon-sellers, the priests and friars and other townspeople who came and went and gathered in the doorways and on the steps to talk and bargain. Sometimes young blades, alone or with companions, would call out to her, half-mockingly, half-amorously, begging to be favoured with a smile, a kiss, an hour alone with her – or not alone, the choice was hers. Sometimes she enjoyed the banter, but sometimes it wearied her and she'd drift back inside to play with her wicked parrot or bid her black dwarf amuse her with some of his magic tricks. Once in the late afternoon she even saw Lorenzo stride across the square below. She felt a little quaking deep inside her then, a tiny, trembling knot of fear and . . . not love exactly, but something more like crushed delight.

If she stood in her sunlit boudoir and looked about her, as she sometimes did, she would say to herself that she was happy: she was cared for generously by the Count; she went to church in a silk cape lined with white fox; she slept in sheets smelling of civet and musk; she dined on oysters and pheasant and pomegranates surrounded by wealthy merchants, wits, poets and travellers . . . yet some clock inside her had stopped ticking, some spring inside her had come uncoiled, some voice almost out of earshot kept whispering something to her about this still not being it. Something was missing that had nothing to do with happiness.

One afternoon late the following summer, when she was strolling with her maid along a street of silversmiths behind St Mark's Square, a young man in a gaudy velvet suit leapt from a window above her and landed at her feet. Camilla gasped with fright and swayed back on her high heels, clutching at her maid's shoulder. The young man grinned foolishly, begged a thousand pardons and, with a quick glance back up at the window, darted off down the street and was soon lost in the throng. When she looked up, the window was a dark square. She was about to walk on, with a wry comment to her maid, when the figure of a woman with a scarlet headband appeared fleetingly above them in the square of the window, peered down anxiously and quickly drew the panes closed, vanishing back into the dark. A narrow escape, she thought to herself, and smiled. They hadn't walked on more than a hundred paces when the young man leapt out in front of her again, bowed theatrically and grinned. 'Please forgive me, signora, I'm sorry I startled you, I was called away suddenly and – how should I put it? – most unexpectedly.' He had an appealing head of bright red curls, fuller lips than a young man usually had, a wiry frame and a slightly slurred accent which Camilla couldn't quite place but found enchanting nonetheless. She laughed. 'I admire your agility,' she said, briefly considering his stockinged calves, 'if not your timing.'

'My timing,' the young man said, a little too quickly, fixing her with his gentian-blue eyes, 'was defter than you might imagine.' Camilla reddened slightly despite herself and flapped her fan. When he asked if he might accompany her and her maid at least as far as the bridge, Camilla felt a flush of pleasure and said he most certainly might not. He might, however, call on her the following evening, joining the company for an entertainment with bagpipes, cornets and viole da braccio and possibly a juggler or two. He said he would. How light his tread was as he made off through the crowd. And how red his curls. Camilla kept them in view — bobbing, ducking, swerving — for far longer than she'd meant to.

As a consequence, it wasn't with the svelte Lorenzo, white-skinned and practised in his passion, that Camilla fell in love; nor was it with Rodrigo, who was always twirling like a top, whipped along by little storms of rapture and strong feeling; nor was it with the eagle-nosed Count with his taste for muted luxury; nor was it with any of the other men who pressed their attentions on her every day. This one was too smooth-tongued, that one too self-admiring, this one's virility too sculpted, that one's charm too unctuous. Or perhaps that wasn't it at all, perhaps none of that really mattered. Whatever the reason for falling or not falling in love, in the course of just two or three days Camilla fell up to her eyebrows in love with the red-headed, blue-eyed Alberto, who had landed at her feet like a wicked, sharp-eyed monkey, up to all sorts of tricks.

At first, like everyone, she fell in love with what she'd seen (the cheek, the litheness, the virile zaniness), so different from the ordered manliness she spent her days manipulating. And then she quickly fell in love with what she had not seen (which was far more dangerous) and hungered to see it. Each day when he called at a time when she knew she would be alone, she sat a little closer to her brightly coloured prey, who always sat by the small table covered in green velvet in the centre of the room. From her divan she gradually moved across the room towards him, first to her deep Spanish armchair, and from there to the Turkish footstool, and from there to a high-backed chair on the opposite side of the velvet-covered table. Once there, she was close enough to reach over once or twice and take his gold neck-chain in her hand to admire it, allowing his long-lashed eyes as she did so to burrow down into the milky depths revealed behind the embroidered damask folds of her dress. Once or twice he leant close enough for her to smell his breath, but that was all he did. Although his eyes never left her, he seemed to be parrying her every thrust.

The feeling of hunger might have passed, as it usually does, if it had been fed. When desire is fed, after all, it either grows fat and spills over into kindness and generosity, or else it is quenched and grows drowsy. Starved, of course, it just withers away. With a taunting insouciance Alberto, in those early days, did neither: on the contrary, he made her ravenous in a thousand little ways — feeding her morsels, touching, smiling, promising, suddenly appearing and then vanishing again — but never offered her a feast. So he might come through the door with two or three friends one afternoon, kiss her hand in a mocking, foreign way, make merry with his friends and then disappear again suddenly, borne away by a larger life; he might give his word that he'd come to see her at a certain hour, then send a breezy note, procrastinating vaguely — affectionately, but always vaguely; he might make her glow with whispered nothings in her ear, but spend the evening noisily playing cards with other visitors. And so Camilla was left with a simmering greediness she despised in herself but could not rise above.

Donna Scamozzi was irritated by her daughter's infatuation and contemplated having the young colt taught a sharp lesson and sent packing. Camilla's value, after all, was in her ability to play at love — to tease and toy and dally, to recite sonnets with feeling, but precisely not to love. The Count, for his part, felt riled by Camilla's inattention and snappish moods and thought of sending her away to one of his estates in the hills for a month or two to distract her and calm her nerves. Their glittering serate were now fraught with sulky silences, long, heart-felt sighs and flimsy excuses to leave the company and flee upstairs. Then something happened to turn their peevishness into dismay.

In desperation one morning, alone with her hairdresser, Maddalena, Camilla gave vent to her misery, hoping Maddalena, with her many skills, might suggest a way out. Standing behind her, Maddalena's eyes narrowed with pleasure and she wound Camilla's hair so tightly her scalp ached. 'You must help me, Maddalena. I know you know about these things,' Camilla said, straining against the pulling of her hair. And, indeed, Maddalena did. In fact, the bleaching and brushing and curling of hair was the least of what Maddalena knew. As a ruffiana of many years' standing, she had a finger in many a juicy Venetian pie, arranging for certain men to dine at certain tables, for certain wives to take interesting advantage of their husbands' occasional absences and for the intimate education at the hands of accomplished teachers of the scions of well-to-do families. A little overpainted, Maddalena looked on her hairdressing as little more than a means to more profitable ends. Although it was none of these skills that interested Camilla that morning – she was pinning her hopes on knowledge of a more arcane kind – it was precisely these skills which made the next few moments so pleasurable for Maddalena and so horrifying for Camilla.

'Do you not know who Alberto is?' Maddalena asked in a low voice just behind Camilla's right ear.

'Who he is? Well, no, not exactly. He travels for his father, I think. I gather he's been living in Flanders. And he paints, he said. He's promised to . . .'

'And do you not know who his father is?'

'His father? No. Cotton or something, I think.'

'Yes, cotton. His father, you see, is Lorenzo Cordellini.' This was whispered right into the ear.

Camilla sat bolt upright as if stung. Her mind swam. 'Lorenzo? But the red hair, the blue eyes . . .' As if they mattered.

'He's the image of his mother.' But even prettier, Maddalena thought, although didn't say so. 'It's the Flemish blood. It's the other son, Aldo, who looks like Lorenzo and has his moods.'

Dizzy with a kind of panicky grief, Camilla tore herself from the chair and went to the window. She stared down into the water in the canal, green at this hour and flecked with sunlight. Above the roofs across from her window the sky was meshed with strands of cloud, as if somebody had been up early raking them. It was impossible. It smelt of blood. She could feel her throat tightening, filling with an aching sweetness.

'Does he know?' she said after a while. 'Does Alberto know who I am?'

'I imagine he does, my dear, yes.'

Camilla groaned. 'But Lorenzo has heard nothing?'

'I imagine not, my dear, no.'

Camilla stood staring at the combed clouds. After some moments she said: 'What shall I do, Maddalena? Tell me what I should do.'

'We'll lock the door, my dear, when we're finished,' Maddalena said, still standing behind the chair, 'and have a little look at what the cards say.' Like a sleepwalker, Camilla drifted back into her chair. In fact, the cards made Maddalena draw her breath in sharply, then widen her eyes, then smile a pursed smile, then call on Jesus and all the saints and then sit back wheezing with her eyes closed.

'Well?' said Camilla, after a little pause, her smooth, young hand on her throat. 'What do they say?'

'They say,' said Maddalena, as if from far away behind a mountain, 'that his soul is wandering in a wasteland swarming with evil spirits, squinting at him with murderous intent. I see soot-black souls hanging like bats from barren branches, twisting and squealing as he passes with delight at his horrid fate. I see a lake of bile and a bloodthirsty boatman, pale as a ghost . . .'

'Yes, yes, Maddalena, but what should I do?' Camilla was feeling ill with fear and hopeless desire. Bloodthirsty boatmen, soot-black souls — this smelt of sulphur and the Devil. Camilla wanted to know what she should now do.

'We must find a lure for his soul, Camilla. We must lure him out of the wasteland and into . . .'

'What sort of lure?'

Maddalena was still fossicking about behind her mountain, and took some time to answer. 'Bring me a thumb-nail clipping, a drop of his sweat and a lock of his hair.* Bring them soon,' she said, her eyes still closed. 'And bring me a pearl and a sliver of amber shaped like a teardrop. And bring them soon.' Then she opened her eyes, scooped up her cards and made ready to leave.

'Maddalena, I'm afraid. If it works and Lorenzo finds out . . .'

'Let us first cast our lure,' she said, casting more than one lure herself, 'and wait to see what happens.'

The pearl and sliver of amber took no more than a moment's thought to obtain, but the hair, the thumb-nail clipping and drop of sweat took a little more scheming. A whole week went by before Camilla could lock the door of her boudoir again and lay the ingredients out for Maddalena on the low inlaid table beside her chair. After drawing the curtains, Maddalena crushed and burnt the hair, the clipping and the sweat-soaked silk handkerchief in a small bowl, added a paste of nightshade, foxglove and musk-seeds, squeezed the mixture into a tiny blue glass phial and told Camilla to bury it in earth until the moon was full and then smear it, while Diana the huntress was riding high in the sky, on the tip of Alberto's penis. 'Plant him quickly inside you, my dear, and watch him rear and buck for you until the next full moon. It's up to you how you use your whip and reins.'

'But how can I be sure of coaxing him to bed me on that night?'

'As the moon rises, drop this pearl and this piece of amber into a glass of wine. Make sure he drinks it looking at the moon. He'll have you on your back, my dear, before he's finished the glass.' Maddalena cackled briefly, remembering the pleasure of being thrown back on a bed in the dark by a trim, half-naked youth. It was a very faded memory.

Camilla did exactly as she'd been instructed. Miraculously, the smell of sulphur turned to orange-blossom and lilac, and Alberto seemed indeed to change and love her. The morsels multiplied and became a banquet. Slowly, step by tiny step, Camilla could feel herself passing into that blissful state where she no longer desired Alberto himself so much as she desired no longer to desire him, just to be with him — or at least she had some inkling of what it might feel like to desire him in that way.

Donna Scamozzi, meanwhile, was beside herself with fury and apprehension. The Count was running out of patience as well, and, when he was told who the red-haired monkey was and how he had been snared, he became rigid with fear, locked Camilla in an upstairs room and told her she would stay there until the Devil had been starved out of her. A gloom seeped into the house and stayed there all winter.

Alberto, less monkeyish now, was at first stricken with despair.

His pride wounded, he cast about for ways to pass word to Camilla of his undying fidelity, his smouldering rage, his oath to free her – he gleaned wonderful phrases for all these emotions from the poets – but she seemed out of reach, immured like a nun. Quite a few of his friends counselled him to leave Camilla to her fate and not tempt his own. Yet there was something in his feelings for her that would not die away like a guttering candle, something innocent. It was as if she were his means of knowing something good. He watched his father's face all through that winter, but noticed nothing. If Lorenzo knew about what had happened, he gave no sign of it at all.

By the same token, with time his love for Camilla became like a poem he kept in his heart as he began to live life to the full again. Even in the fastness of her locked room at the top of the palazzo Camilla eventually heard of his attachments first to this and then to that young lady. She dreamt over and over again of his long-legged, fiery-headed body leaping from a window to land at her feet. She heard him whisper to her again: 'You are my red-hot butterfly!' No one had ever called her anything more beautiful.

When in the early spring Camilla was first allowed to leave the house to take the air, on rounding a crooked corner of the church she found herself staring straight into the eyes of Lorenzo Cordellini, not an arm's length from her nose. 'Lorenzo!' she said, startled, but with a sad eagerness to please, to look into eyes which had looked on Alberto, to touch a hand which had perhaps touched his. Lorenzo hesitated for the blink of an eye, smiled, doffed his cap and gave a shallow bow. 'I hear you've been unwell, Camilla,' he said.

Camilla blushed. Could he know the cause? God forbid. 'Y-yes, I have,' she stammered, 'but it was nothing serious. It's been so damp and cold.' Lorenzo nodded, but scarcely smiled. 'Come and see me, Lorenzo. Why don't you come and see me? You often seem to pass this way'. He appeared to consider her impromptu invitation for a moment or two in his pale, deliberate way and then soften. 'Perhaps I will, Camilla, if that's what you'd like'.

'Do, Lorenzo, please'. Why was she saying these things? What could come of it? Why court danger? Because she must have news. She watched him walk away with the light, almost animal step she knew so well.

When he came to the house not long afterwards, he seemed to be in an oddly heightened mood. Dressed in a loose silk shirt and tight breeches, with his jacket slung over his shoulders, he had a gay air to him which Camilla scarcely recognized. He even kissed her differently, urgently but without deep feeling, with one hand behind her neck, his long fingers in her hair.

'Let's go out on the lagoon', he said, stepping back and looking around him without comment. 'It's sunny, the wind's warm — it will do you good'. Camilla felt her spirits lift.

And so they glided off down the canal, past the gilded and painted palazzi, the floating melon market, the cloisters and towers of St George's Island and out across the busy lagoon, quite choppy in the easterly breeze, towards the low line of the Lido, dodging the water-fowlers and fishermen. Camilla had the feeling everyone whose love is thwarted has at such times: a frantic longing to turn back mixed with a submissive desire for gentleness.

They came at length to a small village towards the southern end of the Lido, and Lorenzo suggested they refresh themselves at a small inn by the water's edge. After a glass of wine or two Camilla felt more at peace. After the eels with spinach in nutmeg she could feel the pull to return slacken. And after the blackberry tarts and Lambrusco with its whiff of violets she felt a fondness growing in her for the smooth-skinned, strong-jawed man who had gently taken her small hands in his, and did not resist when he whispered to her that they might take a room upstairs for an hour or two for old times' sake.

It was a vile room, cramped and smelling of grubby linen, but Camilla felt too drained of strong feelings to make a fuss. She sank onto the bed beside Lorenzo and kissed him almost chastely, pressing her lips into the warm sockets of his eyes. Then she licked him just beneath his jawbone and nibbled the tender skin behind his earlobe. He groaned softly. Then, easing himself off the bed away from her, he held up a finger as if asking her to wait and said: 'I need to have a word with the innkeeper — we don't want to be disturbed. Stay there, don't move! I'll be back in a moment.' Camilla smiled and lay back amongst the pillows. She heard him run lightly down the stairs. For the first time in many months she could feel a cocoon of tenderness being woven around her.

The footsteps that came back up the stairs were heavier on cruder soles. The man who came into the room was taller and dressed in rough fisherman's garb. He flung himself on her and, nuzzling and dribbling in her ear, he raped her with savage fervour. He was followed by his wiry brother, who stank of dead fish and whispered honeyed filth into her ear until he gagged with pleasure. He was followed by his son, who then ground into her face while two of his reeking companions busied themselves between her aching legs. They were followed by the wine-merchant and his spindly assistant and they were followed by the pastry cook and his idiot son. And Camilla bled and retched and wailed, but they stopped her mouth with their thrusting bodies, clawed at her, beat her, spat on her, opening her up again and again and again to their gouging and jabbing and ramming and churning. And as the afternoon turned into night footsteps kept following footsteps up the stairs until Camilla lost count of the men who came into the room to rape and grunt filth at her and hold her for others to do the same.*

When towards midnight the bandy-legged butcher's boy left her and staggered noisily down the stairs, there was silence. Camilla was a tiny leaden ball, no bigger than a pinhead, floating in empty blackness. No clocks told the time where Camilla was. Camilla was no longer Camilla.

No mention was made to the Count of Lorenzo. But not out of Christian charity.

Life at the Count's palazzo returned to its normal flow, to the relief of Donna Scamozzi, the Count and his circle. If anything, Camilla appeared gayer and more self-assured than before her wretched infection with love. There was a certain brittleness, perhaps, to her manners and grace, which had not shown itself before, but a touch of glassiness and fragility is not unattractive in a spirited woman. There was little need for Camilla to spend many hours alone.

A few weeks before St Anthony's Eve Camilla called again for Maddalena. As she braided and decked her hair, Camilla spoke with her about the festivities the Count had planned for the saint's day and certain requirements of her own she believed Maddalena might like to assist her with. This time, however, there was to be no need of potions or unguents, no need of screech-owls' hearts or fennel-stalks sprinkled with blood and urine, no need of any kind of spell or divination. This time the skills she was in need of were far more down-to-earth.

The very day before St Anthony's Eve, with Maddalena's invaluable help, Camilla wrote Alberto Cordellini a carefully worded letter. An hour later, again with Maddalena's help, she wrote another carefully worded letter to his father. Then the two women began their careful preparations for the festivities the following evening. In this intricate dance no dancer must stumble.

By sunset the next evening the crowd in the salone grande was in a frolicsome mood. In the glow of chandeliers and torches women in exquisite gowns from Milan and Mantua drifted amongst men who owned half of Venice, resplendent in silk and satin and African gold. Maids, servants, dwarves and pages of every hue swarmed beneath the Flemish tapestries. Two monkeys chased each other in and out of the doorways, parrots shrieked. Whole roasted swans lay on the table, each feather in place, amongst boars and deer and suckling pigs, pheasants and thrushes and quail by the score, vast dishes of oysters and mountains of melons. Jugglers juggled, fiddlers fiddled, and painted actors sang songs of lust and unrequited passion:

> Stringi'l bramoso amante e stretta aggiungi
> Le labbra a le sue labbra, e'l vivo spirto
> Suggi de l'alma amata, e del tuo spirto . . .*

Soon after midnight there was a ripple of slightly drunken laughter when the Count announced the next divertimento: wondrous wizard, clairvoyant and conjurer, supreme maestro of the magical arts, Claudio Coccola would now demonstrate, before the very eyes of the distinguished signori and signore, a feat never before seen in Venice and known only to a handful of grand masters from the Levant, where Signore Coccola had spent many years studying at the feet of . . . Here there were raucous calls from the throng to stop saucing the goose and to 'bring the trickster on'.

It was only when the magician appeared like a puff of smoke at the far end of the hall that the crowd noticed four large carved coffers standing in a row a few paces out from the wall. 'Signori e signore, for your amusement and edification I am about to work the impossible. Tonight, here under your very eyes, I am about to make one of you disappear.' Here there were several hoots of derision and a surge of disrespectful giggling, but Claudio Coccola swept on undeterred, fixing the crowd lolling at the table and gathered in knots around the walls with a penetrating stare. 'You will observe, ladies and gentlemen,' he went on, 'that at this end of this (magnificent) hall there are no windows.' He strode with one of his black-clad assistants over to the tapestry draping the wall behind him and together they lifted it to show that, indeed, there were no hidden windows, doors or other exits in the white-washed wall. 'And I must have complete silence during the weaving of my spell, ladies and gentleman, or else' – and complete silence actually fell – 'I cannot guarantee that the one who disappears will be able to return – the spirits may take offence.' At this point there was one muffled guffaw from a group of young men clustered by the main doorway, but on the whole the crowd seemed to be entering into the spirit of what was about to happen.

'And so, ladies and gentlemen, I now call upon the following four ladies to come forward and stand each upon one coffer.' The magician closed his eyes and raised one hand to his forehead as if listening for the names to come to him. 'Lucrezia Niccolini!' (Applause from the assembled throng – Venice herself would sooner disappear than Lucrezia Niccolini, one of the city's grandest and most ravishing cortigiane, a must on the itinerary of every visiting Englishman. Lucrezia swished forward in her flowing blue satin and was helped up onto the first chest.) 'Ortensia Campanella!' (Half the room wished Ortensia would disappear – for good. All the same, there was good-natured applause as she tripped across in her black velvet to stand on her allotted chest. Such a vixen.) 'Grazia Sardo!' (She blew farewell kisses to the crowd as she made her way to her chest. The pearls looped through her hair were the fattest in the room.) 'And, lastly, Camilla Scamozzi!' (Roars of approval now – she was, after all, in a sense the evening's *ostessa* – and she looked radiant in her long white gown trimmed with gold. Her hair looked strikingly different this night – Maddalena had evidently been busy: it was parted and fell in heavy, golden loops to each side of her head and across her cheeks. Her expression was utterly serene.) 'One of these lovely ladies will, when I utter the magic syllable, vanish from among us. And I remind you: I must have complete silence during the casting of the spell or else the soul of the disappearing lady will be in mortal danger!' (Breaths were held in anticipation.)

Meanwhile, as instructed, moored below in the shadows on the side canal, was a small, green gondola, and in it was the seated figure of a single man, head cowled. It was Lorenzo Cordellini. And in the pocket of his cape was the letter from Camilla, a letter whose simple womanly words had fired an arrow straight into his seething heart:

My dear Lorenzo! I am without hope – give me hope! I am a prisoner in this house, Lorenzo, chained to the monstrous desires of my master and to my mother's greed. I see now how heartlessly I dishonoured you and why the blemish on your manhood had to be wiped away. But my suffering has its source not just in my slavery to others' passions, nor in the shame I endured that you might be shameless, but in my own aching and unworthy desire to find favour in your sight once more and to tend again to your needs as you deserve.

If you will only rescue me from this prisonhouse, where I am every day misused, I swear in God's name to repay you most sweetly in ways you hardly dare dream of.

Tomorrow, just after midnight, I shall come to the gate on the side canal. Have mercy on me, Lorenzo. C.

Camilla knew that the best lies are shot through with profound truths.

Upstairs in the salone grande Claudio was holding his hands aloft for complete silence. 'Lower the candelabra!' he called, and several servants ran to ring it down. 'Extinguish all other candles and torches!' he cried, and again servants ran to snuff the candles and torches. The candelabra which had hung above him hit the floor at his feet with a jolt. His face floated above the flickering lights as if underwater. 'Alleb afnin!' he suddenly cried out hoarsely, and his two pale hands fluttered above him in the shadows. The crowd shuddered. 'Alleb afnin!' he cried again in the silence, and the strange words ricocheted from wall to wall high up near the ceiling. The four women stood silently behind him in the gloom, their faces like four pale moons.

Then he reached out with a long snuffer and snuffed one candle. 'Alleb afni!' he cried. Again he snuffed out a candle, this time with the cry 'Alleb afn!' And as one by one the candles were extinguished, and the darkness grew thicker, and eyes widened, and breaths were held, he barked into the blackness:

> *Alleb af!*
> *Alleb a!*
> *Alleb!*
> *Alle!*

Alll!

Al!

A!

The last candle went out – pfsst! – and there was a swishing and
rustling – whoooosh! – as of vast rushing wings beating high up
amongst the ceiling-beams. Down tumbled a huge brocaded curtain,
hitting the floor with an echoing thud. Apart from a tiny knf! knf!
knf! (a minor countess sneezing from the dust) all was silence.

In an ill-lit, oak-lined ante-chamber just beyond one of the side
doors Alberto was waiting, shivering in the unheated air, waiting for
his adventure to begin. Like his father in the gondola below, he, too,
had a letter in his pocket. He knew what it said off by heart:

My dearest Alberto! I am without hope – please
give me hope! I am a prisoner in this house, Alberto,
chained to the monstrous desires of my master and to
my mother's greed. If you will only rescue me from
this prisonhouse, where every day I am misused, I
promise to repay you most sweetly in ways you
hardly dare dream of.

Tomorrow, just after midnight, I shall come to you
in disguise in the oak room next to the great hall.
Wait for me there as soon as Claudio the magician
begins his tricks. C.

On the other side of the heavy, carved door from where he stood,
wraith-like figures were scurrying – one, two, three, four, how many
were there? There was cooing and moaning, sighing and groaning.
Then the maestro boomed: 'Light the torches!' As the room filled with

light, slowly, in patches, two of his assistants dragged at the brocaded curtain which came loose from its beam on the ceiling and fell in a crumpled heap on the floor. In the flickering half-light beyond the piles of brocade which his assistants began gathering up, stood the four mysterious trunks. Every eye in the room was fixed on them.

'Lucrezia Niccolini, come forth!' Claudio cried. An assistant lifted the lid and out stepped a dazed Lucrezia, smiling and dusting her breast. 'Ortensia Campanella, come forth!' Claudio cried, and Ortensia rose from her box, looking slightly disappointed not to have disappeared. 'Grazia Sardo, come forth!' Claudio cried, and Grazia, too, stood up and stepped out of her box, adjusting her pearl loops and bowing to the crowd. One box was still closed. Every eye in the room was fixed on it. Claudio paused for effect. 'Camilla Scamozzi, come forth!' he cried. The assistant pushed back the lid, the crowd gasped: out of the box stepped Giulia Giacomini, looking startled in a neck-to-toe puce dress. Giulia, notorious from Santa Chiara to the Arsenal, had not even been invited to the festivities. She looked around her in dazed amazement and began to sob. A wave of spiritual terror passed over the room. Camilla Scamozzi had disappeared.

I smiled indulgently. In the absence of miracles, a touch of legerdemain can be so satisfying.

'Of course, in itself,' said the Professor, 'the magician's tawdry trick was hardly interesting. What was interesting, and scandalized the Venetians for years to come, was that Camilla Scamozzi never reappeared.'

'What do you mean?' I said. 'She clearly didn't vanish into thin air.'

'I mean that from the moment that final *A!* was

uttered and the last candle was snuffed out, no one ever saw Camilla Scamozzi again.' I was impressed.

'But what about Lorenzo and his son? Can we be sure one of them didn't abduct her?'

The Professor smiled. 'Quite sure,' he said. 'We know how the evening ended for them. It ended cruelly – I even feel sorry for the hapless Alberto. Presumably, the little ruse that Camilla and Maddalena worked out between them, with the magician's help, worked like this: one of Claudio's nondescript assistants was in fact the notorious Giulia – a comfort at one time or other to half the youths in Venice and bought, no doubt, for just a few *scudi*. When the curtain dropped, Giulia let her hair out from under her cap and popped into the trunk where her neck-to-toe gown was waiting for her. Once the other three women were safely inside their trunks, Camilla, we must take it, threw off her wig and gown, leaving her dressed in an assistant's black velvet. With Giulia's black cap on her shorn head she was just one of several young lads grappling with the brocade – her gown and wig hidden in its folds – and, distracted by the drama Claudio was orchestrating as the lights came up, no one paid any attention to the boy in black, possibly with Maddalena's help, dragging the brocade into the ante-chamber where Alberto was waiting. Once the door was closed it must be assumed that Camilla convinced Alberto to put on her dress and wig over his shirt and breeches and meet her in the gondola below where she would be waiting for him in a cape and hood – perhaps on the grounds that otherwise he may be recognized and pursued. In any event, he did as he was told, fled down the stairs to the gate on the side canal and joined the caped figure in the gondola. The two figures embraced passionately – indeed, with such passion that within moments each found the man in the other. Stricken with horror, each tore the disguise from his supposed lover and . . . well, you can imagine the heart-wrenching disgust that must have seized them both. Instead of a lover's embrace from his creamy-skinned nymph, Alberto found himself being sexually fondled by his blue-jawed father. And instead of one of Venice's most desirable young women, Lorenzo found himself tongue to tongue with his own treacherous son in women's clothing.' The Professor paused to imagine the scene with what I had the feeling was faint pleasure.

'Lorenzo was appalled, naturally, and, in the heat of the moment, threw himself backwards with a foul curse and fumbled with those long, white hands of his for his knife to kill Alberto on the spot. But the boat capsized and both men tumbled into the water. Only Lorenzo scrambled ashore. Alberto was drowned. It was later alleged by a passing gondolier that Lorenzo had poled his son under until he drowned, but no one knows for sure. He left Venice for good just a few days later. Camilla destroyed him and destroyed his family. Of course, from my point of view, he was repaid very much in his own coin.'

'And the Count? Maddalena? The magician? What happened to them?'

'Well, at first, as you might expect, the festivities simply went on in much the same vein for a while – there was dancing, more eating and drinking, some larking about by the younger guests – but then the Count became anxious: where was Camilla? Why had she not come back? To begin with, he blamed the magician who, also to begin with, thinking it was all just a lark, blamed the minor countess for sneezing. (She never sneezed again, by the way – I've read her memoirs.) The Count then threatened to have Claudio seized for sorcery – a serious offence in early Renaissance Venice, you understand – at which point Claudio ceased to be a magician and blamed everything on Maddalena, the *ruffiana*. Just as the Count was about to have Maddalena seized and unpleasantly questioned, Camilla's body was found drowned in the canal – except that it wasn't Camilla, of course, it was Alberto Cordellini. There was uproar, naturally, from the rafters to the waterline. Why was Alberto freakishly dressed in Camilla's clothes? For that matter, why was he dead? He hadn't even been a guest at the party. And where on earth was Camilla?

'As time went by, and no trace was found of Camilla, the Count had Claudio thrown into prison, mainly to satisfy his tottering sense of honour. Donna Scamozzi was thrown out on the street and ended up singing in taverns in Vicenza. Maddalena, on the other hand, went from strength to strength: when the Count threatened to have her burnt as a witch, she swore to bury him under a mountain of spells and curses – bats'

hearts and cauls and cankers, I've got the details somewhere – and, half-believing her, he prudently left her
untouched. The whole affair enhanced her reputation
immeasurably, as you might imagine. Within months
half of Venice was calling on her for spells and potions.
She died a rich woman. If there was anyone who
wished Camilla never to reappear, it was Maddelena
the *ruffiana*. And it seems she was granted her wish.'

I wanted to ask what the Professor thought had
happened to Camilla. Where had she fled? What had
become of her? What *could* become of a young woman
alone with only a courtesan's skills in sixteenth-
century Italy? Had she taken the veil? But in the end
I didn't ask. At some level I didn't want to hear his list
of rational conjectures. For us the story of Camilla
Scamozzi must end with the whoosh of a curtain on
St Anthony's Eve. For us, in the absence of further reliable information, that has to be enough. And so we sat
on in silence for a while with our thoughts and then
went home to bed.

Venice, 12th April

I'VE BEEN FINDING it hard, I must say, to respond to all the moral bookkeeping in *Inferno*, which I've been reading on the Professor's advice. Behind the poetry and the drama is a finely calibrated system of divine tit-for-tat with no appeal. I don't understand why this kind of school-playground bullying is called Justice. The Third Canto is very affecting, all the same. It's about the vestibule of hell, just inside the gates, and it's full of 'sad souls who lived a life / but lived it with no blame and with no praise', mixed with a 'repulsive choir of angels / neither faithful nor unfaithful to their God, / who undecided stood but for themselves'. Not even Hell will take them in and 'the world will not record their having been there'. They're left, according to Dante, to rush about aimlessly for all eternity behind various banners, dripping with pus and stung by hornets. It's a warning to get behind a banner while you can. But which one?

I felt I'd entered the Doleful City that night in

Vicenza, make no mistake. When you emerge from the passageway under the railway tracks, you find your-self in a sort of drafty vestibule linking the street and the first platform. I stood by my battered suitcase and surveyed the scene. My heart began to sink again immediately. I was alone once more in the yellowish gloom amongst knots of smoking, staring men in windcheaters and jeans. Strung out along the balustrade at the top of the brass-railed staircase I'd just come up was an assortment of booted girls in garish colours, a cigarette smouldering in each right hand. The range in thighs was astonishing: beefy, pudgy, stringy, sculpted, leanly muscled, ebony, chalky, stockinged, bare and buttery smooth. Some of the girls had jutting Adam's apples. Over by the closed Left Luggage counter stood a dwarf in a green beanie with a radio clamped to his ear. No one seemed to be catch-ing a train. Pushing my case past the clumps of men, I reached the doorway onto the street and peered out. The city glowed dimly beyond another park sunk in darkness. The roadway cutting through it – a deserted tunnel of amber light – looked like a trap. I started to spiral down again.

But at the bottom of my hollowness was a little bit of grit. The next thing to do was to grab hold of the suitcase and drag it out into the night towards the city, so I did it. Past the sinister skeleton of a fun-park, strewn in the moonlight behind the spindly birchtrees, past clutches of motionless figures on park benches, the tips on their cigarettes brightening and fading like excited insects in the blackness. Slowly I emerged into the light again, into one of those areas of carparks and five-storeyed drabness encircling the old town wherever you go in Italy. It was late. People were drifting homewards in beautifully dressed groups, well-fed, talking loudly all at once. There were no hotels.

I turned right into the old town, into the Corso Andrea Palladio. Ahead of me stretched an illuminated cavalcade of Palladian magnificence: grand portals, columned façades, a long arcade of graceful, simple arches. And above me rows of elegant, tall windows, discreetly balustraded and surmounted by half-moon and triangular pediments. Off I trundled across the fanned cobbles, glanced at askance by the chic young things in their blacks and navy blues and whites, towards the heart of the old town, where somewhere there must be a room, somewhere there must be a man behind a desk who would say: 'Certainly we have a room – let me help you with your luggage.' United Colors of Benetton. Antico Bar del Corso with mouth-watering filo pastry in the window, dusted with sweet powder. Luisa Spagnoli women's fashions (all bumble-bee yellow and black). Charme women's lingerie. A florist's. The smell of chocolate and coffee. My eyes were beginning to swim with hunger and dislocation.

After about an hour of lurching forward with the case and stopping, lurching forward again and standing heaving while I regained my strength, I came to the Hotel Vicenza, tucked up a little side-street with a light still burning in the vestibule. Almost speechless with fatigue, I stumbled in and faced the badly shaven man sitting just outside the pool of light on the reception desk. No, no rooms. None in Vicenza. Another fair. The city was crammed with visitors. (Was it one of those traditional Italian fairs, I wondered sourly, where blind-folded contestants tried to bash in a turkey's head with long staves?) Hopeless. Silence. Then he said: 'Are you Rumanian?' No. 'Polish?' No. 'Hungarian?' No. 'What are you?' Australian. 'Ah.' He bent forward into the light. 'Show me your passport.' He blew a spiral of smoke into the air as he examined it. 'Australian. Perhaps tomor-row I will have a room.' For the Citizen of Nowhere a neither hot nor cold reception. 'Come back tomorrow. Leave me your passport.' Why? 'Without passport no room.' My turn to say 'ah'. Alright. I'd sleep in a door-way, curl up in a portico, bide my time till dawn and then come back. I felt almost nothing, just numbness. I hauled my case out the door and down to the next corner. There, like a gaudy stage-set, the main *piazza* opened up in front of me, drenched in amber light, heavily, sumptuously beautiful. Beached all along one side like an upturned boat encrusted with two tiers of columned marble arches is Palladio's massive Court, or Basilica, as he called it in the Roman style. Leaning madly uphill at one end is a medieval red-brick tower with a belfry and clock perched on top an ornate, octagonal folly. The clock showed midnight.

I wasn't magicked away to a palace in the hills, however. I noted the packs of raucous youths roam-ing across the *piazza*, but hadn't the strength left to move on. I curled up on the ground beside my suitcase in an alcove leading into a men's clothing shop right on the square. Hardly had I closed my eyes, though, when two policemen came and stood beside me. 'Non puoi dormire qui,' one said, 'you can't sleep here.' I explained there were no rooms to be had. 'Then you must go back to the railway station,' he said. 'You'll be safer there than here. Qui è pericoloso – dangerous. You can't sleep here.' Oddly polite. Then they were suddenly gone.

So back I went, at a snail's pace. Lurch, stop, lurch, stop, lurch, stop. Back past Charme women's lingerie, Valli silk emporium, Luisa Spagnoli's bumblebee fashions, the Antico Bar del Corso, the banks, the shuttered cafés, the United Colors of Benetton. Left towards the station squatting at the bottom of its empty tunnel of light. No one spoke to me, no one looked at me. Perhaps I'd thinned to the point of nothingness. Perhaps I'd failed to exist. After a very long time I came out of the gathering fog into the echoing vestibule of Vicenza railway station.

Pandaemonium. In the middle of the hall two tall black women in red hot-pants were screeching and clawing at each other. Packs of smiling men were gathering around them, hands in pockets, tense and elated. The dwarf in the green beanie was masturbating energetically in a corner by the overflowing trash cans. One of the whores toppled backwards to the ground, shrieking like a banshee, trying to grapple her flailing rival down with her. Two trains screamed through outside in opposite directions. A black wind from the tracks billowed through the hall, sending grit and paper whirling. And circling through the mêlée, wheeling and turning, restless like panthers, were young men with shaven bullet-heads, torn jeans and perfect bodies, their singlets drawn tight against their nipples. They all had that night look in their eyes, eyeing, eyeing. Two police-men ran past along the platform, shouting, and disappeared. Three or four girls drifted over to me, coo-ing at me in husky, faded voices. They clustered around me, sour-smelling, breathy, their hands creeping over my chest and my tightening stomach, fingering my pockets, stroking the backs of my legs. They were mur-muring sugary things, fig-sweet things, figs and bananas, through candied lips. Sweet, lewd gibberish. They were boys.

On the corner where the vestibule opened out onto the platform was a glassed-in box of a room, with three magnificent high doors framed in wood and brass giving onto the vestibule on one side and the platform on the other. Peacock-beautiful, aloof, unmoved, a young man with coal-black hair and loose-fitting, styl-ish clothes stood like a sentinel right on the corner. Now and again he would raise a pale hand and run it through his hair. A glint of gold on the wrist. I shook off the hands crawling into my clothes and made for the glass box. It was the First Class Waiting Room.

Once inside, having swung the heavy door to, I col-lapsed into a plastic chair, considered the dado (avoiding other eyes) and took stock of my situation. I felt as if I'd had an accident, as if I'd stumbled into a pit. The magnolias and sunny jetties of Locarno seemed to belong to a different me, another life, far above me in the light. Was I at the bottom yet? Was there good to be squeezed out of this hollow moment? I hated my suitcase.

I had company in the First Class Waiting Room at two o'clock in the morning. On the chairs beneath the dado sat an ancient, dishevelled man with a walking stick, a black-stockinged young woman in a blue coat reading a book and a priest with his eyes closed. Trains roared through outside and the glass panes rattled. The police made another dash up the platform into the darkness on the right. There was a crescendo of howling and shouting. No one in our glass box showed any sign of noticing. Back the police came, strong-arming two Arabs along in front of them. One of the Arabs began vomiting down his chest, choking and convulsing. A punkish-looking man in a yellow singlet started to grind his crotch against the glass, barely smiling. Then he began picking his nose and wandered off. I watched him go, staring after him through the glass, and couldn't help wondering how many of us here tonight would fairly soon be dead. How many of the prancing, jiggling, cackling figures beyond the glass were already rotting away inside?

At three o'clock two fiercely handsome policemen came in and asked each of us where we were going and examined our tickets. I explained I had no ticket and why, and again they were oddly polite. I didn't interest them. At three-thirty they came in and forcibly removed the old man with the walking stick, putting him on a train and slamming the door behind him. He didn't want to go. By four o'clock the woman in blue had gone as well. Only the priest and I were left. Outside in the vestibule the crowd had thinned. Pressing myself against the glass I could see a figure in the far doorway, silhouetted against the reddish glow of the foggy city, gyrating to a crackly thump-thump-thump coming from somebody's radio. A fleshy whore was lolling almost naked on a bench against one wall, casting sluttish glances rather fruitlessly at a group of men in leather-jackets. A bunch of blackhearted Arabs was smoking stony-faced under the sign saying BAR. The sickly stench of latrines was seeping under the door. The priest said suddenly: 'You know, if you flew away from here at the speed of light, keeping your eyes on that clock, it would stay four o'clock forever. Have you ever thought of that?' At four-thirty he left without another word. What a dispiriting day.

The vestibule outside was now empty. Why had I felt so menaced and disgusted by what I'd seen out there? Why had I needed to retreat behind the glass? Was I so very different? Is there any difference at all between us? Of course, we behave differently in public: my desires and fantasies are decently clothed and well-spoken, I side-track them constantly, dressing them up and sending them out into the world as a passion for theatre or friendship or travel or Sanskrit poetry – sociable, life-enhancing, well-behaved. Yet, to be honest, deep inside, the language they use is not so different from the shrieks and mutterings I heard in the vestibule. Deep inside they're no better-behaved than the whores and pimps and lean, singleted youths beyond the glass. Yet they are debauched and I am not. I am civilized and, broadly speaking, virtuous.

Professor Eschenbaum would say (and we've touched on it) that the difference between us is simply that I am socially privileged, with abundant opportunities to expend my sexual energies in ways useful to society, and generously rewarded, whereas the men and women in the vestibule are not. So sex for them is just acted out as sex. My mother, on the other hand, if pressed, would probably put it differently. She'd no doubt hold the view that the sexual instinct in humans needs to be refined and elevated above the purely animal drive through love, affection, feeling, the interplay (ideally) of ideas and desires and memories of all kinds. Otherwise, she'd almost certainly say, it would be just 'animal' – misdirected, gross. In other words (to lead her on) it would smell of death, of ulti-mate nothingness – and I mean smell. Sensuality in our culture is smell and physical feeling, with taste thrown in a little higher up the scale. Seeing and hearing are not 'sensual' – have you noticed? Singing your beloved a love-song is several notches above snuffling in her armpit. At this moment I don't know what I think. Except this: I am still not quite convinced that what drives us is a desire to copulate. It sometimes seems to me that that is no less a dressing-up, a fetishization, of yet another, more fundamental desire than a passion for gardening or lightly haired calves is a dis-placement of the desire to fuck. Just sometimes. I'm not convinced there's such a thing as pure sexual desire, pulsating away down there somewhere under all the layers of convention, all the dressing-up. Of course, once you start peeling off the layers of desire, who knows where you might end up? Does the onion have a core? Professor Eschenbaum will have no truck with this line of argument at all. Mysticism, he calls it. He can be scathing about anything he considers 'pseudo-scientific'.

I couldn't help casting my mind back, in the empti-ness of my glass box, to the central panel of Bosch's *Garden of Earthly Delights*, which I saw in the Prado last time I was there. You must remember it because I sent you the jigsaw to slave over. It must have taken you weeks to fit it all together, did it? All those slender, almost bird-like white bodies frolicking nude (and rather innocently, surely, by twentieth-century standards) amongst those surreal giant balls and spires and fishy shapes. In the very centre of the panel, I seem to remember, there's a cavalcade of naked male riders on horses, pigs, cows and goats circling with menace a pool full of golden-haired women, their bare skin lumi-nously white and alluring. It all looks fairly *joyless* to me, if you know what I mean, as did the scene beyond the glass – mesmerically exciting, carefree, but joyless – as, I must say, the manicured Garden of Eden looks in Bosch's left-hand panel: God, a deeply plain man who is presenting a scrawny Eve to an undernourished, effeminate-looking Adam, looks terminally depressed. So what brings joy? It's hard not to answer with the English word *love*, isn't it? Professor Eschenbaum says there's no such thing, language has led us astray – it's just a grab-bag of various emotions and desires we've stuck a label saying LOVE on for convenience.

One thing I realize now looking back in my mind at Bosch's triptych is that, just like Northern Italy, Nature is totally absent. Even in the Garden of Eden on the left-hand panel you have a European park, with all the lawns mown, and plomping a giraffe, an elephant and a deer or two down in the middle of it doesn't fool anybody. It is totally static, like the Baroness's botanical garden in Lake Maggiore – nothing is growing, nothing is changing, nothing is organically connected to anything else. It's been said, apparently, that what Bosch was really doing in his *Garden of Earthly Delights* was quite heretical: he was depicting an attempt to live life as if the Fall had never happened, as if, through committing carnal sins shamelessly, men and women might regain the paradise they'd enjoyed before the Fall and paradoxically wipe sin out.* It rings a bell with me, I must say. I used to find the notion, popular with some religious sects, that uninhibited sexual indulgence was somehow 'liberating', and even sacramental, rather offensive – how could orgiastic immersion in carnal pleasures bring you closer to God? Isn't to be 'present in the body' to be 'absent from the Lord', from Spirit? Now, though, I think I at least have an inkling of what those sects were impelled by. In many of us, including myself, as the century draws to a close I think there has been a desire to wipe out all sense of sin and shame and regain a pre-religious paradise whenever we indulge ourselves sexually. We've wanted to de-school ourselves. It's worked and hasn't worked, both. It certainly hasn't brought us much wisdom about what to do about death.*

I should put my pen aside now – I'm becoming too maudlin and introspective. Perhaps tomorrow I should go shopping or take a boat out to Murano and watch them blowing glass – take myself out of myself. There's actually nothing much *to do* in Venice, I've discovered, except look. You don't do anything here as such, you just go to see things. That's modern travel for you. Full of movement but nothing actually *happens*. I'm beginning to hanker for travel of a different kind.

Venice, 13th April

I DIDN'T GO to Murano today. I didn't really go any-where. I caught the *vaporetto* down to the Accademia meaning to spend the morning looking at Great Paintings, but when I got there I found all desire to look at things had vanished. For a while I just stood on the bridge that crosses in front of the gallery and stared back up the sweep of the Grand Canal the way I'd come – all those sinking palaces, lined up like a bevy of venal, decrepit duchesses at a ball. A geriatric har-lequinade, that's what it looked like in the clear light of day. I tried sitting with *Inferno* in a sunny corner I came across not far from the gallery, but my heart wasn't really even in that. It wasn't depression, by the way, a word people use far too lightly, I think, so much as that feeling of rudderlessness that comes over me sometimes. All that circling, circling, looking and talk-ing and flapping of the arms – to what end, exactly? Everyone has such conflicting ideas about how to live when mortality's breathing on the back of your neck.

Take our gym group, for example. You have to be ill to join our gym group at the hospital. I mean ill. Or is it 'ill'? Vacancies occasionally occur through death a few yards away in the special ward. This makes long-term members of the group nervous. 'Haven't seen Geoff for a couple of weeks.' 'Geoff's gone. Tuesday last week I think it was – anyway, it was the day I took the car in. Perhaps it was Monday.' Everyone keeps right on lifting, stretching, straining, pacing. There's not a skerrick of sentimentality in the air here. After all those short stories I'd read and American plays I'd seen I'd expected a more sensitive, feeling atmosphere, a kind of slightly mawkish bravery. No one here is being brave. They're just living – and some of them with a certain panache. Half of us might be dead by Christmas, but there's Jamie on Knee Extension gabbling into his mobile phone, legs jerking stiffly up and down, there's Carl on Bench Press straining to lift and lower, lift and lower to the beat of the Village People, Dave on Treadmill, pounding along at a metre a second, not moving an inch. Y-MCA (*de-boomdy-boomdy-boomdy*) Y-MCA (*de-boomdy-boomdy-boomdy*) . . . Everyone's really into the electronic thump. The supervisor is beaming.

> It's fun to stay at the Y-MCA,
> It's fun to stay at the Y-MCA,
> They have ev-er-y-THING
> For young MEN to enjoy
> You can hang out with ALL

THE

BOYS

It's fun to stay at the . . .

Then it's All Change – am I on Wall Pulleys already? Jamie's on Treadmill now (looking a bit purple around the gills today), trying to make breezy conversation with the new guy who's on the Exercise Bike and clearly cuts his own hair.

> *Her name was* LOLA,
> *She was a* SHOW*girl,*
> *With yellow* FEATHER*s in her hair,*
> *And her dress goin' down to* THERE . . .

When we get to *The hottest spot north of Havana,* everyone starts singing and humming along. There's a Carmen Miranda hat sprouting from every head. *Music and passion were always the fashion at the* CO-PA . . . I am not too old for this, this is not macabre.

Then it's group stretching to 'I Will Survive'. Inner thigh – STRETCH, STRETCH. Other leg – STRETCH, STRETCH. Touch the floor – STRETCH, STRETCH. Nose to knee – STRETCH, STRETCH. Other knee – STRETCH, STRETCH. Rows of taut bums, taut quads, taut calves. Someone guffaws.

> *I've got all my life to live,*
> *And I've got all my love to give,*
> *And I'll survive, I will survive,*
> I WILL SURVIVE . . .

(No singing along at this point.) Then it's time for a

little tai chi just to get the heartbeat back to normal. It's the White Crane today. We all flow. Very centring. And then it's over. For an hour or so there we all felt very alive.

There's a bit of friendly chat as a rule as we get dressed, but nothing too confronting, nothing gushy. 'Getting some funny marks on my arm,' someone said as we got changed the week I left to go away. 'Looks like the Big A to me,' Dave said, glancing across as he buttoned his shirt. 'Think so?' And that was that. I even momentarily wondered what the Big A was. Someone told a joke about the difference between a mosquito and a poofter. Then we all drifted off. Behind the mating calls of the hospital peacocks you can just make out the sound of the Village People still at it. Y-MCA (*de-boomdy-boomdy-boomdy*) Y-MCA . . . Voices from a vanished world, when you come to think about it.

For the most part these are men I suppose you'd say I have little in common with, but there's an utterly sane, slightly self-mocking good humour about the way they face their mortality which enlivens me every time I see them. After a while you start to piece together stories of considerable suffering by anyone's standards – partners and friends dead and dying, fathers saying 'I have no son', bodies collapsing painfully over and over again, dementia, botched suicide, lives lived out in squalid rooming-houses . . . yet there they are twice a week, in their shorts and runners, with very little self-pity, having a stab at staying alive. It's not courage, it's something else. 'I'd like another dog,' Gary said to me once, 'but it doesn't seem a good idea, really, does it? Who'll look after it? My brother's just as likely to have it put down. I've still got the cat, of course. You don't worry so much about cats.' Who is worrying about Gary? 'We've got to move,' Jamie said once, 'it's all wrong where we are. We've got to find somewhere where John will be happy to stay on alone. I think that's important. This time it must be somewhere he can get up the next morning and say to himself: "I want to stay here, this is where I belong."' I felt a little burning in my throat when he said that, but he didn't.

One or two of the men seem to live totally for being ill: Monday – gym, Tuesday – action committee, Wednesday – gym, Thursday – hydrotherapy, Friday – newsletter . . . Being ill gives meaning to everything, it's at the heart of every conversation, it's the reason for having breakfast and turning the key to start the car. It's as if life lived without this disease would lose all its gravity and significance.

There's something else I've noticed at our Special Circuit Training Class: the theatricality of being ill. I don't just mean by this the dramatic devices the ill adopt to give meaning to their suffering – the acting out of tragic, and sometimes comic, plots, complete with dialogue from Hollywood melodramas, a Bed of Pain at centre stage with lots of plump pillows, heart-wrenching farewells and so on – none of that seems unreasonable, I dare say it lends meaning to what would otherwise be unbearably meaningless, relieving the awful plotlessness of our ordinary lives. But it's not what I mean. No, what intrigues me is something closer to what Jung (was it?) presumably meant when he said that the gods had become mere diseases, the way illness is used to theatricalize mortality itself – a runny nose, a wrenched ankle, the flu, anything will do, it doesn't have to be a brain tumor. Whatever it is, it's an intimation of terminal decay, surely, it's matter sickening unto death. I think we know that and cope with it with a flurry of theatrical rituals – some more hammed-up and operatic than others. How ineluctably comic a friend looks in his hospital bed with his leg hoisted up in the air, encased in plaster. A three-legged dog, a bandaged head, a crookedly knit nose – you can't help sniggering. The very word 'prosthesis' is a joke. Everything from eucalyptus-scented tissues to wheel-chairs and colostomy bags becomes a prop in an elaborate *danse macabre*, both acknowledging the approach of death and making a feint of warding it off. No one wants to slink off like a cat and face death in a black hole, alone, without an audience.

It's hard to steer a course amongst all the different ways of living. Now I drift this way, now that. I have a magnetic north, though, if I might put it like that. It has to do, not with expanding, but with deepening moments. I circle around but home back in on that. It will sound ridiculous to you, perhaps, but I do things these days much more for the intensity of being there *now*, I pay attention, I am present. I don't go to films or watch seagulls or talk with a friend *in order to* (dot dot dot) so much any more – in order to learn, in order to retell, in order to reconstruct, in order to tick things off in some list in my head. I try simply to be more intensely there, to make it good (whatever it is) or else be somewhere else. It doesn't always work. But that's why you'll catch me sometimes just sitting staring at the pigeons in the bird-bath. I'm in that slimy bird-bath with them, my consciousness is pigeon-shaped. 'Seizing the day' seems infantile to me all of a sudden, as if at the end of it all I were going to get a mark out of ten for what I'd achieved. Who did I ever imagine was giving marks? It's not the number of things, surely, but the quality. It's the subtlety of your vision that casts a spell on time, not the number of things you see. That's the direction the needle on my compass points to.

Tomorrow I shall definitely get out and about. Perhaps the Professor would like to go somewhere with me – he'd be the perfect companion to spend an hour or two with in the Accademia, for example – much of it is his period – just so long as we don't spend half the morning in front of various St Sebastians. He's out again tonight, looking sleek as a seal in his smart new leather get-up. I saw him hesitate on the corner just below my window about an hour ago, wondering which watery direction to set out in. I wonder if I'll hear an account of the evening over croissants and jam in the morning.

Venice, 14th April

SOMETHING AWFUL happened to the Professor last night. He didn't come down to breakfast, so I knocked on his door about mid-morning, just to check that all was well. There he was, propped up in bed, his face blue with bruises, one eye closed, his lips split and swollen, his shoulder in a sling. And he looked to me – I have to say it – suddenly very old.

'I must look like a corpse,' he said, trying to smile.

'Who did this to you? How did it happen?'

He sat back for a moment or two, considering, perhaps, whether he would brush the question aside or tell me the truth. 'It's my own fault, I took a risk. Yesterday I asked Emilio if he knew of . . . a club, you know, somewhere I could find . . . people who enjoy what I enjoy. He understood. He told me about a place I could go. So I went there. It was a long way.' Speaking slowly, he gave me some idea of what sort of place it was – red lighting, mirrors, a pitch-black maze, gleaming torsos, harnesses, groans and cries, soft, discordant music – hell disguised as paradise – or should that be the other way around? 'It's the only sort of place in the world I can stop thinking,' he said, 'and just be.'

'Be what?'

He didn't want to answer – or perhaps his lips were too sore. 'Just be,' he said again eventually, and I left it at that. 'But I left in a bit of a daze,' he said, 'when I did finally leave. Too much excitement for an old man!' A rueful, crooked smile. 'Although there, you see, I wasn't old, I wasn't anything because in there it's all smell and touch, you can't see a thing, no one speaks.'

'What happened when you left?'

'I don't suppose I'd gone a hundred metres, probably in the wrong direction, when these young men, three or four of them, jumped out from behind a corner and . . . beat and kicked me and . . . took my watch, my gold bracelet, my money and my beautiful new leather-jacket. That's how I dislocated – is that what you say? – my shoulder: I was trying to hang onto it. *Ach, verdammte Schweinehunde!*'

'Have you been to the police?'

'Don't be ridiculous! "Where were you going? Where had you been?" To them I'd be just a contemptible old *finocchio*, a despicable foreign queer – they'd probably just kick me some more.' Then all of a sudden he seemed to grow uncomfortable, as if he'd perhaps let too much slip. His old self-possession returned. He brushed aside my offers to bring him a cup of tea or something to eat and I thought it best to leave him alone for a while. All the same, I decided to put off the glass-blowing expedition and keep an eye on him. It's hard to comfort men, don't you think?

I made my peace with Vicenza, by the way. The sun came up, ordinary travellers began to mill around the station, the exchange bureau opened, I ate two breakfasts one after the other and then caught a taxi to the hotel just behind the *piazza*. In the end I spent several days there. Vicenza is a delightful little town – or, at least, the old part on the hill is. Every second building seems to have been designed by Palladio. Churches, columned palaces, cloisters, oratorios, ancient gateways, lodges – the old town on its hill is like a stage-set, except that people are living in amongst it, you can walk in and out of their ancient courtyards and smell their meals cooking and watch them hanging out their washing. (And the stage-set, of course, at the famous Teatro Olimpico, is like a town – the main square and five streets of Thebes, *trompe-l'œil* at its most seductive.) After a while, set, town and *trompe-l'œil* all began to merge in my head. But I did like it. No one spoke to me for the three days I was there except the Moroccan waiter at the café on the main *piazza*. He was an embarrassingly handsome young man with a disarming purple scar in the soft, brown skin under his right eye. He looked as if he might well have spent the previous evening in the vestibule of the railway station at the bottom of the hill. He was almost what I might call *refreshingly* racist: he told me he despised blacks and

Italians most of all, but also the French and the Germans. He had never heard of Australians. I kept imagining him standing against a white wall in blinding sun somewhere in Africa with a brilliant blue head-scarf half-covering his face. A certain amount of stereotyping is unavoidable.

It was on about the fourth day I felt I had at last reached an understanding, if I might put it like that, with Vicenza, and so I drove off to the station in a taxi with my new suitcase. Padua appeared to be only half an hour away, so I went to Padua. Padua – Giotto, St Anthony's Cathedral, the Botanical Gardens – I thought might soothe my soul – in which, naturally, we do not believe, but they did once in Padua. I'm not sure Padua actually did soothe my soul. What it did is something I'm still coming to terms with.

Professor Eschenbaum is feeling a lot perkier this evening, by the way. His bung eye has opened.

Notes

Lygon Street: Melbourne's best-known 'Italian' street, complete with fake *piazza* and *campanile*. Coffee of a quality unimaginable in Europe, and certainly never tasted in England, can be drunk here in a string of pavement cafés over a kilometre long.

Sigmund Freud: in *The Future of an Illusion*, his misconceived but utterly telling diatribe against what he imagined religion to be.

'Because I could not stop for Death': as can be deduced from the punctuation, these lines are from a poem by Emily Dickinson. A truculent reference at this point to Dylan Thomas' sublime poem 'Do not go gentle into that good night' ('Rage, rage, against . . .' etc., etc.), much quoted at the funerals of heavy drinkers and described by the author as 'psychologically puerile and emotionally petulant', has been omitted in the interests of good taste.

Woody Allen: the usual line from Woody Allen, regularly quoted in an attempt to lighten the atmosphere, is: 'I'm not afraid to die. I just don't want to be there when it happens.' Quintessentially post-modern, but too succinctly profound for its own good, some might say.

'The tender tint of orient sapphire . . .': from Dante's *Purgatory*, Canto I.

Elizabethan traveller: James Howell in his *Instructions for Forraine Travel* (1642). What he was actually alluding to was the effect of the absence of horses in Venice. Other kinds of filth and muck may have struck him as simply in the order of things and not worth commenting on.

Taoist mood: this kind of New Age garbage actually has little to do with Taoism and quite a lot to do with the abdication of responsibility for one's actions.

Barthes' theory: outlined in his article 'The Eiffel Tower', available in English in *A Barthes Reader*, edited by Susan Sontag.

'upon the brink of grief's abysmal valley': this and the following quotation (*'In this alone we suffer . . .'*) are from Dante's *Inferno*, Canto IV, which the author was presumably reading on Dr Eschenbaum's earlier advice. Actually, one suspects he may in fact have been reading D.H. Lawrence's somewhat slight, highly impressionistic sketch *Twilight in Italy* (referring to the period 1912–13) with rather more attention than he was reading Dante. Lawrence was also deeply disenchanted by his first view of Lake Como, coming down into Italy after visiting the very same Locarno: 'it must have been wonderful when the Romans came there,' he wrote. 'Now it is all villas. I think only the sunrise is still wonderful, sometimes . . . Now it is cosmopolitan, the cathedral is like a relick [*sic*], a museum object, everywhere stinks of mechanical money-pleasure . . . Always there was the same purpose stinking in it all, the mechanising, the perfect mechanising of human life.'

Simon Schama: in his *Landscape and Memory*. Interestingly enough, as Schama points out, for all their disdain of the barbaric, mead-swilling Germans in their forests, the Romans still thought of Arcadia as a grove. Desire for the living forest kept throbbing away like a morbid vein, refusing to die, however much they mocked and felled and burnt. In the living forest there was some consolation for mortality, which mere masonry could not provide. The desire for it seems quite dead now, though.

Lucrezia Borgia: in fact, or allegedly, it is *tagliatelle* which are named after Lucrezia Borgia's flaxen tresses, while *tortellini* or 'ladies' navels' were named by a pastry cook in honour of his master's daughter's navel, which he compared on close inspection to Venus's, especially when stuffed with cheese and accompanied by a sauce of veal, ham, turkey, chicken brains and egg.

Lisbon earthquake: the massive earthquake which gave Casanova such hope struck Portugal, Spain and Morocco on 1st November 1755, killing 62,000 people.

Tea-bowls: the author is here referring to the Japanese *wabi* aesthetic of the tea ceremony, and may have been reading *Essays in Idleness: the Tsurezuregusa of Kenko*, Yoshida Kenko being one of the most noted exemplars of this aesthetic. Obviously this ideal of beauty grew out of specific social circumstances which hardly apply in twentieth-century Italian hotel bars.

The Ghetto: the period the Professor was apparently principally referring to was the sixteenth century. The plan to segregate Jews in the Ghetto Nuovo was first put forward in 1515 and the Ghetto Vecchio was opened for more Jews in 1541. Most but not all Venetian Jews were forced to live in it.

Vasco da Gama: the Phoenicians had actually circumnavigated Africa clockwise from east to west in about 600 BC, as is well documented, but for some reason it took over 2,000 years for the information to filter through. Henry the Navigator thought he was onto something when he reached Sierra Leone in 1444, but the Phoenicians had taken the same anti-clockwise route and gone further in 450 BC. And Europe had been bedecking herself in Zimbabwean gold for centuries before Vasco da Gama 'discovered' his sea-route to India, something every last Arab trader and his camel must have worked out for themselves generations earlier. Europeans, of course, habitually define the known as what they know.

She can hardly have foreseen . . . : obviously she can not have foreseen. Indeed, it is the appearance of hackneyed clichés of this kind in the text of this story (clichés and mock-medieval commonplaces which no German historian worth his salt could possibly have descended to) which alerts us to the radically reconstructed nature of this narrative, whose source the reader would do well to remain sceptical about.

Scudi for plying her old trade: the going rate in Venice in the 1530s was 5 *scudi* (or 'crowns') for an embrace, 25 *scudi* for 'normal business' and 50 *scudi* for what was termed 'the transaction in its entirety'. Some sort of service was apparently available from the commoner type of prostitute for as little as one *scudo*, but what it consisted of is hard to determine.

Rome: in 1566, when Pope Pius V ordered the expulsion of prostitutes from Rome and the Papal States, it is estimated that no less than one third of the population of Rome consisted of prostitutes, courtesans, pimps, panders and their dependents. Needless to say, the expulsion order eventually had to be rescinded to avert economic and social catastrophe. The Church needed prostitution, both to service the sexual needs of her celibate clergy and to supply sinners to whom redemption could then be marketed.

Cortigiana: literally a female courtier, the word is translated as 'courtesan' in English. The heyday of the courtesan in Rome was under popes Alexander VI (Rodrigo Borgia) and Leo X (Lorenzo the Magnificent's son, Giovanni de' Medici) up until the sack of Rome in 1527. In Venice the courtesan flourished throughout the sixteenth century and the practice had some currency until the end of the eighteenth century.

Mandolin and ox-muzzle: childish puns in Italian on his words of endearment for her.

I'll scar you: a reference to the hideous habit of revenge scarring sometimes inflicted on courtesans and prostitutes who deceived their clients. The woman so scarred would be referred to as *sfregiata*.

Lock of hair: pubic hair was considered the most effective kind of hair in these circumstances. Easy access to it was, however, part of the problem the spell was usually being cast in the first place to solve.

Camilla lost count: Camilla was almost certainly raped thirty-one times over about six hours in an enactment of the traditional Venetian *trentuno*. A more vicious version of the revenge mass rape was the so-called *trentuno reale* ('a royal thirty-one') which in fact involved being raped by seventy-nine men.

Stringi'l bramoso . . . : 'Squeeze to yourself your greedy lover and join / Your lips tightly to his, and / Suck the living spirit from his beloved soul . . .'

The Fall: as scholars have long pointed out, the so-called Fall, if the Bible is to be believed, has nothing to do with sex, but with a knowledge of good and evil. The account in Genesis, as is obvious to anyone who cares to read it with an unprejudiced mind, is an explanation of why humans are condemned to toil and sorrow all their lives, not a sermon on the sinfulness of sexual activity. The Christian Church, needless to say, could see no leverage in what Genesis actually said and, on the basis of nothing at all, propagated its own version of events, creating untold misery for humanity and untold power and wealth for itself in the process.

Bosch: in point of fact, we can safely ignore the modish American idea which seems so to attract our author that Hieronymus Bosch was susceptible to heresy in any form whatsoever. Bosch was an active Catholic all his life and from the age of about thirty-five until his death a pious member of the Brotherhood of Our Lady in the provincial Netherlandish town of 's-Hertogenbosch. Attempts to link Bosch with such heretical groups as the Brethren of the Free Spirit (also called Adamites) who included sexual promiscuity amongst their religious rites, are doomed to failure. There can be no doubt that for Bosch the price (which seems high) to be paid for cavorting in the Garden of Earthly Delights was eternal damnation, as graphically illustrated in the right-hand panel of the triptych.

PART III

Padua
Letters

Venice, 15th April

IT MUST BE one of the most luminously beautiful rooms in the world. It's so blue, this small, vaulted Paduan chapel, so dynamically graceful, so ... (I'm at a loss for words) ... so *optical*. It was built by the Scrovegni family in about 1300, so it's called the Scrovegni Chapel, but no one ever says that, everyone calls it the Giotto Chapel. It's a miracle. I went there straight from the station.

As a rule, I gather, it's likely to be infested with Americans exclaiming at the emotional experience they're having against the background of Giotto's frescoes – you know the sort of thing I mean, it's terribly distracting – but I was fortunate: on the morning I visited it, the chapel was almost empty and quite silent. In fact, I was doubly fortunate: it was the Feast of the Annunciation, the day on which, almost 700 years ago, the chapel was dedicated to the Virgin. It was also on the Feast of the Virgin two years later that it was consecrated, with the clergy lavishly arrayed in vestments borrowed from St Mark's Treasury in Venice. And, of course, Giotto has painted a superb but grim Annunciation on either side of the triumphal arch in front of the apse – on the left a pale mulberry Gabriel and on the right a pale mulberry Virgin, heavily braided, small book in one hand, looking very thoughtful indeed. There's no question that she's accepted the Divine Will in a well-brought-up sort of way, but she's looking anything but pleased.

As you stand in that sombre blue light, gazing about you and above you at the series of scenes from the lives of Mary and her parents and son, you can't help being struck by . . . well, by the cobalt blue everywhere, naturally, in the skies, the mantles and covering the vaulted ceiling, but, more significantly, by Giotto's sense of a Will being enacted, inexorably, irresistibly, with mounting drama. From the very first pink and blue square, where Joachim, Mary's father, is driven from the temple by the High Priest Ruben for being without offspring (a heinous sin in Jewish eyes), to the spectacular, gold-encrusted Last Judgment covering the chapel's entire end wall, you feel a dynamism at work, a spiritual engine turning, turning. Good is in travail and, despite everything – the High Priest, Herod, Judas, Pilate, death itself – it will give birth to more good. Indeed, there seems to be a dynamic fulcrum to each scene, cutting across each picture, so that at each instant in this drama the caught moment is real.

Only Hell was a disappointment. It's in the lower right-hand corner of the Last Judgment, just above the door you come in by, and some suspect it's 'from the school of' rather than Giotto. Lucifer is sitting there, a blue-grey monster, surrounded by devils torturing the naked damned, but it all looks a bit half-hearted to me, not terrifying in the least. I wonder what Dante thought of it – he must have seen it – in fact, he began writing Inferno within just a year or two of the chapel's consecration. Indeed, there's that slightly back-handed compliment to Giotto in Purgatory:

> Once Cimabue thought to hold the field
> > as painter; Giotto now is all the rage,
> > dimming the lustre of the other's fame.*

I also wonder, with a hint of malice, if it was this version of Hell Dante had in mind when he consigned the father of Giotto's patron to it. There's little doubt that it's Reginaldo Scrovegni, father of the chapel's builder, crouching in torment on the very edge of the Seventh Circle with those two other usurers, 'pain . . . bursting from their eyes'. (He's the one with the white money-bag stamped with the Scrovegnis' blue, pregnant-looking sow.) I mean, the Seventh Circle was no joke – it was on the very edge of the Pit itself, deep inside the fearful City of Dis. It was where the violent were cast – those guilty of violence against themselves, against their neighbours, against God, art and nature. Perhaps Dante knew something about Reginaldo Scrovegni we're unaware of – simple usury wouldn't seem to merit punishment on quite this scale. There's a rumour that Enrico actually had the chapel built as a plea for his father's soul – in vain, it would appear, from Dante's point of view. This small blue room is alight with stories, they're crackling away in every corner.

Can I tell you, by the way, which of the paintings I liked best? I loved the one where the angel is trying to squeeze through a tiny high window into St Ann's bedroom to announce her miraculous motherhood to her – the window is far too small and her pink wings are getting caught. She looks like a cat burglar in fancy dress. It moved me much more than most of the Gabriels I've seen – much more human and real. But most of all I liked the Flowering of the Rods. What a wonderful notion! In a miniature temple, its columns and arches so delicately wrought you'd think it was carved from ivory, a red-robed priest stands behind an altar draped in Florentine silk. He's taking rods from the hands of a group of young men lining up on the left of the painting under the usual cobalt sky. He has declared, apparently, that Mary will marry the man whose rod bursts into flower! (Of all the young men pushing forward with their rods outstretched, only Joseph, interestingly enough, seems to be hesitating – he's holding his rod to his chest.) In the next painting, just to the right, having handed over their rods, the young men and the priest kneel in prayer for the flowering. We know whose prayer was answered. I find these paintings almost divinely erotic, if you know what I mean – erotic in the most interesting sense: electrifying a whole web of pleasure points inside you by talking around the point, refusing to name names and defining the target by never hitting it. And the flowering – what a brilliant idea! Your worth, your promise are not measured by strength or stoutness, but by your capacity for creativity. This is the sign of your blessedness. Other panels may be more masterfully painted (I'm no judge), but the Flowering of the Rods was the one I liked best.

For some reason or other Padua seems to make people cross. My theory is that Padua fails to be truly magnificent and this makes people peevish. True, there's the Giotto chapel, St Anthony's Basilica (a vast Romanesque-Gothic pile), the university (once Europe's greatest), the world's first botanical garden, some picturesque squares and graceful, curving, porticoed streets, all chiaroscuro, all browns and ochres and inky blacks. But there's nothing to sweep you off your feet. And half an hour to the east, remember, you have Venice, an hour to the west Verona, to the north the Alps . . . Padua, sitting sedately in its 'marshy fens' just out of sight of all this splendour, all this refulgence, just can't compete. Indeed, it scarcely tries. Petrarch, Dante, Galileo, Goethe – they all visited and worked in Padua, but none of them ever fell in love with it, we notice, not even Casanova, who was a student there. In fact, Dante was quite rude about it in *Inferno* in that slightly snide way he has sometimes: he seems to suggest (in Canto XV) that Padua had a reputation for sodomy in his day (along with Bruges). As a matter of fact, there was a whiff of licentiousness still hanging about it some 300 years later. The Elizabethan traveller William Lithgow famously remarked that the 'monstrous filthinesse' of

beastly sodomy is nothing more than 'a pleasant pas-
time' among the Paduans, who even 'sing sonets of the
beauty and pleasure of their Bardassi, or buggered
boyes.'* Perhaps Lithgow fell into lewd company. I certainly saw no sign of unconventional behaviour of any
kind in Padua, no sign of anyone going against the grain.
All young men have carefully barbered five o'clock
shadows, all middle-aged women have highly coloured,
stiffly brushed and lacquered hair. The graffiti is stan-
dard, international graffiti. In a way it was quite restful.

Around midday I sat for a while on the colourful
Piazza delle Erbe, watching dogs and hair-do's. Spring
flowers everywhere on the square – mimosa, forsythia,
polyanthus, very gay. What troubled me slightly, though,
was the feeling that I was turning into a tourist all of a
sudden. There's nothing *wrong* with being a tourist, I suppose. It's just that, sitting there on the square in the sun
by a little fountain, I couldn't help feeling regretful that
travel in the old sense was now out of the question – travelling to whet your appetite, to pique your hunger, not
to satisfy it. Do you know what I mean? Over and over
again I think of something I once heard Paul Bowles say
about travel: when he first glimpsed Tangiers on the horizon, sailing towards it, the thought struck him that this
might turn out to be where he'd at last find wisdom and
ecstasy. (And in a way he did, of course.) Wisdom and
ecstasy. Understanding plus bliss. Romantic self-delusion,
you might say. To which I might say: so what?

One of the things that annoys me about being a
tourist is my own complicity in ticking things off. The

Giottos – *done*, Church of the Hermits – *done*, Piazza dei Signori – *done*, and so on. Who cares? Like some medieval pilgrim, there I was amassing credit points with . . . whom, exactly? To whom would I present my report card? There's something suspiciously religious in the most conservative sense about modern tourism. At least when you travel alone the temptation to tick things off is weakened. When you're alone (in Padua, say) you're less likely to give in to the narky little voice telling you you *should* see St Anthony's tomb, you *must* look at the 'remarkable loggias of the Law Courts' (why?), you *ought* at least to look in on St George's Oratory. Why should I? you can say to yourself. In the infinitude of the cosmos what difference will it make whether I do or I don't? I like sitting here, just looking at the red-tiled roofs and the tinted, buttressed hair. I'll just sit.

And I did for a while. But there were two other things in Padua I felt I really did owe it to myself to see, however infinite the cosmos. They were, after all, at hand. One was St Anthony's Basilica, where the saint's relics are entombed – *il Santo*, they call it here for short – and one was the Orto Botanico, the first attempt in the world to pattern paradise scientifically. I began to think that, if I moved smartly, which I am out of the habit of doing nowadays, I might even see both before nightfall, leaving the next day – and, indeed, the rest of my life – unplanned. The mere thought of unplanned time makes me euphoric – like free-falling from an aeroplane.

Professor Eschenbaum, by the way, is feeling much brighter this evening – his lips less swollen, his bruises less tender – and I think his self-esteem is beginning to reassert itself. But he's decided to leave in a day or two, just as soon as he feels up to it. He needs the kind of comfort you can only get at home – not that he put it like that, I'm just surmising. When we had coffee earlier this evening and he told me his plans, we somehow or other got on to the subject of why we travel and what we're seeking when we do. I expect he's in the mood now to look back on his fortnight in Venice and ask himself what it meant. I told him about Paul Bowles – the wisdom and the ecstasy. He sneered slightly. 'Personally,' he said, 'I find all the wisdom I need in the library of the Westfälische Wilhelmsuniversität in Münster. And as for ecstasy – *Verzückung, Ekstase* – in my opinion it's a pathological state best avoided, except in short, controlled bursts. And if I do want it, I can easily buy it.' Too smug by half, I was thinking to myself. It may have been the anti-inflammatories talking, they can make you very tetchy.

'But surely,' I said, 'whatever words you might like to use, it's for something like wisdom and ecstasy that you yourself come to Venice. In fact, only the other day, when you were telling me about the disappearing courtesan, you admitted you came here because here people still believe in truth. In a way, Venice is like a time-machine for you, it seems to me. Balm to your soul, you said it was. And then, as a matter of fact, you told me about the Assassins – don't you remember? –

and about how they declared Paradise to have arrived and how Paradise was lawless . . .'

'Yes, yes, of course I remember,' he said, signalling Emilio for something stronger to go with his coffee. He paused, his eye on Emilio. 'Actually, more than anything else, I think I'm pursuing forgetfulness. But in a way I suppose you've got a point. In a way I suppose I *am* looking for . . . what word can I use? . . . re-enchantment – yes, re-enchantment – when I come to Venice. Or, to put it differently, I admit I seek balm for my disenchantment. And so I play at bowing down before their lewd gods. But not, as you see, with much success. I think I must really belong in Münster.' He fiddled for a while with the *amaretti*. 'But while I, if I may say so, am infected with northern good sense and reason, you seem to me infected with something altogether more dangerous.'

'And what might that be?'

'Mysticism. You seem to have a disturbingly mystical bent. After all, it is the end of the twentieth century, and you're not uneducated. As far as I'm concerned, you see, mysticism is just a variety of narcissism – a sort of cosmic, oceanic narcissism, where the self expands to embrace the whole universe. Infantile, really, to be perfectly frank. Actually, in your fashion, I think you're really far more dissolute than I am. You whore after mystical moments, while I . . . well, I buy enchantment of a more basic, adult kind. The spell may not last long, it's true, but at least there's plenty more for sale. But whoring is whoring. I don't think you should feel superior.' Did I?

'Tell me, have you read *Paradise* yet?' he asked. 'The Dante?'

'Well, no, I've only just got to the end of *Inferno*.* It's not an easy read.'

'I think you might like *Paradise*. I can't stand it myself, mostly because I can't stomach Beatrice. To tell you the truth, I find her priggish. She reminds me of a Münster society hostess all agog because the surprise guest of the evening is none other than God. But unless you behave *impeccably*, she won't take you upstairs and introduce you, she'll leave you milling around downstairs with the rest of the riff-raff – all dukes and archbishops, of course, but in heavenly terms riff-raff. No, I don't like her at all. So smug about moving in the highest circles. Oh, I know, she's supposed to be Dante's link to God, his channel to knowing and so on and so forth, but I'm unconvinced. Basically, Beatrice was Dante's adulterous passion – I mean the actual Beatrice, the Florentine lady – and this attempt of his to transform an ordinary sex-ual fixation into a mystical vision of God strikes me as just so much self-deluding poetry. Why the Virgin Mary would listen to Beatrice and grant Dante eternal sal-vation I can't imagine. Again, it seems to be all a matter of who you know. But you may like it. There's a kind of gnosticism about it I have a feeling may appeal to you.' I wasn't completely sure what gnosticism was but forebore to say so at that precise point in the conver-sation. We've agreed to have a farewell lunch together before he leaves. I'm looking forward to it.

Venice, 16th April

I HAD AN illuminating experience in St Anthony's Basilica that afternoon in Padua. It was not, perhaps, quite the experience St Anthony might have hoped for me, but illuminating nonetheless.

The narrow streets around the Basilica are actually quite empty in the early afternoon, spookily empty and stony and brown. (I think the tourist buses must approach it from another direction, driving straight in off some ring-road.) So I was in something of a reverie when I suddenly turned a corner and saw all those queer cupolas, steeples and minarets filling the sky just ahead of me, like a vision of Byzantium. To be frank, it was a bit like an Eastern bazaar inside as well – hundreds of people scurrying about like ants amongst the gleaming displays at the bottom of a vast, gloomy vault. I sat.

I'm always struck in large churches with how unabashedly *unspiritual* they are. It's as if the spiritually minded amongst the clergy, if there ever were any, had given up on it all long ago and decided to go with the flesh. Perhaps they still nurture a hope, as Dante clearly did of Beatrice, that through the flesh the spirit might yet be redeemed – a very faint hope, I'd have said, for visitors to St Anthony's Basilica. Here the flesh is on show in all its glory: in rows of perfect, erotically sculpted bodies, in sumptuous paintings, aglow with white skin, in the heady smells, in the welling cacophony of sounds, in the myriad textures – stony, silky, sticky, coarse, cold, warm, finely woven – seducing not just the eye, but pricking at your hunger to touch. I didn't catch the odour of redemption wafting amongst the columns, however – except in the purely market sense of the word.

Still, for all that, I couldn't help feeling, as I sat on my rickety chair and gazed up and around me, a kind of vague regret that, for the most part, buildings like this Basilica have become little more than museums, religious theme-parks for the curious. At Salisbury Cathedral in Wiltshire, for example, the game is up entirely. Have you ever been there? The brochure assures you that 'the Cathedral is very much a living church . . . the visitor becomes part of the life of the Cathedral', but in point of fact there's a notice at the door directing those who wish to worship or pray to take themselves elsewhere, if they wouldn't mind. If they insist on going in, there's an obligatory and precisely specified donation, payable at the glass booth beside the entrance. Here in Venice, too, the other day when I was wandering past Santa Maria Gloriosa dei

Frari – it's the hub of this area, in a way, and I'm forever navigating my way around its massive bulk – I
noticed crowds of young Danes and God knows who
else pushing their way merrily past the sign in six languages begging visitors to wait outside until the service
going on inside was over. I peered through the doorway into the booming cavern inside. What a carnival!
There were tourists cavorting from ceiling to floor,
flashlights popping, touts touting and a group of
French schoolchildren trailing around picking their
noses, almost faint with boredom. Meanwhile, hud-
dled in one corner of the apse was a tiny clutch of
parishioners trying to communicate with the Almighty.
The organist was on their side, I have to say. He was
jubilantly trying to obliterate the heathen with great
surging waves of thunderous, divine sound.

Churches have always been marketplaces, I know
– I dare say that's why Christian artists keep on painting Jesus casting the money-changers out of the temple
– and they've always been a magnet for the unholy, for
all the shysters and knaves in the city. That's not what
made me feel regretful, sitting at the bottom of that
vault in St Anthony's in Padua. Let them all come. No,
what stirred my feelings of regret was the overwhelming impression that some sort of living
continuity has been broken, irreparably, that what
brought all this alive and gave it a developing meaning is no longer there. It can't be experienced as alive
any more. You can restore the frescoes as much as you
like, print guidebooks, rid the church of inauthentic

accretions – it won't ultimately make any difference because it's dead now, the spirit that inhabited the place and grew with it has fled. Tourists want an embalmed body, not a body brought back to life. Not that I'd probably have much liked the spirit of the place if I'd encountered it. All the same, I have a feeling that its loss goes part of the way to explaining why the streets in behind the Basilica are unutterably beautiful, embodying a shared love of the city and what it stood for, while the streets around the station are, as they are everywhere, alienating, sharing nothing.

Actually, there was one point in the church, not so far from where I was sitting, where a tiny pulse still seemed to be beating. In an ornate alcove in the northern wall stood St Anthony's carved tomb. I might well have overlooked it if it hadn't been for two things: the line of serious-looking people forming to the left of it and passing in behind it, and a conversation that was going on in the row directly behind me.

'That must be his tomb over there.' It was a middle-aged woman's voice and the accent struck me as regional – Leeds? Sheffield?

'Yes, I can see that.' A woman travelling companion, by the sound of it, from somewhere close to home.

'There's no notice, but that must be it.'

'Yes, I can see that.'

'Why do you suppose they're all lining up?'

'Well, how would I know? I'm not a mind-reader. I'll look it up in the book if you like.'

'Yes, look it up, Doris, they're obviously up to

something. We might as well know what it is.'

'*According to ancient tradition to kiss the . . .*'

'Don't read it all out, Doris, for God's sake – just tell me.'

'Well, *apparently*, if you kiss the sarc . . . sarc . . . if you kiss the tomb, the saint may heal you of your ills. Or so it says here.'

'*May* heal you? Do you mean he'll consider it?'

'I'm only reading out what it says in the book. Don't get thingy with me about it.'

'For goodness' sake, the things people will believe! Talk about hoodwinking the public. Just look at them all – daft, every last one of them. The Church has got a lot to answer for, in my opinion.'

'You don't feel inclined, then?'

'Inclined? Certainly not. As if I would.'

'No, I'm not inclined, either. Although I suppose some might say you'd have nothing to lose.'

'Your self-respect, that's what you'd have to lose, Doris. Self-respect.'

'I think I lost that a long time ago. No, actually, I suppose you're right. There'd be no point.'

'*Obviously* there'd be no point. He's stone dead. And even if he *was* listening, I don't expect he'd put himself out over my ingrowing toenails, do you?'

'Well, you don't know, do you, unless you give it a go. He might. For all you know he might be sick to death of blindness and lung-cancer and quite fancy a quick . . .'

'Oh, Doris, don't try to be facetious, it's hardly the

time nor the place. I'm not going up and that's that. You do what you like, but, personally, if you do, I don't know how you'll live with yourself.'

'I suppose you're right.'

'*Obviously* I'm right. Now, do you want to see the High Altar or not? Give me the book. *Bronze bas-reliefs by Donatello*. It says here it's magnificent.'

'Alright, I suppose we should, then. Isn't Donatello the one who did the horse out the front?'

'Well, it'll be in the book – I'm not a walking encyclopaedia.'

And off they set, with much scraping of chairs and groaning about backs and legs, to inspect the magnificent High Altar by Donatello. I didn't have a book – mine was in my luggage at the station.

I'd followed their reasoning with close attention, as it happened, because, when you're quite alone and haven't spoken with anyone for hours (as can happen all too often when you travel alone), others' conversations can fill your head as if they were your own. And so they left me on my chair feeling both drawn, like Doris, and not inclined at all, like her companion, both at the same time. As Doris had pointed out, what was there to lose? And as her companion had retorted, there was your self-respect. I kept my eye on the line of believers, but didn't budge. On the one hand I didn't believe, even for a moment, that kissing a slab of marble behind which were gathered the bones of a thirteenth-century Portuguese cleric could effect even a minor miracle – it couldn't because the universe didn't work like that. (As far as I knew.) On the other hand, perhaps the change of heart it would take to plant the kiss might indeed do a tiny bit of good – might open up my mind to the possibility of good, or, to be completely cynical, send a spurt of some chemical or other surging through my veins, giving a quick boost to the immune system. Not that one has to be completely rational all the time, surely. I suddenly fancied an irrational escapade. I went up and joined the queue.

As we inched our way towards the rear of the sarcophagus, a friar in a black robe with a white cord around his waist was standing watching us, not wholly benevolently, as if he suspected some of us might be plotting a wild act of sacrilege. With each step towards the tomb the voices in my head grew more agitated: 'It's a farce! Go away!' 'Kiss it – what does it matter? A blinding shaft of light may . . .' 'Rubbish! You know it's rubbish. Why pander to superstition? Have some self-respect.' 'Now you're here, just do it, throw your hat in the ring.' Was the friar eyeing me with particular apprehension?

Then it was my turn. I stepped up, stared at the lifeless marble for a moment – and walked on out past the lugubrious friar. I couldn't do it. It wasn't my way. Newly emboldened, with a definite spring in my step, I crossed the nave and made my way out into the cloisters.

Cloisters – I love them. That's probably partly because, to all intents and purposes, we don't have them in Australia, so they're strange and exotic to me, like Balinese temples.* But it's also partly because of my (no doubt Freudian) love of the enclosed garden, the *hortus conclusus*, and the permission it gives you to be alone with your thoughts, to spiral inwards for a change, to take your time, detached from the time-keeping of the world outside. You secretly hope, in a cloister, that your monologue might prove to be a dialogue with God, but our cleverest minds assure us that this is a vain and dim-witted hope. No doubt they're right, at least in their own terms.

The cloistered garden, if I might put it like this, is like another, more intact self. '*A garden inclosed is my sister, my spouse; a spring shut up, a fountain sealed . . . Awake, O north wind; and come, thou south; blow upon my garden, that the spices thereof may flow out.*' From Solomon's Song.* It is also a little Eden, reminding you of what you once were or might have been, and sheltering you while you contemplate it. Ideally, of course, like the walled garden I sat in a few weeks ago with Rachel on Lake Maggiore, there's a window in the wall, or perhaps a gated doorway, reminding you of the wilderness outside. Yes, the perfect medieval *hortus conclusus* always had a *claire voie* to the outside world. And, in fact, as time went on, people began to look out more than in, wondering if Paradise might lie more in untouched wilderness than in the miniature mirroring of God's perfection. Certainly, in Australia nowadays the Garden of Eden is sought in the rainforests of Far North Queensland and the deserts of Central Australia, not in the Royal Botanic Gardens in Melbourne, however idyllic they may be.

As you know, I'm having trouble adapting to this more modern view, but I *am* trying.

As I've come to expect, St Anthony's cloisters turned out to be no more spiritually nourishing than cloisters anywhere in Europe these days, despite the fragments of Giotto's frescoes on the walls. On Sunday mornings in Westminster Abbey, for example, they're full of tourists sampling coffees of the world as part of the Coffee Club's activities, and here in Padua the cloisters were littered with notices about the video display, the souvenir shop, the museum and the toilets. Taiwanese and Swedish tourists sat about reading their guide-books and taking photographs of each other against a background they had no background in. It was dispiriting. I felt what used to be called *disconsolate*. With a vague sense of foreboding I headed off towards the museum.

By the time I came out of the museum I was feeling positively *merry*. If you ever go to Padua, don't miss the museum at the Basilica. All I knew about St Anthony before I went in was that he was the patron saint of people in dire straits, especially the shipwrecked, but, given the paucity of shipwrecked Catholics nowadays, I'd imagined (if I'd thought about it at all) that the saint's uses must have become severely restricted. Nothing could be further from the truth. Apart from a few glass cases full of ecclesiastical regalia, which didn't much interest me, the museum was mainly given over to works of art sent in by people from all over the world who had been rescued from adversity by the intercession of the saint. It was fascinating: there were paintings of people falling from balconies, falling under trains and cars, falling into fires, falling into the sea – falling, falling, but always scooped up at the last minute by St Anthony. And dotted about amongst the paintings and samplers and sketches were various crutches and other aids to the infirm, discarded thanks to the saint's intervention. For the most part the paintings were dreadful – naïve, amateurish, often garish – but at the same time they were somehow utterly disarming, touching, animating, deeply felt. These people, from Nigeria, China, Italy, India, Peru, perhaps even Sweden, I don't remember, were speaking to me from a world I'd hardly known existed, a world with completely different laws from my world's, where good could suddenly irrupt into a scene of evil and despair and triumph absolutely. And in one corner of each work the artists had inscribed PGR, which means, apparently, *per grazie ricevute* – for grace received.*

I was moved to pop into the St Anthony shop attached to the church and get a tract or pamphlet about him. I don't believe in saints, of course, or supernatural presences or intercession with God, but I felt that while I was there I'd just like to see the picture filled out a little. Armed with a little red-covered booklet I'd come upon amongst all the slides and videos and other devotional material in the shop, I sat down in a café across the square from the Basilica and began to peruse it. I was actually quite keen to get on, as I thought of it, and visit the famous botanical gardens

tucked away just in behind the Basilica not two minutes' walk away, but I became quickly engrossed in St
Anthony.

First of all, I'm terribly glad I didn't kiss the sarcophagus. St Anthony, it turned out, is not my kind of
saint at all. Well, no one is my kind of saint, but least
of all this Portuguese. I'd be the last person on earth
he'd have bothered to bless. And, secondly, whoever
writes this kind of gumpf should be shot.* Apart from
the odd male adolescent battling with the temptation
to masturbate, it could convince nobody. And, speaking of temptation, by the way, this is not the St Anthony
who was so famously tempted – that was St Anthony
the hermit and hog-keeper, who lived a thousand years
earlier in Egypt. No relation. This St Anthony, St Anthony
of Padua, was, in my view, an altogether unsavoury
character.

Apparently his mother used to croon songs of devo-
tion to the Virgin Mary to him in his cradle. That was
in Lisbon in 1195. In a sense, he never recovered. At
the age of fifteen, as we might expect of the son of
pious nobles, he was prostrating himself at the feet of
his Heavenly Mother before the altar of Lisbon
Cathedral, begging to be saved from 'temptation' – by
which I take it the booklet's author meant the urgent
desire to copulate. Lisbon, as he points out, was a
remarkably 'dissolute' city at the time, literally pullu-
lating with fleshly enticements, mainly, he says, because
of the rule of the Saracens, who had been pushed further south only a few decades earlier. So all the

necessary elements were present for the young Ferdinand (as he was christened) to convert his personal neurosis into something grander, something more universal, and to deflect his carefully cultivated hatred of himself onto Christendom's two greatest enemies at the time: the Muslims and the heretics.

A few years later at the Holy Cross Monastery at Coimbra in the north, where the mountains meet the plain, he happened to meet five Franciscan friars who were about to set out for Morocco to preach to the heathen. This was a fateful meeting, steadying his flapping libido and harnessing it to the great and magnificent purpose he hungered for. When the bodies of the five friars arrived back in Coimbra a short while later, their skulls brutally cloven by the scimitar of the Emir of Morocco himself, the young Anthony – and he now called himself Anthony, having become a Franciscan friar himself at a monastery about a mile from the Holy Cross – resolved to become a Christian martyr in the pitched battle against the Saracens. His self-renunciation, in other words, or, if you like, his denial of life, was about to take the extreme form (from my point of view), in the fervent hope of the richest reward on offer in the universe. 'For our light affliction,' as Paul wrote to the Corinthians, 'which is but for a moment, worketh for us a far more exceeding and eternal weight of glory.' But isn't this then lust under another name?

Whatever the case, God was not fooled. The Mohammedan Mission to Morocco was a complete disaster. Young Anthony failed to convert a single

Muslim soul to Christ – in fact, he failed to deliver a single sermon. In the end he fell ill with a 'fever' – a cover-all term we don't allow any more, I notice – and set out for home. At least his skull was intact. Providence decreed, however, that he never reach Portugal. Instead, a storm blew his ship onto rocks on the Sicilian coast. After resting up in Messina for a while – at exactly the time the Baroness's amulet found its brief resting place there, by the way, it's odd the patterns that appear in hindsight, although they mean nothing – he made his way to Assisi where he became involved in the Church's campaign against its other enemy, the heretic. So, as I would see it, at this point the masochist was transformed into the sadist. In either case something was very wrong with the way he loved both himself and the world.

This is really what I can't forgive him for. Well, it's hardly a matter of forgiveness, of course – who am I to forgive or not to forgive? It's beside the point. But this is what turns me right against him. Heresy to me is sacred. Heresy is the rogue genetic mutation that makes the species multiply. Heresy is the very source of all the colours and shapes and pain and joy in the world. Those who would stamp it out are my enemies.

In point of fact, no one in Assisi paid much attention to the young Portuguese for a while, not until the Bishop of Bologna took a liking to him and sent him to Forlì. That's where he really got into his stride, apparently, after stepping in one day to give an impromptu sermon when the preacher fell ill. Before long, tens of thousands of people were crowding out the church and the square beyond to hear him thunder against the heretics. They'd cover whole hillsides, according to my booklet, straining to hear his inspired fulminations. The Hammer of the Heretics, they called him, and his anvil was Catholic doctrine.

In the short term, as we know, the campaign was marvellously successful. These were the years, after all, when the evil flower of the Albigensian heresy was blooming lushly all over southern France and north-ern Italy – the Cathars, the Waldensians, as well as various minor sects. By 1200, for instance, the Waldensians had no fewer than six bishoprics in north-ern Italy. Mere preaching, however, proved insufficient – it was physical extermination, encouraged and in part organized by the Church, which was most effective (the good old wholesale massacre), as well as the tight-ening noose of the Inquisition a little later. Anthony preached all over southern France and northern Italy during the most crucial years of this murderous cru-sade and so, in my eyes, must share in the blame for the horrendous and, ultimately, pointless suffering it caused. (Pointless because in the long term, of course, the campaign failed utterly – heresy, although not in the Albigensian form, has triumphed.)

My moral outrage is the product of the times I live in, I know. It's interesting to note that in Dante's *Inferno* no one is damned for killing. In other words, in the early fourteenth century in northern Italy, a hundred years or so after St Anthony died, killing human beings does not seem to have been regarded as much of a sin in itself, unless basely motivated, motivated by misplaced love, for example – of money, fame, possessions, self and so on. So suicides, pimps, adulterers, the fraudulent, the proud, the gluttonous, the violent, sodomites, those who forgot to say 'Mary' as they died – all these are damned for all eternity to unspeakable tortures, while killing *as such*, despite the Ten Commandments, doesn't seem to offend anyone. It clearly failed to offend St Anthony. For that matter, of course, millions of ideologues in our own times, including lots of charming, well-educated people we all enjoy having dinner with, have failed to be *deeply* offended by the massacres carried out in the name of their own ideology in their own lifetimes. Regretful, saddened, made uneasy – but not outraged. When you chop wood, they explain tranquilly, pouring themselves a little more chardonnay, chips fly.

Oblivious of his complicity in mass murder, the populations of the towns the saint visited were impressed with a series of miracles: at Rimini, for instance, when the Waldensian heretics rudely walked out on his sermon, he called on the fishes of the sea to listen to him instead – and, indeed, the fishes did line up to lend an ear, their little fishy heads poking up above the waves of the Adriatic; in Bourges in France, the mule belonging to some doubting Jews preferred the host St Anthony offered it to the oats its owners thrust at it – and the Jews of Bourges rejoiced and were converted; he drank poison given him by heretics with no ill effect; the Lord of Châteauneuf was amazed to see him cradling the Christ Child in his arms. And so it goes on, degenerating in our times into finding lost pen-knives and golf-balls. It all smacks of something I deeply dislike.

Just before he died (of dropsy) Anthony is said to have burst into song:

> Hail, Glorious Lady, Virgin seated above the stars.
> Hail, Mother of my Saviour.

Presumably, it has more of a ring to it in Italian – or was it in Portuguese? At any rate, this last song rounds off the narrative very nicely, I think, returning us to his first musical experience in his mother's arms in Lisbon. He died just outside Padua, according to my booklet, 'his face irradiated by a sweet smile'. He was declared a saint practically on the spot and in 1946 the Pope awarded him the posthumous title of *Doctor evangelicus*. Sitting there at that café table across the square from the Basilica's ornate façade, I could have wept. From disenchantment.*

Professor Eschenbaum, by the way, was not at all interested in hearing about St Anthony of Padua – he's strictly *Renaissance*, whereas the saint was Middle Ages. (I love the way he says *Renaissance* with a German accent – delicious.) He was more interested in my moment of temptation at the Basilica, since his whole purpose in coming to Italy, as I've mentioned, is to give in to temptation. Not, I think, that St Anthony would have much tempted him. It's instinct he's more lured by, not the renunciation of instinct. I told him about my experience in the Basilica this afternoon in the hotel bar. He's decided not to leave until tomorrow, by the way, when he hopes his arm will be a little stronger – you need all the arms you can get when you're lugging suitcases on and off trains. It's the ideal place to sit and talk, that bar. For my part, I have a perfect view out over the embankment and the canal and I can watch the Venetians walking by. (It's one of the unacknowledged delights of Venice, in my opinion, watching people walking. Everyone has to walk – up and down, in and out, along, across. It's endlessly diverting.) And the Professor, for his part, has a perfect view of Emilio. I watched him watching Emilio easing one finger down between his collar and his neck, rubbing at the spot where the starched edge of the collar bites into his skin. The Professor's attitude to Emilio seems to have changed a fraction over the past day or two. Perhaps it's because he's leaving, perhaps it's something else. It's not something I can easily put my finger on, but the old peremptoriness has faded, there's almost a hint of meekness in his behaviour towards him, while at the same time Emilio seems increasingly off-hand, but on purpose. It makes me slightly uncomfortable.

Venice, 17th April

ALL I HAD to do to see the Botanical Garden that afternoon in Padua was get up from my table and walk across the square. I'd found it on the map and it was tantalizingly close, in behind the Basilica, just a stone's throw away. But I didn't do it. I'd read about it, thought about it, imagined it and made a mental note to visit it one day, but when the moment came – and there were still a couple of hours of daylight left – I stayed glued to my seat in the shadow of St Anthony's.

It's not unlike not wanting to finish Dante's *Paradise* (which I *am* quite enjoying, the Professor was right, I'm afraid). I do like to postpone culmination. And the Orto Botanico in Padua was conceived as the culmination of something – what, exactly, it's hard to say at this distance. But in 1545, when Padua was Venice's centre of learning – it's just across the fields, after all, from the seat of the Most Serene Republic – someone had the idea of 'collecting the whole world in a single chamber'.* Needless to say, the *idea* of the botanical garden had existed for thousands of years – Aristotle had one, as did Montezuma in Mexico, not to mention every second Renaissance prince in Italy – but it was the Paduans who conceived of the first truly *modern* botanical garden, a garden which, now that the whole world was known, could reflect both the wondrous breadth of God's creation and its order, both at the same time. (The 'whole world', I need scarcely add, did not, to the European mind, include Australia – nor does it to this day, to all intents and purposes. We remain a kind of Estonia of the South Seas, a not wholly unsatisfactory state of affairs.) Hence in Padua the almost mystical patterning of the parterres: circles within squares within circles – infinite variety, but enclosed infinitude, which is geometrically possible, by the way, and not a contradiction in terms. And the circles and squares were arranged in this circular garden in four squared-off groups: Asia, Africa, Europe and the Americas, across which continents God had apparently, in His wisdom, scattered the glories of the original Garden of Eden, since no explorer, not even Columbus, had succeeded in locating it in one place – Mesopotamia, Venezuela, they looked everywhere. And, although it took forty years to complete, the gardens were even designed in one fell swoop, in conscious imitation of God's dramatically sudden creation of the Garden of Eden.

So make no mistake about it: what was beckoning me from beyond St Anthony's spires and domes was nothing less than the recreation of Paradise. Here, as the Paduans might have seen it, innocence and sin-lessness had been reconstituted, here we might all become new Adams before the fall, wandering amongst God's trees and flowers (no fanged animals in evidence, and certainly no rutting) before sex, before greed, before toil. But I turned away, I didn't go. I just sat there with my cappuccino and thought glumly about how I didn't believe in Edenic visions or regained innocence. Nor did I believe that the Orto Botanico had much to do with Nature – it was a book about Nature, an ency-clopaedia of Nature, not Nature itself. I felt that was a book I'd already leafed through more than once. In fact, botanical gardens aren't really gardens at all, of any kind. They somehow contrive to be neither orchards, nor flower gardens, nor kitchen gardens, nor physick gardens, nor even parks. They're static, nothing's hap-pening – no flowers are being picked, no fruit eaten, no medicines boiled up, there's no one picnicking or admiring the view. It's a museum, not a garden. Paradise was never a museum. So, instead of heading off across the square towards the garden, I went the other way, back through the old city towards the sta-tion. Nothing diverted me, so I eventually came to the station. I retrieved my luggage, went up onto the plat-form and got on the first train that came along – to Venice.

A couple of hundred years ago, I seem to remem-ber reading somewhere, the stylish way to approach Venice from Padua, especially in summer and autumn, was by saloon-barge along the River Brenta, drifting past all those Renaissance mansions with their elaborate topiary, fountains and frescoed walls. As evening fell the waterway was transformed into a tunnel lit by glow-worms. The approach by rail is more prosaic, to say the very least, but even crossing the lagoon to Venice by train filled me with a kind of warm excitement, a peaceful exuberance I've felt nowhere else.

I've got wheels on my new suitcase, so when I got to Venice, hardly half an hour's journey away, I was able to walk away from the station as if I knew where I was going and lose myself in that dizzying maze of laneways and canals across the bridge from the station forecourt, looking for a hotel. There's a flamboyant vulgarity, a sort of decadent, almost camp theatricality about the scene that greets you when you walk out of the station and find yourself standing right on the Grand Canal – it's invigorating, but it also makes you want to laugh. The set is grand opera but the action is pure vaudeville. When you leave the embankment and wander off up one of the drab side-streets, it's almost like suddenly turning off a rattling film-projector – in an instant there's silence, sobriety and age-old serenity. Only the smells seem to waft in after you. Bliss.

I've actually been back to the station tonight to say goodbye to Professor Eschenbaum. I put him on the Paganini Express to Dortmund. It wasn't sad – everything that needed to be said had been said. He didn't want me to bother accompanying him, but with his delicate arm I could see he was going to have trouble with his cases, so I insisted. I don't imagine we'll ever meet again. These days I try hard to make things worthwhile for what they are now, without considering what they may lead to or whether what I've been experiencing can be recaptured. Needless to say, I should have lived more like that all along, but you don't, do you, when you think of your life as an almost infinitely long continuum. I hate to think how often I've failed to notice what was happening to me at the time because my mind was taken up with preparing to retell it or repeat it or in some other way consider its ramifications. Too often I've been like those people you get trapped with at cocktail parties, forever looking over your shoulder to see who they might talk to next.

It isn't putting the Professor on the train my mind goes back to tonight, all the same, although I've been thinking about him all evening, rattling along, no doubt, somewhere up in the mountains north of Milan. No, it's our last conversation that will stay with me, the one we had over our farewell lunch earlier this afternoon. It turned out to be all about Casanova. Although he wasn't *Renaissance* (he was the eighteenth century incarnate), I knew the Professor was interested in him because of the conversation we had about prisons a few days ago – do you remember? Casanova was the most famous prisoner ever incarcerated under the notorious Leads. And, in fact, it was the question of his fame that sparked our conversation. It was a paradox, surely, I said, that the two most famous Venetians of

all time, Marco Polo and Casanova, were virtually forgotten in Venice itself – just try to buy a book about
either of them in a Venetian bookshop, for example,
it's far easier in Melbourne. The Professor objected that
there were plenty of other famous Venetians – Vivaldi,
Titian, Tintoretto, he reeled off a whole list of them
in that slightly tiresome, academic way of his – to
which I said that, yes, they were all famous, millions
had heard of them, but it was only Marco Polo and
Casanova who had become, as it were, symbols of
something much larger than themselves. 'Iconic, you
mean,' said the Professor and I reluctantly agreed that
that probably was what I meant. Vivaldi was famous
for his music, let's say, but Casanova and Marco Polo
had come to represent entire ... '*Mentalités*,' said the
Professor. Exactly.

'Why do you think that is?'

The Professor neatly detached one side of his sole
from its skeleton. We'd decided to lunch somewhere
Very Expensive to mark what was a rather special occasion and were sitting behind glass on the very edge of
the Grand Canal. While he considered carefully how
to respond, I drank in the scene beyond the glass, that
astonishing cavalcade of dainty stone façades, wheeling slowly round towards the Rialto to disappear in
an explosion of domes, towers and crazed roof-lines.
'I think,' he said, chewing thoughtfully, 'it's because each
of them represents one important kind of journeying.
Yes, I'm sure that's why. Almost opposite kinds, in fact.
And journeying is, after all, so fundamental to the way

we humans think of ourselves and assign our lives a meaning. Every second book you read is about some kind of journey, really, isn't it? And we constantly talk about paths in life – ways, roads, progress, stages and so on – all travel metaphors, when you think about it. I would say that Marco Polo and Casanova have come to stand for completely different ways of travelling – and therefore of living out your life.' I was wondering how I could provoke him to say more.

Watching an overloaded *vaporetto* chugging towards the station, I tried to recall for a moment that very funny passage in *A Sentimental Journey* where Sterne lists all the different kinds of travellers he's observed – you must have read it, it's a delicious little burst of pseudo-scientific nonsense. It came to mind because I've been picking Sterne up and reading bits and pieces from the journey almost every day for weeks – on trains, over lunch, before I fall asleep – he's a marvellous antidote to Dante.

The writing is so nervy and self-mocking that it's almost impossible to work out exactly what he's saying, to be honest, although clearly at some level he's mounting a defence of his own kind of travelling – the *sentimental* kind. Most people (he seems to be saying) travel (and he means to the Continent) out of boredom ('idleness', he calls it, so much more aristocratic), curiosity (which is never properly fed), imbecility (I suppose he means people who can't think of anything better to do) or else some kind of necessity – to escape creditors, to improve their minds, because they have been sent abroad by someone else and so on. You get the feeling Sterne finds all these reasons for travel in some way or other vain and misguided and thinks these kinds of travellers would do just as well to stay at home – especially if they're English. (Lesser breeds are hardly considered – this was 1768 or thereabouts.) Now, the *sentimental traveller*, on the other hand, such as Sterne himself was, or affected to be, is an altogether more modern creature – in fact, Laurence Sterne may well have been the first true example of the species. The sentimental traveller travels simply in order to observe the motion of his own sensibilities. (People are awfully snooty about the word 'sensibilities' these days. Do you mean 'feelings'? they ask querulously. If so, say 'feelings'. But I think it's quite a useful word, I think it indicates, as the simple word 'feelings' doesn't, a self-awareness and even appreciation of what you feel, as well as a kind of pleasure, which may indeed be unwholesomely effete, in the way the different currents of feeling you experience work together and against each other to produce a whole – an emotional self, if you like. And so I tend to think what Sterne really meant by 'sentimental traveller' was 'sensible traveller' in the old-fashioned sense.) Sterne's ostensible purpose in rabbiting on to the point of incoherence about all these categories and sub-categories of traveller is to make his reader reflect on what kind of traveller he (again, this was 1768) might be.

Another thing: when you step back from that single passage in *A Sentimental Journey* and consider the picture of the sentimental traveller which emerges (a little dishevelled) from the record as a whole, you can't help noticing how suffused with eroticism this Yorkshire parson's account of the voyaging of his sensibilities turned out to be. I don't mean this in just the obvious sense that the book is full of quivering encounters with *filles de chambre* and seductive ladies, but also in the less obvious sense that his use of English is never less than flirtatious: dotted with innocent *double-entendres*, it constantly promises satisfaction and then abruptly twirls around lightly and trips off in the opposite direction. He teases his reader like a lover on every page, turning his chastity into something almost positively lewd.

None of this is particularly interesting in itself, I suppose, but I remember suspecting when I read this passage that sentimental travelling is probably *always* erotic – in some sense. But which one? Actually, what my companion went on to say, silhouetted as he was against the shimmering, swarming arch of the Ponte degli Scalzi, happened to chime in very aptly with my reflections on sentimental travelling. Perhaps that was not a complete coincidence since Sterne was a contemporary of Casanova's – and, for that matter, Polo was a contemporary of Dante's, who has also been very much on my mind these past few days, as you'll have gathered. (Interestingly enough, Dante contrived to ignore his illustrious contemporary utterly, although he managed to get in a line or two on almost every other Italian who had ever lived. I'm sure there are theories about why.)

'Have you ever read Marco Polo's *Travels?*' the

Professor asked, detaching the second side of his sole from the skeleton.

'Well, no, I've only read about him, really.'

'You probably shouldn't bother – I'm sure you'd be disappointed. In any case, you wouldn't be reading Marco Polo, you'd be reading Rustichello, the scribe he recounted his travels to in prison in Genoa, and Rustichello, who wrote it all down in a strange Italianate sort of French, took enormous liberties with the text. He even went so far as to plagiarize himself – without any acknowledgement he stuck bits of other things he'd written, especially about King Arthur, right into the middle of the Marco Polo. Mind you, if anyone needed recasting in the role of knight errant, it was Marco Polo. Deep down he seems to have been an unforgivably dull man – even Rustichello couldn't disguise that.' Professor Eschenbaum picked very lightly at a tooth with a toothpick, his other hand dangling over the back of his chair. He was waiting, I felt, for me to register some surprise. 'He was amongst the first Europeans ever to penetrate the Mongol court at Karakorum, that's so, and perhaps the very first to visit Peking. He served Kubilai Khan – the Khan of Khans – for seventeen years, he travelled all over China as his envoy, took part in sieges and battles, and by the time he returned home had travelled more widely across the earth than any other human being in history. Palestine, Persia, Kashmir, China, Burma, Java, India . . . it was a staggering achievement. As a matter of fact, some of the paths he took were not trodden again by Europeans until the nineteenth century.

'Yet what he *felt* about crossing the Pamirs or the Gobi Desert or living in thirteenth-century Peking he doesn't say. In fact, he gives little indication of what anyone felt or thought about anything. He barely even mentions what Kubilai Khan looked like! No, what Messer Marco Polo travelled for was to assess the trade possibilities of the countries he passed through and not much more. Productivity, and the local customs that might affect it, how each state was ruled, who was a Saracen, an idolater, a Christian and so on – all politically important – these were the things Marco Polo noted down and very little else. There's no sign at all that his thinking changed about anything – he left Italy as an Italian teenager and returned to Italy twenty years later as Italian as he'd left it. Nothing he saw seems to have had the slightest effect on his medieval Italian view of the world. This to me is almost as amazing as his itinerary. He hears ghost armies in the desert, wanders through Buddhist monasteries, finds a lake full of pearls, escapes from brigands and wild animals, meets yogis, lives amongst people so different from Venetians he might as well have been on Mars, is surrounded by every kind of wonder and curiosity (one of his favourite words) – yet you have almost no sense of his being *present* in these places. So weak is the sense of his presence that it's almost impossible to work out what parts of his story reflected his own experience and what parts borrowed reports. Did he ever go to Madagascar or just hear tales about it? Was he ever in Japan? Or in Zanzibar? Did he ever fall in love? Was he ever afraid? Impossible now to say. He travelled to compile a dossier on trading with the East, so it hardly matters whether he's speaking from personal experience or just passing on information from other sources. He just started at the beginning and ended at the end – all very linear. You couldn't write a book like his nowadays.'

'All the same, it sent Columbus out across the Atlantic.'

'Yes, that's true, but, again, not in search of experience, but of wealth. These men travelled to *accumulate* things, not to experience being alive.'

'Surely you're being a little harsh?'

'Of course I am – I'm having lunch with you, not writing a book. You're confusing genres.' He smiled. His lip must be on the mend. 'All I'm saying is that out of this rather narrow-minded but observant Venetian trader we've constructed someone much more to our liking: an adventuring knight errant, braving unimaginable perils to bring the light of Europe to the pagan East, discovering treasure troves so vast Europe had no time to plunder them all, returning home after twenty years, virtue intact, the banner of Christ soiled but still unfurled, to a tumultuous welcome. Rustichello records diamonds, rubies and emeralds spilling from the seams of the Polos' garments when they got back to Venice – proof that *they had travelled well*. And, in a way, I suppose they had. Essentially, though, what I'm saying is that Messer Marco Polo had not *been* anywhere.' (A bit precious, I thought.) 'And it may sound churlish of me to say so, but, on the subject of his powers of observation, he failed to remark on the fact that the Chinese drank tea, had discovered printing and built the Great Wall.' He called the waiter over and ordered a selection of *gelati*.

'And Casanova? How was he different, in your opinion?'

The Professor considered me carefully. 'In every way, my friend, in *every* way – in how he wrote, in what he looked for, in how he loved, in his notion of happiness. I suspect you might like Casanova very much.'

'What makes you think so?'

'Because his obsessions were your obsessions, that's why.' I was surprised – I'd thought Casanova was mainly obsessed with seducing nuns.

'And what were his obsessions, would you say?'

'Time, for a start. In fact, above all – time. Of course, on the face of it, he was little more than a wandering philanderer. From Rome to St Petersburg, from Paris to Prague, if you play his life back like a film, all you'll see is a series of seductions – nuns, maids, prostitutes, duchesses, he was even ready to have a go at Catherine the Great, but the arrangement fell through. He had an unquenchable hunger for sexual experience, there's no doubt about it, and to most people today – and we must remember we live in far more rigorously moral times than he did – his attitude to sexual experience must appear gross. But beneath the surface something much more ... yes, I would even say "refined", was going on. You have the impression, when you read his memoirs, that much more than the mere accumulation of orgasms was going on – that could have been achieved in much simpler, more straightforward ways, after all, without all that theatricality and danger and those wild dashes across Europe. And I'm convinced that at the root of all these copulations in carriages and palaces and inns all over Europe was an obsession with the secret of time.'

The Professor was gesturing with his spoon as he warmed to his subject and little flecks of ice-cream were landing on the tablecloth and my ironed, cream shirt.

'I see,' I said.

'Yes, I'm completely convinced of it. You see, when Casanova was just a small boy of seven or eight, his mother took him to see a sorcerer on the island of Murano to cure him of nosebleeds. Interestingly, it worked – the mumbojumbo worked, the nosebleeds stopped, the boy was cured. Now, I think this experience had a profound effect on Casanova. I think it sowed the seed of certainty in his mind that there was a secret knowledge he was attuned to which would reveal quite a different meaning behind everyday functions and events. I don't think that certainty ever left him. You must remember that apart from being a card-sharp, swindler and unprincipled adventurer, Casanova was also highly adept in astrology and the cabbalistic arts. In fact, what the Inquisitors claimed they were most outraged by in the Casanova case was his corruption of prominent Venetians with occult knowledge. They sent their spy, the jeweller Manucci, to his house here in Venice to borrow books on the cabbala and Casanova fell straight into their trap, enthusiastically showing Manucci his extensive library on these subjects. So, all through his life, right up until he died as librarian to a minor count in Bohemia, I think he pursued sexual pleasure, not so much for its own sake (although an orgasm is an orgasm), as in the hope of breaking through somehow to a different order of bliss.' He glanced across at me here to see if this new turn in the conversation had caught my attention.

'You see, apart from anything else, his sexual tastes invited difficulty and a certain amount of fairly complicated choreography. For public consumption, needless to say, he's been presented as an indefatigable devourer of women, one after another, quite indiscriminately – whore, novice, mother of ten, it made no difference, according to the traditional picture of him. But, in point of fact, Casanova's predilections were quite specific: he always preferred what have been referred to as 'side-dishes', women with some kind of handicap – physical, social, it made little difference – the lesbian, the chaperoned maiden, the nun, the transvestite, the one-eyed and so on. He also found talking during sex highly erotic – sexually stimulating talk, I mean, which is much harder to come by than most people imagine – and that's why he didn't bother sleeping with England's most famous courtesan, Kitty Fisher: they had no tongue in common. In any case, it appears the self-assured, attractive woman of the world held little interest for him, except as a rung on the social ladder he was always climbing. Nor did he have much stomach for seducing women affected by alcohol or courtesans for whom he would be simply another customer. Even at this level, I would contend, there was some motif of "breaking through".'

I was feeling less than convinced by the picture the Professor was painting of Casanova. Not a philandering ratbag, apparently, but yet another subverter of paradigms. There was little point in saying anything, though, because the Professor was in full flight.

'Yet, as we now know, his sexuality was even more transgressive than that.' (I knew the word 'transgressive' would come up eventually.) 'In modern terms Casanova was at the very least bisexual and possibly even that word doesn't adequately describe his sexual shape.' If I looked sceptical at the turn the monologue had taken, it was because I had heard this line so often before – everyone from Jesus to Tom Cruise, it turns out, was 'one of us'. Really? Who would be next? Mao Tse Tung and Charles de Gaulle? 'It's *documented*,' Professor Eschenbaum said, having noted my expression, 'extensively *documented*. In fact, it's in his memoirs in his own hand. There's the delicious incident in St Petersburg where he politely pushes a willing French adventuress aside to address himself to a certain Captain Lunin who was employing all the time-honoured methods to arouse his drinking companion – military shirt open to the navel, progressive display of other "treasures", as Casanova puts it, a little manly horseplay. "I wasn't indifferent," he wrote later, "and saw no reason to pretend I was." Two hundred years later few public figures would write about themselves with such refreshing candour. And before the white-chested Captain Lunin there'd been a swarthy Turk or two in Constantinople – a certain Ismail in particular, I seem to remember, caught his fancy there – and he was on intimate terms with several notorious sodomites, including both the Duc d'Elbœuf and the Duke of Maddaloni, not to mention a fellow-prisoner called Camille (a man's name in French, as you may know) and a certain X at Dunkirk. No, it's quite clear that Casanova took voluptuous pleasure in both male and female bodies – as did his more famous prototype Don Juan, by the way. Did you know that? Oh, yes, the Spanish kept it quiet for centuries, but the awkward fact is that their famous Don Juan de Tassis, Count of Villamediana and living icon of male heterosexual desire – he was supposedly executed by Philip IV for sniffing around the queen – was in fact the chief, *el jefe supremo*, of a secret homosexual ring discovered in Madrid in 1622.' That was a surprising tidbit.

'But what does it matter?' I said. 'What is your point?'

'*Matter?* Of course it matters.' He pushed back his chair and stared for a moment over his shoulder at the teeming canal beyond the glass. 'In the first place, it's clear now that Giacomo Casanova was imprisoned under the Leads not just for corrupting the youth of Venice with atheism and Freemasonry, not just for "outrages against the holy religion" and practising necromancy, but also, quite importantly, because he was homosexually involved with three powerful Venetian men – Senator Bragadin, of course, a blind donkey could see that, as well as the two Marcos – Dandalo and Barbaro. These were his three Venetian . . . what is the word I'm looking for?'

'Sugar-daddies, perhaps?'

'That sounds right, yes. The Inquisition, you see, while it could tolerate murder, robbery, greed and corruption quite happily, could not tolerate such a flagrant attack on the very foundation of Venetian society: the heterosexual family. All power and wealth relied on the maintenance of its forms.'

'And Casanova cocked a snook at them.'

'I beg your pardon?'

'Transgressed.'

'Exactly.'

'But what has any of that to do with time?'

'Ah!' he said, obviously pleased I'd not lost track of his argument. 'Yes, time. This is where I think Marco Polo and Casanova represent such different types of traveller, such different mentalities. Polo discovered paradise *over there*, you see, he travelled there and then came back. Casanova discovered paradise *in the travelling*, if you see what I mean – it wasn't somewhere you *could* come back from. Polo flew with the arrow of time, he pointed forward and simply lived one day after the next. As we all do, at least most of us most of the time. Today he is in Kashmir, he travels forty days and arrives in Kashgar. He spends so many days in

Kashgar and then travels so many days to the next town – and so on. He experiences life as a sequence of events, episodically. Casanova, by way of contrast, I think experienced life quite differently. My impression is that he zigzagged through time in search of timeless moments, blissful instants when the past and future ceased to exist for him – the only kind of spiritual perfection he could conceive of. His lust for another moment, always another moment, was his way of trying to blur these timeless points into continuous, amorphous rapture. He wasn't hunting for happiness, in other words, which is always episodic, he was trying to experience bliss.' He paused to see what kind of effect his reasoning had had on me. 'And more than that, I would maintain that this difference between the two men was connected with their sexuality.'

'Well, nowadays *everything* is supposed to be connected with your sexuality.'

The Professor was undeterred by any faint bleats from my side of the table. 'Although sex is never mentioned by Polo, except from time to time as a strange foreign custom, like worshipping idols, we can be sure without being told that Marco Polo's sexuality was entirely conventional. You know as you read him that this man has a sense of cause and effect, indeed of responsibility and consequence, which is inseparable from the patriarchal mentality.'

'Why do you emphasise responsibility like that? Surely you're not suggesting that a sense of responsibility has anything to do with sexual orientation?'

'Because one of the first things you notice about Casanova is the lack of any idea of consequence or responsibility – and, as I say, this is connected with his sexual identity. At each seduction he seemed to draw a magic circle around himself, a circle of rapture and voluptuous pleasure, with no links to anyone or anything outside it. In fact, I suspect one of the reasons he had to keep escaping from city to city was to make sure these moments *had* no consequences, at least for him. And yes, I *am* suggesting some connection between responsibility and sexual identity, I suppose. It's a cliché, I know, a tedious suburban platitude, but not totally without foundation. The androgyne, the homosexual, the sexual delinquent is always looked at askance by neighbours and aunts as behaving irresponsibly. They're always so relieved when you buy a house, take on commitments, get a loan from the bank, *settle down* – act responsibly, like other people. There will always be something about the bisexual and homosexual male which favours a picaresque existence – and something about a picaresque existence which will always have homosexual overtones.'

I was about to object that this sounded highly dubious to me, if not complete hogwash, when the tea arrived. It wasn't tea at all, of course, in our sense of the word, but the Professor seemed quite happy with it, enjoying the little rituals accompanying tea which coffee can't compete with. There were a couple of those bone-dry Italian biscuits to go with it.

'And, speaking of escaping from place to place, I

don't think Casanova's astonishing escape from the Leads makes much sense, either, unless you understand how driven he was to keep circulating, keep flowing, keep letting things happen to him. No one, naturally, wants to be shut up in prison, everyone wants to be set free, but no one had ever escaped from the Doge's prisons before, not a single prisoner had ever bribed or dug or bored his way out of those hideous cells. You did visit them, by the way, didn't you?'

'Yes, I did. I must say it was a little hard to picture what it must have been like to be a prisoner there, with all those strapping Finns and Canadians striding through them with knapsacks on their backs, but still, yes . . .'

'Well, did you notice how low the ceilings were, for instance? Now, Casanova was extremely tall – that's partly why he was thought to be so "handsome", an almost meaningless term in the abstract – he was almost half a metre taller than the ceiling in his cell. Can you imagine the torture of spending month after month bent over like that, listening to the constant screaming and cursing, watching the stream of fellow prisoners passing your cell on their way to execution, not to mention the filthy food, the foul-smelling dis-eased bodies, the scorpions, rats and spiders? And the shocking thing was that this cesspool lay festering beneath buildings of such astoundingly graceful beauty at the heart of Europe's most magically beautiful city. As you suffered you knew that just a few steps away – literally half a dozen steps away on the other side of

those massive walls – princes and dukes were confer-
ring in panelled rooms hung with magnificent
paintings, tourists were parading up and down the
embankment watching ships glide into port from cities
half a world away, life in all its richness was in full
swing. Who wouldn't want to escape?' The Professor
paused again and gazed over his shoulder for a moment
at the huge green dome of St Simeon Piccolo a little
further up the canal on the opposite side. There were
dozens of black gondolas with brightly coloured cushions bobbing about in front of the church steps.

'But it was impossible,' he said, turning back to face
me again, 'not just difficult, but impossible. Men far
more powerful than Casanova had failed. Men far
stronger and more athletic than Casanova had failed.
Everyone had failed. Yet it was Casanova, the dandy, the
effete bookworm and degenerate scoundrel who succeeded. Why? Well, he was lucky, of course, but, over
and above that, he was driven by his spinning nature
to keep spinning – or else topple onto his side and die.
He also developed appalling piles in prison, which, as
you may know, can drive you to any extremity. Piles
have been unaccountably overlooked in the history of
compulsive personalities, in my opinion. As a matter
of fact, I personally believe there's such a thing as a
haemorrhoidal character and, until we come to terms
with that, a lot of strange behaviour in human history
will remain a mystery.

'Haemorrhoids apart, however, I still think Casanova
could somehow not conceive of himself as a prisoner.

Have you heard the story of the dead arm? It's trivial, really, but everyone mentions it because, subconsciously, we all know it has a larger meaning than at first appears. Soon after he was incarcerated, Casanova woke up one night horror-struck because there seemed to be a dead man lying beside him. Crying out in shock, he tried to push the corpse away from him, but it wouldn't budge, it seemed bound to him. He broke into a cold sweat. Then, grappling with the dead flesh, he realized all of a sudden that it wasn't a corpse, it was his own numb arm. A nasty moment, but only worth recording, surely, because Casanova's real fear was that prison had killed off his vital parts. That bits of him were dead.'

'Which bits?'

'Haven't you been listening?' I had been, but the Professor's mind darted about all over the place with such alacrity that I was beginning to get left behind. Prison, his point seemed to be, or at least the Doge's prison, was death to seduction. 'You can forget the prison pornography you may have come across,' he said airily, gesturing dismissively, 'that's just a sado-masochistic fantasy.' There was, he said, clearly room for a certain amount of rape and sexual assault in the Doge's cells, apparently, but Casanova, despite his diverse tastes, seems to have been interested less in coercion than in seduction, and for that there was almost no opportunity at all. You were locked in your cell with a stinking companion or two for months on end and under those conditions seduction can't work – there's nowhere to escape to afterwards and the professional seducer must always be able to move on. But it wasn't just the directly sexual parts of him which were threatened with death, according to the Professor, it was those other sides of his nature he'd been speaking about – his picaresque side, his constant need for contingency, for things to happen to him. Prison, I could quite see, puts an end to contingency, every minute of the day being more or less predictable, scheduled. 'And, of course, I would say that prison is an utterly sequential experience, in the Marco Polo sense,' the Professor said. 'One day follows another, dates are crossed off one after another on the wall. Prison is time.' For Casanova, if the Professor's view was the right one, this, above all, was intolerable.

'So he escaped. To this day no one quite believes his story – the drilling, the sheets, the lead tiles, the gondola – it seems impossible. Yet it is true that one day he was in prison and the next he was not. This at least is true. And do you know where he spent his first night of freedom? In the house of a policeman who was out all night looking for him. What flair! What panache!' And for the first time since we'd met Professor Eschenbaum laughed – a short little bark of a laugh, but not a humourless one.

'He was cocking a snook.'

'I beg your pardon?'

'Just an expression. Tell me, what sort of traveller are you?'

He smiled, more to himself than for me and a

little ruefully. I thought how much I liked him. 'Sadly,' he said, 'I don't think I'm any kind of traveller, really. I wish I were. But I think I've turned out to be just a vacationer. Perhaps when I retire . . .' But I could see he didn't really believe it would happen. 'Speaking of travelling, I think it's time I went back to the hotel. There are still a few things I need to attend to.'

So we drifted off back across the bridge towards the hotel and I could feel something I'd taken great pleasure in coming to an end.

Sitting at my desk here tonight in my room, thinking back over all these things, I even feel a little bereft. It will pass. Professor Eschenbaum, like Rachel and like writing to you, has helped me befriend a part of myself I only had a nodding acquaintance with before. And they've helped ease my constant anxiety, too, that no words can be found to say certain difficult things. No words may be quite adequate, but there are words and they're worth saying. Tomorrow, I'm quite convinced, everything will look painted in fresh colours.